CAUS

CAUSE OF DEATH

SIMON WESTON

and Patrick Hill

I would like to thank all those involved in Ireland, both legally and illegally, in the researching of this story.

Simon Weston, 1995

First published in Great Britain in 1995
22 Books, Invicta House, Sir Thomas Longley Road, Rochester, Kent

This edition published 1996

A CIP catalogue record for this book is available from the British Library

ISBN 1 898125 92 9

10 9 8 7 6 5 4 3 2 1

Typeset by Hewer Text Composition Services, Edinburgh
Printed by Cox and Wyman Ltd, Reading

Prologue

The telephone burst into life, its shrill tones reverberating through the empty room. Outside, the heavy thrash of the Chinook's rotor blades almost drowned the sound of its ringing. Cursing, the small group scurried through the drizzle as, ushered by three uniformed soldiers, they moved from the building to board the waiting helicopter. The flashing light on its underbelly reflected off the wet tarmac that was the take-off spot. The ageing machine was lucky to be flying that night, in those conditions. The pilot cursed his luck at being chosen for this job.

Slowly the five men and two women, all in civilian clothes, hauled themselves aboard. Just as the last of their group was hoisted in and the sound of the engine gathered momentum, a uniformed orderly burst from the building which they had just left and dashed up to the doorway of the Chinook.

'Is there a Mr Philip McGann here? Please, sir, there's an urgent telephone call ... it's the police, sir ... it's your wife, sir ... you're needed on the phone,' blurted the excited, breathless, corporal of the Royal Air Force Regiment.

All eyes in the helicopter turned towards the dark-eyed man who sat at the rear.

'I'm McGann. What's this you're saying?' he said.

'Urgent telephone call for you, sir. You can take it in the waiting lounge over there, sir. It's your office – something about your wife, sir.' repeated the corporal.

The smartly dressed man who sat in front of McGann turned to his fellow passenger. 'You'd best go, Philip. We'll sort all this lot out. Catch us up later.'

Philip McGann, Deputy Chief Constable of the Royal Ulster Constabulary, hastily jumped out and ran back to the building behind the orderly through the spray that rose from the force

1

of the chopper blades. Behind him, he could hear the door of the helicopter being closed.

The telephone lay on the table in front of him in the empty, smoke-filled room. 'McGann here. What's the problem?' he enquired in his deep Ulster tones.

The roar of the helicopter's engines increased as the pilot finally lifted off through the gloom of a wet night at Aldergrove Airport.

*   *   *

The news wasn't good. Commander Colin Jacobson, Head of Special Intelligence Gathering for MI6, had guessed as much when the telephone had woken him from a deep sleep at 2 a.m. Seven hours later, things were looking even worse. A briefing had been urgently arranged, and a call to see the boss, Home Secretary Douglas Hamilton. Now Jacobson sat impatiently in the wood-panelled room, waiting to be summoned. Rolling and unrolling the lunchtime edition of the London *Evening Standard*, he scanned the lead story time and again without interest.

An army helicopter carrying a party of high-ranking security chiefs had crashed on take-off from Aldergrove Airport in Belfast some fifteen hours earlier, but the cause of the crash remained a mystery. Four male passengers and their two female assistants had been killed, as well as the pilot and co-pilot. Accident investigators were on the scene and an inquiry was already under way. Initial reports had blamed adverse weather conditions or pilot error. It was well known that the Chinook did not have the necessary night-flying equipment that made other types of army helicopters safer in bad visibility and weather conditions. According to the report in the newspaper, security heads had ruled out any links with terrorism.

Jacobson contemplated lighting a cigarette but thought better of it – the boss didn't like smokers. He attempted to comfort himself with the knowledge that Fleet Street had been fobbed off with the cock and bull story that he and his assistant had helped the Press Office prepare. Now it was time for him to drop the bombshell. He had waited for the right moment.

'Well, it's a little strange, but there is a possibility that neither of the sides might be behind this.' He had Hamilton's attention.

'The last couple of months,' he went on, have seen a few incidents that we didn't connect until recently. There have been some killings and a few incendiary explosions throughout the region that no one has admitted to. By and large we've kept them at a very low profile – didn't want to interfere with the peace process and so on. We put them down to sectarian killings or even simple criminal acts – you know, a few shoot-outs from unemployed gunmen who didn't have their weapons and just wanted to keep their hand in. However, he continued, the army intelligence-gatherers had heard a different story.

'But the chaps in Fourteen Int have been coming back with rumours from the pubs and the streets that these incidents are all down to someone else. Both the Army Council of the IRA and the UVF bods have been baffled as well. But it's given them a chance to start beating their chests again. The other month a Catholic bricklayer was bumped off – shot in the head at close range. A few days later, a Protestant milkman was shot in his home. The RUC were reluctant to turn round and say they were sectarian killings in case they got the war drums going again. They claimed that the two separate incidents were crime-related.'

Jacobson paused, cleared his throat. 'Go on, Colin,' said Hamilton tersely.

'A month ago a tout, known regularly to the RUC, dropped a bit of a bombshell, although he didn't have any real proof. He said he had heard of a third party that were behind a string of goings on. He called them a "wild bunch" who were actually led by an outsider from across the water. He claimed that this outsider was an expert. It all seemed a bit far-fetched.'

Jacobson paused again, but the Boss's eyes never left his face.

'Then, a fortnight ago,' he continued, 'there was an attack on a businessman's home. This chap James O'Donnell has been rumoured to be dabbling in the drug scene, but no one has been able to prove it. Two weeks ago his home was sprayed by gunfire. The police and ourselves put it down initially to a drug squabble. But afterwards the local army intelligence lads received reports from neighbours who swear to God that they heard an Englishman there. They insist that the orders for the attack were all given by a man with an English accent, someone who seemed to know what he was talking about – as if he was a professional. Let's face it, O'Donnell's house wasn't an easy target – behind it's a big wall, with security cameras and the works. But, even according to the RUC, the whole thing seemed to be carried out with military precision.'

Hamilton stiffened. 'So what you're saying is that we've got a bloody loose cannon in there. Good God, that's all we need – some damn mental retard of a mercenary going around stirring things up!' His eyes narrowed. 'I want this bugger, Colin. I don't care what it costs – get him before things get out of hand! We're too far down the line to allow some gung-ho little bastard like this to screw things up for us now. *I want him!*'

Chapter One

They had come at night. There had been no warning. The whole village would have been asleep, just another end to a perfectly ordinary day. The twenty or so tiny white-walled houses positioned at varying angles around the tree-lined square that formed the centre of the village had stood silent in the blackness of the mountain night. The troubles of the rest of the country had seemed light years away from this tranquil scene. Time had not laid its finger on this untouched spot at the end of the valley smothered on three sides by the vastness of the tree-covered slopes which surrounded it.

Life was simple but hard. The locals had scratched a living from the land there for generations. Few had travelled to the towns and cities. Why should they? Everything they wanted was here. All they had hoped for was to be left in peace. Life had been good for two centuries. The events and troubles of history had ignored the people of Velika Kupa. Not even the Nazi invaders had paid this spot much attention over fifty years earlier. The place had been too insignificant to bother about.

The first snowflakes of winter were floating lazily down to begin settling on the red-tiled roofs of the village and the surrounding mountain slopes when death came from the sky – from the battery of mortars on the bluffs 1200 feet above. The bombs rained down to shatter the fairy-tale scene with a hail of fire, noise and destruction. The first crashed into the centre of the square, showering the surrounding area with white-hot shrapnel and debris. A second, landing a split second later, erupted by the side of a fragile wooden barn which housed two mules brought in to shelter from the expected snow. The barn and its contents were lost in a ball of flame which quickly engulfed the building. Another landed directly on the largest of the white-walled houses around the square. Its shuttered windows and wooden door were spat out at the end of tongues of orange flame as the tiles and timber of its roof were hurled skywards in a mushroom of fire and smoke.

The panic-stricken inhabitants began to spew from their homes into the freezing night. Some were half-dressed; mothers clutched tiny children to their breasts; men pathetically attempted to shield their women and loved ones by covering them with their own bodies from the missiles that bore down on them. Shrieks of fear and agonizing pain filled the air that only minutes earlier had been so silent. As suddenly as they had started, the mortars stopped. It had taken only a minute for the fifteen bombs to fall. Then the soldiers had come . . .

*   *   *

The first rays of bright winter sunlight were starting to focus on Velika Kupa. Virgin snow now lay thick on the ground, shrouding gruesome clues to the savagery of a few hours earlier. Two dark figures in green combat fatigues and woollen hats emerged cautiously from the undergrowth that surrounded the outskirts of the village. Bent low, they ducked behind a stone wall which had once been used by a farmer to pen goats, hugging the ragged rocks for protection. A fine haze of smoke hung over the building, and the smell of burning wood, tinged with the sickly sweet odour of burning flesh, wafted through the crisp air.

Silently the two men scurried towards the adjoining cottage. Its front door swung lazily open, as if inviting them to enter. The taller of the two figures peered cautiously over the wall at the open door. He took off his huge backpack and rested it against the wall, then shot a sideways glance at the other crouching figure, who was nervously scratching his week-old stubble.

'Oh well, here bleedin' well goes . . .' sighed the tall man. With one fluid movement he sprang to his feet, vaulted the wall and dashed for the open doorway. He slammed himself against the house wall by the side of the door and waited to catch his breath.

In the eerie silence that gripped this spot, all he was aware of was the sound of his own heart slamming against his chest.

The fingers of his left hand groped forward; with his other hand he gripped the handle of the sub-machine gun that was slung around his neck. From the corner of his eye he was aware that, without being told, the other man had raised his own weapon above the rock of the wall to offer covering fire if needed. Gulping down an intake of breath, the figure by the doorway then lunged forward through the open gap and into the building. The split-second action as the figure charged through the doorway into the darkness within the building was greeted by what seemed an eternity of silence.

Once inside he instinctively sank to one knee, offering a smaller target to any would-be attacker. The dying embers of the log fire in the corner of the room still glowed defiantly. Through the sharp shaft of daylight that came through the open doorway, the crouching figure spotted a half-burnt candle and metal tray on the floor. He rummaged through the pockets of his combat jacket, pulled out a scratched lighter and lit the candle. The light from its flame created a sinister glow which revealed a scene of violent struggle. A solid farmhouse table lay on its side, the accompanying chairs smashed to pieces. Pots and pans were strewn around the floor, and the few meagre possessions that had been stored in a battered sideboard now lay scattered around the room. In an adjoining room, the mattress of a simple wooden bed had been ripped to shreds and the mirror of an aged dressing table had been smashed. There was no sign of life.

The figure turned to leave the building and signalled to his companion. Together the men edged their way to the outer corner of the building, to a narrow path which led to the centre of the village. Just twenty feet along the path they came to an abrupt halt as they reached the entrance to what had been the square. Smoke still billowed from the charred windows of the simple stone-built houses. The remains of various wooden buildings were but smouldering skeletons. As the two men stepped into the square they were greeted with a sight which would haunt them for the rest of their lives. To each tree was tied one of the male villagers, with his hands bound behind him around the trunk. Then each had had a crude rope garotte placed around his neck and the trunk of the tree. The rope had slowly been tightened, gradually strangling the victim until his eyes had bulged, his tongue protruded from his mouth and his entire face was distorted like some ghastly, gruesome caricature. Finally his neck had snapped, bringing the blessed release of death. The grisly faces of the dead men seemed to stare at the two silent figures who stood in the centre of the square, their eyes following them as they began to walk towards the remnants of some of the gutted buildings.

As they stumbled through the snow, the smaller of the two stopped suddenly and glanced into the open doorway of a building they assumed to have been a small store. He stiffened as he looked down and saw the body of a woman shot through the head. Her eyes were still open, staring blindly upwards, her face frozen in an expression of terror and bewilderment. Elsewhere the scenes of carnage were identical. The corpses of women lay like bundles of rags in the middle of the road, now half covered in snow. Some were still half-naked from their abrupt awakening when the bombs had started to fall. Those who had survived the bombs had been unable to survive the soldiers who followed.

The two men walked in silence, their weapons lowered as if in recognition that now only the dead inhabited this place. There was no living threat to them.

A narrow alleyway led from the square to where an opening had been cleared in the dense line of trees. In the middle of the opening stood the only building that still had its roof intact. Above the corrugated iron archway attached to its facade stood a stone belltower. The tall man walked slowly towards the building. He pulled off his woollen hat, oblivious now to the freezing temperatures of the mountains. Guessing that the building might have been a school he stepped forward gingerly, steeling himself for the horrors he feared he might find inside. Nervously he placed his weight against the huge double doors, which slowly creaked open.

The single whitewashed room behind the doors was illuminated by the sunlight that shone through the two leaded windows on either side. At the far end stood a solid oak table strewn with papers. By its side stood a blackboard. This was certainly the schoolhouse. And it was the place where the soldiers had given their own lesson in mindless barbarity.

For Sergeant Jim Scala, it was an image he knew he would

carry to his own grave. He had been trained in death, surrounded by it for the last thirteen years, ever since he had chosen a life of action and adventure and violence; ever since he had opted to give himself to the regiment. He had walked with death all round the globe, from the deserts of Iraq to the green fields of South Armagh. But never had he gazed upon a sight such as this.

The Serbian soldiers who had come to this village had known no compassion. The adults had paid the price for being born Muslim. And then it had been the turn of the children. Wide-eyed with terror, screaming and crying, they had been systematically rounded up and dragged helplessly from the desperate grasp of their mothers to the schoolhouse. Before that night it had been a place where they had learned together, where they had laughed and played the innocent pranks that children play on each other.

But that night the air had been filled with screams as they were herded into the single room with its rows of wooden benches. The Serb soldiers had gone about their work efficiently. Three of them had rolled the grenades along the wooden floor towards the huddled children and slammed the doors shut. The men had quickly taken shelter and waited for the explosions. Then they had pushed open the doors and sprayed bullets from their automatic weapons into the thick smoke that belched from the room. They had continued firing until the crying stopped and there was silence. A whimper emerged from the darkness, a single shot rang out – and there was silence again.

Scala had seen violent death in all its brutal forms and believed himself to be immune to it by now. But this was truly different. He could not fight back the tears that welled in his eyes as he surveyed the carnage, the pitiful sight of the tiny smashed bodies flung around the room like grotesque broken dolls, many without limbs. Some had been mere babies snatched from their mothers' arms in the mindless savagery that had gripped this village. He took one step further into the nightmarish room, glanced into the corner and startled himself as he caught sight of the face of a small girl, her corpse propped against the bloodied wall. Her deep, dark eyes seemed to stare directly into his, her features strangely peaceful in this ghoulish scene. As he stared, his mind conjured up an image of his own daughter, Gemma. They were both about the same age; four or five years old, he reckoned. They even looked similar. He thought of Gemma playing peacefully in their garden back in Hereford, worlds away from this godless place.

Then his son Sean sprang to his mind. Two years older, he would be at school now, thinking about the Christmas that would soon be upon them, dreaming of toys and happiness. Scala looked around the room and wondered if these children had enjoyed similar dreams . . . He counted twenty-three bodies, but it was almost impossible to say if that was a true figure – such had been the violence and hatred that had ended their short lives.

'Oh, Jesus fuckin' Christ!' came a voice from behind as his partner, Corporal Peter Kearns from Manchester, entered the doorway. 'Not the fuckin' kids as well!' he whispered. 'And these bastard do-gooding politicians reckon there's no such thing as "ethnic cleansing" in Bosnia. They should get off their arses and come and see this fuckin' lot. This would teach them about "ethnic cleansing". Where's the fuckin' TV cameras when you really want 'em? I tell you, Jim, you've got to be a really sick bastard to do summat like this. The grown-ups are one thing, but to take it out on the little 'uns as well is really bleedin' sick! What the hell did they ever do except get themselves born? What the fuck did they know about soddin' Serbs and Muslims and all this shit?'

Scala had difficulty finding his voice. Still haunted by the visions of his own children, he could only nod his head in agreement. Finally he shook these images from his thoughts, and forced himself to return to the reality of his surroundings.

'Did you find anyone alive?' he grunted to Kearns.

'No, mate, not a bleedin' one. They really turned the place over good and proper,' he replied. 'Do you think they're the same bastards that we're lookin' for?'

'Could be – I wouldn't be at all surprised. They could simply have come across this lot while pushing up towards Donji Vakuf. I can't see any real strategic importance for this place, so I reckon they just got unlucky. They were Muslims who got in the way of these Serbs – simple as that. I tell you, Pete, I've seen some things in my time, but this thing with the kids has got to me. I know they hate each other's guts and all that, but to do that to kids is something else. They don't care about the bloody politics of it all – these bastards really *like* what they do!'

The two men left the schoolhouse and greedily breathed in the clear air. It was starting to snow again.

'What are we going to do, Jimbo?' asked Kearns. 'Are we going to bury them?'

Scala glanced behind him to take a last look at the horror of the schoolhouse. 'Nope! We can't afford the time. Just record it and radio it in when we get to our next stopping point. The lot at base will probably call up the UNHCR or something. Let them sort it out. But remember what you saw here, Pete. I know I will, for a bloody long time . . . Now let's push on.'

There had been 147 people living in Velika Kupa before the soldiers came. Scala and Kearns counted 131 bodies the day after the soldiers left. No one knew what had happened to the others. Perhaps they had escaped into the night. Or maybe they too had been caught and butchered and left among the undergrowth and trees that covered the mountain slopes. Perhaps no one would ever know what became of them.

Scala and Kearns gathered up their belongings. Kearns winced under the weight of his radio set and slung his rifle over his shoulder. The pair passed to the edge of the village and found a track, marked on their map, which would take them high into the mountainous area where they would carry out the reconnaissance task they had been sent here to undertake. They trudged on in silence, leaving Velika Kupa behind. To the outside world, it was a name that would probably never be heard of. To the two men, it was a place they would never forget.

*   *   *

The first traces of dusk were already starting to appear in the sky when Scala and Kearns next stopped. It had been a hard march. Both were breathing heavily as a result of their exertions at this unaccustomed altitude. They had hauled themselves up the steep, narrow mountain trail for the last four hours. It had felt like longer. Even after this time they had barely covered three miles, but their efforts had got them to the high mountain path that traversed the almost sheer sides of the range. From here on, it should be easier to stalk their quarry.

The pair had been in the field for six days since leaving base at Travnik. Their task was, on the face of it, simple. They were to be the eyes of the NATO pilots who were attempting to seek out the positions of the Serbian heavy guns that were now pounding the central Bosnian town of Donji Vakuf. If won, this strategic prize would present the Serbs with a good road running from the Adriatic to important towns in the hinterland such as Zenica and Travnik itself. The casualty figures were already high but the Bosnians were virtually powerless to respond, for their artillery was no match for that of the well-armed Serb forces. The Serbian troops could in fact have taken Donji Vakuf whenever they had wanted. But local UN officials were still stubbornly attempting to halt the advance with proposals to protect the civilian population. Meanwhile the Serb guns, hidden deep in the hills to the north of the town, continued to ignore this war of words.

The British peacekeeping force in the region was becoming increasingly desperate. Their attempts to negotiate between the two sides had failed, and they were now taking casualties themselves from the big guns. The Serbs had ignored UN pleas not to use their heaviest weapons – they were winning, after all. Now, as a protective measure, the undercover and behind-the-lines experts of the legendary SAS in the persons of Scala and Kearns had been drafted in to seek out those guns and relay their positions back to base for possible retaliation by air strikes.

For the two veteran soldiers, the task had seemed simple enough. But the reality was harder than they could have imagined. The Serbs were masters at disguising the location of their precious armour. And if the UN forces were lucky enough to track them down the weapons were often spirited away before any air strike could be called up.

Scala now appreciated the impossible task that the German troops had faced during World War II, when they waged a constant losing battle against Tito's guerrilla army. How could they kill them if they couldn't even find them? Seeking out the

Iraqi Scud missile sites in the vast wastes of the desert during the Gulf War had been comparatively easy compared with this place. But this time Scala and Kearns felt they were close to making contact. The massacre in the village proved that Serbian troops were operating in the area.

Now they had reached the top of the heights they stood a vastly improved chance of discovering the hidden Serbs. To Scala they were the 'enemy', despite the UN's complicated role as 'peacekeepers'. The Serbs were undoubtedly the 'bad guys': he had seen enough suffering in Bosnia to know that.

Neither Kearns nor Scala had spoken much during their four-hour trek. There had been no need to – they each knew the routine. Both had been lost in their own thoughts as they trudged silently up the slippery track. Scala still found it difficult to dodge the images of the schoolhouse that regularly flashed across his mind. In the discussion that he was having with himself in his own mind he was amazed to find that he was actually starting to feel the same way as his wife. Angie could be right, he thought. Maybe it was time to get out and have some kind of proper life. But what? He knew she was disenchanted with the army and the knowledge that her only prospect in life was that of being a soldier's wife – probably waiting for him to come home in a body bag. The arguments for and against had rolled around in his head throughout the march.

As he and Kearns huddled at the base of one of the tall pine trees that covered the slopes Scala pulled down his headover – a tube of thermal knitted material that could be worn around the neck or as a balaclava – against the biting cold. Each broke open one of his twenty-four-hour ration packs, known as 'rat packs', and began to eat. They would rest near the top here for half an hour before pressing on.

'I wonder how the lads got on this afternoon?' pondered Kearns, a soccer fanatic since first being taken to see Manchester United as a boy. 'Should have been easy for 'em – they were playing Sheffield Wednesday. But you can never tell with that bloody lot.' He shook his head.

Scala reflected. Of course, it was Saturday. He'd forgotten. Elsewhere in the world dads were taking their youngsters to football matches, or maybe having a few pints before watching

Match of the Day. And there he was, stuck up some mountain in the arsehole of Europe.

'What team is young 'un going to foller?' enquired Kearns in the hope of kindling some form of conversation.

'Dunno yet. He's a bit young to make up his mind – can't see it being Hereford, though!' grinned Scala.

Suddenly the pair became conscious of a shift in the wind direction. It had been behind them as they clambered along the path, and now it had changed. A slight breeze was blowing straight into their faces. With it came an unexpected smell of smoke. Not just ordinary smoke. There was also a slight but distinct smell of cooking in the air. Someone not too far away, perhaps just over the rise, was using a cooking fire. The two men stiffened. They stood up and adjusted their equipment before Scala silently motioned to Kearns to follow him further along the track that led to the ridge some thirty yards ahead.

At the end of the path they stopped. The snow on the ridge was deep, but the whiteness of the covering provided additional light as the two men peered into the distance. The smell of smoke was stronger now. A few more paces further they crouched low, hiding behind a fallen tree trunk and listening intently for the slightest sound.

At first they imagined the voices. But as they strained their ears the sounds became more audible. They were Serb voices well enough – and a lot of them, too. Gradually Scala and Kearns worked their way down the slope on the far side of the ridge. The slope led down to a deep valley where a fast-running stream cut through the landscape. Through the dense forest that shrouded the hillside the pair could see the glow of firelight against the darkening background. They half slithered, half scurried through the snow to fresh positions in the undergrowth less than two hundred yards from the commotion ahead.

In the faint light they saw a jagged lip of rock jutting from the hillside some twenty yards away. From there they would have a perfect view of the proceedings below. Scala led the way, scampering across the untouched snow; the short, stocky figure of Kearns followed a split second behind. The two lay belly down on the rock, looking down the slope towards the base of the valley. Scala scanned the area in front with his

H80 laser rangefinder, flicking to night vision to obtain a clearer view.

'Look at those bastards!' muttered Scala, passing the glasses to Kearns. 'No wonder our blokes had a job to find this little lot, hidden among this woodwork.'

Kearns took the glasses and blew a low whistle. They had found what they had come for. In front of them lay more than twenty heavy artillery pieces of mixed calibre. There were the same number of tanks. They were accompanied by what Scala estimated to be five hundred infantrymen, all clad in the rag-tag uniforms of the Bosnian Serb army, plus a battery of 120mm mortars and a string of support vehicles.

The Serbs must have used the single-track road which snaked up the hillside from the north-east to sneak the armour towards Donji Vakuf, hugging the tree-line to avoid detection. Safe in the belief that no one for miles knew of their existence the gunners had prepared the emplacements for the artillery, which could now shower down shells directly on to the town. To the two SAS men it was obvious that the guns had been in place for the last three or four days, hidden from the outside world. It crossed Scala's mind that the people of Velika Kupa had probably been eliminated for the sake of the Serbs' anonymity.

'Got the bastards!' whispered Scala. 'Look at 'em sitting around, drinking cups of coffee and getting ready to knock three colours of shit out of some other unsuspecting poor bugger. I'll bet you a month's bloody wages that they were the bastards that knocked off that village.'

'How do you know that? You can't know that for certain,' snapped Kearns. 'What we do know is that there's some good news and some bad news. The good news is that we've found this little lot. But now let me remind you of the bad news. Firstly, those guns are surrounded by a whole lot of infantry. Now I don't care how clever these so-called "smart bombs" are today – they can't tell the difference between artillery and infantry. Everything is just too close together down there. And you know that our winged heroes up there are not supposed to go blitzing some bloody foot-slogger. We're only supposed to knock off 'eavy stuff. The other bad news is that the Flying Tigers are still going to find it hard to sight their targets amongst all these trees, even after we've given them the right coordinates. It's just too dense down there. In order to make sure that our lads were bang-smack on target you and me would virtually have to be sitting amongst the enemy in order to direct 'em – and pardon me, but I still want to be around to see if United make it to Wembley this year!'

'Listen,' said Scala, 'let's just assume that these were the bastards that wiped out that village. Don't you think they deserve to have a taste of their own shit? If we don't give the air strike boys all the help we can, most of those sods are going to get away again. Okay, I know we'd have to sit a bit close, but we've been in tight places before and there's a lot of protection here, isn't there? And who bloody cares if some of their infantry happen to go sky-high with their guns? I bloody well don't. And I'm sure those poor little kids in the schoolhouse won't be too bothered either!'

Kearns glared at Scala. 'Oh yeah! That's right, start pulling me bleedin' heartstrings again! I know they deserve it, but we've got orders . . .'

He did not get a chance to finish his sentence before Scala turned on him. 'All right, then. If it's an order you want don't forget I'm in charge here, and while I'm still a sergeant and you're a corporal I'm telling you what we're going to do.' He glared at Kearns. 'If there's any shit to be taken over this, then okay, I'll take it – when we get back. Until then, you do what I say. If we play our cards right I don't think we'll be compromised here. I'm saying that we're going to whistle up the fly boys and take this lot out, infantry or no infantry. Now get on the blower and tell base where we are, and that we plan to direct the strike from as near as possible.'

Kearns slammed his fist on the rock. 'Oh, great! My bloody 'ero – all we 'ave to do is to get the old Dam Busters lot up there to come in and drop bombs right down our own throat. I tell you, sarge, if I survive this little trip I will definitely *not* be inviting you to my bloody box at Old Trafford!'

Scala, ignoring the jibe, turned and looked down at the Serbian positions. He could make out groups of gunners sitting around a smoking fire, sipping from tin mugs. They were talking and laughing with other soldiers who had AK-47 assault weapons slung around their backs – storm troops by the look of them. He wondered if they had laughed when they had dropped the bombs on the village, or when they had tossed the grenades among the terrified children trapped in the schoolhouse. Once again in his mind he saw the faces of his own children . . . then he returned to reality as he heard Kearns speaking quietly and clearly over the radio to base, giving precise coordinates for an air strike.

'Don't worry,' muttered Kearns into the handset, 'we'll be here to see them in on target . . . we don't seem to be going anywhere,' he added in a resigned tone.

The attack, led by American bombers stationed in Italy, would come at first light once the details of the strike had been worked out. All Scala and Kearns could do now was watch and wait: they shuffled further round the outcrop of rock to a better vantage point. Kearns figured that they must be only about one hundred and fifty yards from the first gun positions – too close for comfort to his mind.

After watching the bulk of the Serb force bed down for the night, Scala snatched an hour's sleep. He awoke in the early hours to allow Kearns a spell of sleep, but Kearns found it impossible even to close his eyes. In just a few short hours the jets would come screeching in, delivering their parcels of flame and destruction – right next to him! The hours seemed endless until the first glow of dawn reached over the mountains. It would be a clear, bright day. But the streaks of sunlight were having to battle their way through the dense forest on the slopes. Under the trees, it was still to all intent and purpose dark.

Just minutes after the first rays of sunshine showed themselves above the ridges, Kearns' radio crackled into life. An American voice with a Southern accent blurted news of his imminent arrival.

'Hawkeye to Delta 30. Are you receiving?' boomed the voice. 'Hawkeye to –'

'Yes, yes, Hawkeye! Delta 30 receiving you loud and clear,' Kearns snapped back. 'I should think everybody within twenty bloody miles can hear,' he muttered to himself.

'Hawkeye to Delta 30, please identify the target and provide coordinates. Please acknowledge! Delta 30, we're ready to commence attack.'

Scala had written down the exact coordinates for attack and passed them to Kearns, who relayed the numbers and references to the aircraft which were still several miles away.

'Now please, Hawkeye, if you could just let the gentlemen down in the valley have their Christmas presents early,' said Kearns, grinning. 'Then we can all go home.'

The Serbian camp was just stirring into life when the first of the jets flew over the slopes. The soldiers stared at the sky, trying to catch glimpses of the flashes as they passed overhead. At first the two F-15s and two F-18s merely flew over the positions to familiarize themselves with the terrain. A minute later, while the troops on the ground were still stretching into life and rubbing their sleepy eyes, the first F-15 struck. The two 1,000lb laser control cluster bombs streaked through the trees to land some two hundred yards to the right of where Scala and Kearns lay concealed on their ledge. The two men could feel the heat and fiery wind of the explosion as the missiles struck two tanks on the outskirts of the position. The tanks erupted in a volcano of fire and smoke, their crews burnt alive as they sheltered beneath them.

Kearns gave corrective coordinates to the pilot leader above, in the hope that the next attack could be directed more at the artillery that lay deep in their camouflaged gun pits. The correction worked. The bombs from the next F-15 tore through the centre of the positions and exploded in balls of orange and yellow flame to shatter two of the M-1983 rocket lauchers into hundreds of pieces.

The two F-18s met with similar success, to be followed seconds later by the two F-15s beginning their second run. Each rocket and each bomb brought fresh devastation: guns and tanks were reduced to twisted scalding metal, while the men who operated them died by their sides. Each time the jets came the attack seemed to grow more ferocious. Scala grinned as he saw two bombs land in the midst of the biggest concentration of troops, where he had seen them laughing and joking the night before. Engrossed in the hellish scene unfolding before him he was oblivious of the fact that the explosions were creeping their way towards their own position and the missiles were now falling perilously close.

'That's it, Kearnsy, you're off,' said his partner as he hurriedly gathered up his radio and weapon in preparation for a life-saving dash from the ledge up the hillside. Scala, startled by Kearns' sudden movements, spun round and agreed. They had done their bit.

The F-18 had circled to begin its final run over the target. The pilot could see the plumes of smoke rising from the ground and had watched the explosions tear the heart out of the green carpet of trees beneath. He was certain that they had been successful this morning. Just one more run and that would be it; then back home for breakfast. He would concentrate this last attack on the far edge of the target, because it looked like his buddies had already ripped the heart out of the remainder. Just two more bombs to go . . .

Scala and Kearns were already on their feet and running when the first bomb exploded. It had overshot the target by a hundred yards and landed fifty feet behind them. The blast lifted them both and threw them to the ground like discarded toy soldiers.

Immediately they began to raise themselves again, ready to make that final dash up the slope away from the death and destruction that they had brought down on the Serbian gunners behind them. Kearns rose just before Scala – just before the second bomb crashed into the trees by his right side. The blast tossed him thirty feet into the air, spinning his body round in mid-air cartwheels. Scala, who had just started to lift himself, had been mostly shielded from the blast by his partner's body. But he could still feel himself being scorched by the searing heat from the bomb and the excruciating agony of the the pain from his twisted and bleeding legs. The world was spinning in Scala's mind. He lay helpless, thrown against the side of a shattered tree, the taste of blood in his mouth. He shot a sideways glance and glimpsed the torn body of Kearns spread-eagled on the hillside twenty feet in front of him, his side sliced open and his right leg blown away. The noise of death and his own pain whirled around in Scala's head. Then there was only blackness.

Chapter Two

Jacobson stepped into the lift and pressed the button for the fifteenth floor. He turned and caught a glimpse of himself in the full-length mirror behind him. Stroking his dark wavy hair down with his gloved hand, he adjusted his blue and white spotted tie as if preparing for parade. As he stared in the mirror, he looked for any increasing signs of his forty-six years. Seconds later, the lift shuddered to a halt and he stepped out into a long, featureless white corridor where the smell of the new blue carpet, freshly laid, still clung to the air.

He walked quickly to his left, unbuttoning his navy blue cashmere overcoat as he walked. To his right the plain white walls gave way to a series of individual offices. Some of the doors were open and Jacobson glanced into the occasional one to nod and utter a cheery 'Good morning' to the occupants.

As he strode along the corridor he silently mused over how bland and boring the building was. He hated coming here. Travelling south of the river never really agreed with him – he much preferred the familiar surroundings of his own office near Victoria. At least one could enjoy a civilized working environment there, a stone's throw from Westminster, Whitehall or even the Palace. And there was never any shortage of places to lunch. But life south of the river was a different ball game. Here, you were lucky if you could find a decent pub. The decision to fragment the operations units had been taken at a much higher level than his own, and he acknowledged that there was some merit in not putting all one's eggs in one basket. But the idea of having one of his prime intelligence units based on the fifteenth floor of one of these god-forsaken new office blocks in London's Docklands still infuriated him, even though he knew that few people were likely to question the goings-on of a nondescript 'security firm' here.

He stopped at the door marked 'D. Matherson' and gave a

gentle rap on the wood before opening it and entering the tiny reception area, where a smiling brunette in a crisp white blouse beamed at him from the far side of a desk.

'Good morning, sir! Please come straight through. Colonel Matherson is expecting you.' She took Jacobson's coat, then opened an adjoining door into a spacious, newly furnished office.

A short, fair-haired man in a smart charcoal-grey suit walked across to greet his visitor.

'Morning, David. Good to see you again. Sorry for pouncing on you like this!' said Jacobson, placing his briefcase on the desk.

'Not at all, sir! Always good to see you. It's nice to know that we're not forgotten over here anyway,' smiled the smaller man as he brushed his thin moustache, a relic of his army service days.

Jacobson put his hands in his trouser pockets and strolled over to the huge window which offered an uninterrupted view of the giant Canary Wharf complex opposite. He looked up at the flashing light on the roof which acted as a beacon and dominated the London skyline. Small puffs of white cloud sailed over the tower on this bright, clear December day.

'I think we've got a job that's just about up your street, David.' Jacobson turned and looked his Special Director of Covert Operations straight in the eyes. 'But it's going to be bloody tricky. We think we've got a problem with the Micks again.'

Matherson looked up as if to speak, but Jacobson continued. 'I know, just when you think everything has gone quiet off they go again. But we've had reports that maybe someone else is stirring them up this time, for whatever bloody reason. There's a possibility that a recent string of incidents over the water might be linked. On the face of it, they look like the usual kind of sectarian killing jobs. But neither side is owning up. The PM's worried that the whole thing could blow up again, even after all this time. I know we all reckon that each day the ceasefire lasts it gets harder for either side to break. The truth is, there are already rumblings. Both sides have had people killed. The Army Council are putting pressure on Sinn Fein to come up with something, and the UVF are just itching to have another pop. They've got some real mad dogs in their ranks, as we know. At the moment the Unionists and Sinn Fein are keeping their troublemakers under control – but it's bloody shaky.'

Matherson listened intently as Jacobson filled him in on the series of incidents, including the background to the Chinook crash a week earlier.

'To sum up, it looks as though we might have a loose cannon wandering around,' said Jacobson grimly. 'And I've been told to look into it. That's why I'm here.

'By all accounts he could be an old soldier. So I need you to find me someone who can get into the mind of this bastard, someone who can track him and deal with him before the whole province starts kicking the hell out of each other again. We need our own wild card in there. If this guy *is* a soldier I want to set a thief to catch a thief, so to speak. It'll be too bad if he doesn't make it back – we'll just put that down to experience.' Jacobson threw down on to Matherson's desk a file detailing the situation.

'Study it, David. Come to me in three days with a list of candidates and some kind of scheme. And we can't afford to go public on this one – it would be far too embarrassing if the press found out that a one-time "good guy" had gone off his bloody head and was about to bollocks things up. I want you and you alone to run our guy. Keep us out of it. No one else will know anything about him.'

The briefing was over. Matherson had begun the process of accumulating the files on possible candidates before Jacobson had even stepped out of the lift on the ground floor.

* * *

The room had certainly seen better days, she thought. Over the years an army of impatient children had defied their mothers and had continued to draw bizarre cartoon figures and one-dimensional houses on the bare blue walls. Served them right for offering up giant drawing boards for walls, she thought. She wondered how her own two children were. They were probably driving her mother to distraction. Still, it was only for the one night.

She was suddenly aware of being alone in the room. Everyone else who had sat patiently sifting through the pile of aged magazines for the last hour had since left. Strangely, she was now conscious of the heavy sound of her own heart pumping louder. How many times had she waited like this? Alone, terrified, steeling herself for someone to tell her that her man was about to die or would be crippled for life.

She looked at her hands and considered how old and dry they looked for a woman of twenty-nine. They were old maid's hands. She was growing old, and hardly graciously – simply spending her life waiting and hoping.

Throwing down the torn and crumpled woman's magazine with its cover picture of a smiling soap star, she stared out through the full-length glass windows that made up the wall to the waiting room. The flow of people passing by included nurses, people in white coats and the occasional figure in uniform; few paid her any attention.

It was well past lunch, and over seven hours since she had received the call from the base to say that her husband was being treated at this hospital and was now able to have visitors. It had been the first call in six weeks.

An hour later she had been on the road, passing by Ross-on-Wye, heading through Oxfordshire and then along the M40 towards London. Three hours later after leaving Hereford she had arrived at the Royal Military Hospital in Woolwich. She had been asked to wait, and that was precisely all she had done. But it had been a good time to think – to think about all the arguments that had gone on between them. She was sure he loved her, but she had told him that there could be no future for them if things remained as they were. Yet she was still here, waiting like the faithful puppy dog she feared she was becoming. This was it. She would tell him it was over.

The glass door to the waiting room suddenly sprang open, abruptly cutting into her thoughts. A uniformed officer with the pips that told her he was a captain held out his hand in greeting.

'Mrs Scala, I do apologise for the fact that you've been kept here, but no one told me you had actually arrived. Still, these things do happen, as I'm sure you appreciate,' said the young officer, wearing a practised smile. 'I'm Captain Young. I've been dealing with your husband. I'm not certain what you've been told about the extent of his – '

'I've been told nothing,' she interrupted. 'I'm assuming that it must be something quite bad, though, if he's in here.' Her small figure almost bristled with indignation – an act to hide her personal fears. But the weeks of pent-up emotion were now beginning to take their toll, and she was fighting back in her own way.

The captain flushed with embarrassment, realizing the ignorance in which Angela Scala had been kept. 'Well, I can tell you that we've been treating him for the last three weeks or so. He was transported here from Sarajevo, where I think you know he's been working . . .' The officer looked directly into the dark brown eyes of the woman in front of him.

She nodded. She knew he had been in Bosnia, but that was where her knowledge ended.

'There was an incident,' he continued. 'I don't know if you read the newspapers, but . . .' He considered telling her more about the 'incident', but decided not to. 'Well, whilst on a mission, Sergeant Scala was injured – severe leg injuries actually, which was the reason that he was sent to us here.' The self-assurance on his face faded when he saw the stern look on her face.

'What kind of injuries?' she demanded.

Captain Young consulted his notes. 'He received severe injuries to both the tibia and the fibula where it enters into the ankle joint – in fact it was shattered. We've been able to rebuild most of the damage, and have pinned most of the area together, but I'm afraid – '

Angela Scala virtually leaped at the young doctor. 'So you're telling me he's crippled?' she blurted.

'No! Absolutely not!' the startled captain retorted. 'He's far from being a cripple. But there are problems which we feel Sergeant Scala may have difficulty coming to terms with.'

'What problems?' demanded Angela.

'Well, without beating about the bush, we feel that they may be psychological, because . . . well, you see we believe that there is no way that Sergeant Scala will be able to continue serving with his regiment. He may be physically strong, but his leg and ankle joints will never achieve the high level of physical strength that his special duties are bound to demand. I'm afraid we and the powers that be have had to recommend that your husband be transferred from the regiment. That's why we've asked you to come here. Sergeant Scala knows the score, and I'm afraid he hasn't taken the news too well. We had hoped that you might be able – '

Before the flustered young officer could complete his embarrassed summing up she shook his hand and thanked him profusely, unable to hide the broad grin that had spread across her face. The doctor, both startled and relieved, quickly gave her directions to the small ward along the corridor where her husband was.

Fighting to regain her composure, Angela Scala almost sprinted down the corridor. It was as if an invisible weight had been lifted from her heart. He was to leave the regiment behind. He was to be free of his mistress – the mistress that for years had dominated their lives and left nothing for a loyal wife or children; the mistress that had robbed them of a normal married life and had so often almost taken him from her completely. Now, at last, she was getting her man back!

* * *

The three other beds in the side ward were empty. Only the one farthest from the door, next to the window, was occupied. Jim Scala sat propped against three huge pillows, attempting to read one of the stack of paperback novels on his bedside cabinet. He turned the pages, but the words that he scanned failed to register in his brain. His thoughts were elsewhere. The memory banks of his mind flashed into his brain a random string of recollections from previous years. They varied from images of his children, his parents and his own childhood on the grim working-class estates of Merthyr Tydfil to a flashback of a bloody life-or-death firefight somewhere in Iraq or on one of the numerous other battlefields that had been his life since joining the army. Then he had thought of Angie, of their life together and the possibilities for their future.

He had had plenty of time to contemplate his life since being brought to Woolwich three weeks earlier. He looked down to the end of the bed and gazed at the steel frame that gripped the end of his leg, holding the shattered pieces of bone and muscle together. He stroked his hand over the dressing on the right side of his face which ran from the corner of his eye a full six inches down his cheek – the effect of a searing piece of shrapnel from the bomb that had killed his mate Peter Kearns. Jim Scala knew he had been lucky. An inch higher and he would have been blinded for life, or even killed. All he would now have to contend with was going through life with a scarred right cheek. For three weeks he had carefully monitored his ankle: at first, after the surgeons had planted the network of steel pins into the bones to join the limb together, the wound had been left open to encourage healing then it had developed a hideous swelling that had made his foot resemble a grotesque balloon. But now, from the outside at least, the ankle and foot looked decidedly more normal – except of the scaffolding that still gripped the end of his leg.

A sudden movement in the doorway attracted his attention. Turning his head sharply to the left – so hard that it brought a stabbing pain to the injured right side of his face – he levelled his eyes on the figure of Angie hurrying through the door towards him. Her face was flushed, but her long dark hair was swept back behind her head to reveal her full beaming smile.

Scala momentarily studied her as she walked to his bedside, surveying the contours of her small, slim figure in the tight-fitting green skirt and white silk shirt. It had been over two months since he had last set eyes on her, during which time the image of her body had often been blotted out by the horrors that he had witnessed. God, she looks good, he thought. He could not disguise the smile that erupted across his face. He wanted to touch her and feel her against him again.

Without looking at the wound on his face or even glancing at the injured leg, Angie gently held out her hands and took his head in her arms to cradle her man. They kissed. There was a lot to talk about, but she felt they had all the time in the world. She pulled up a chair and sat looking into his blue eyes. She had forgotten what power those eyes held over her. They appeared to burn deep into her own soul. Once they were fixed upon her, she felt almost powerless to deny this man anything he wanted. It had been like this ever since they had first met ten years earlier.

At first, despite the intimacy of their years of marriage, they could only speak in the small talk of long-lost friends as they explored areas of mutual ground.

Jim asked about the children. How had they spent Christmas? Had she heard from his parents? Angie asked if he was suffering much pain. How were the hospital staff treating him? Had he always been in the ward on his own? They chatted for half an hour in this way, like a boy and girl on their first date; neither raised the topic of how he had been injured. Then the small talk was exhausted and a sudden silence fell. Angie broached the subject at last.

'So what happened? Can you tell me? How did you get hurt? . . . Was it bad? . . . I mean . . . if you can't talk about it, then I'll understand,' she spluttered, her smile leaving her lips.

Scala glared at her. Oh Christ! She really doesn't know. No one's told her yet! he thought. But surely she must have read the newspapers or seen the telly.

He considered for a while, then began a brief outline of the mission that he and Peter Kearns had embarked upon. Painfully he recalled the horror they had discovered at Velika Kupa; how they had set off to track the Serb troops; how they had discovered the guns; and his decision to call in the air strike, despite the fact that he and Kearns had been so close; how they had been found afterwards and brought out by a French UN patrol.

She shuffled in her seat as she listened. It was almost as if Scala had been waiting to unburden his pent-up memories of the incident on someone else.

'I made the decision to call the strike in on us,' he whispered. His bright eyes looked beyond her, unblinking, as he recalled the moment when Kearns was killed by 'friendly fire'. Still staring over her shoulder, he murmured: 'I suppose I more or less killed Kearnsy. If I hadn't been so bloody . . .' he searched for the word '. . . so bloody emotional . . . so bloody righteous . . . then Pete would still be alive and I wouldn't be here without a future. I suppose they told you about my injury and what it means? I mean, about leaving the regiment and all that. They reckon my leg will never be strong enough to jump out of a plane again.'

Angie nodded.

'The trouble was . . . after the bombing there was all hell to pay, because as well as taking out the Serb guns the planes also took out about a hundred infantry . . . I didn't tell the air boys that there were any infantry around. I didn't care – I wanted them dead.

'Anyway, there were dramas all over the place, because according to the rules of engagement over there we're not supposed to bomb infantrymen. The Serbs complained – they said that the United Nation forces were now openly siding with the Muslims. I called those planes in, Angie . . . it was me. I kept seeing that schoolhouse . . . so I took it upon myself to call in the bombers. I let my emotions get in the way of the mission.

'Because of all the shit that was flying, my boss and the UN over there decided that it would be better that I was shipped out with as little fuss as possible. They didn't want the press or TV getting to me. That's why you weren't told that I was here, in case you said anything and people put two and two together.'

Now at last Angie began to recollect the headlines of the recent weeks. Certainly she had read about the protests from the Bosnian Serb government over the killing of their soldiers. She had paid little attention, never thinking that her husband might have caused the furore. She gripped his hand to comfort him in his obvious torment.

Scala looked down at his ankle, then said, cynically, 'Anyway, it doesn't matter a toss any more, does it? They're kicking me out after ten years. It's all over. They reckon I could join another regiment or quit the army altogether. Just tossed out like that . . .'

Angie wanted to say, 'Thank God', and tell him how grateful she was that they now had a chance of a life together . . . of a proper marriage. But she resisted the temptation and clutched his hand even more tightly.

Suddenly Scala turned his attention to Angie, grinned and, in an exaggerated Welsh accent, went on: 'So, my luvverly, the quacks reckon that they can take the scaffolding off my foot tomorrow. They're going to strap me up, and they say I should be able to get up and about in a day or two on sticks. I should be okay to be let out next week, so it looks like you've got me all to yourself.'

For the first time in years Angela Scala felt a surge of hope enter her body. She had travelled to the hospital prepared to end their marriage, to end the years of torment. At the very last moment her patience had paid off and she had won a reprieve. Now, as a family, they could plan for the future.

* * *

The brilliant winter sunshine brought a deceptive air of spring as it glinted off the car roofs and brightened even this most dismal part of south Birmingham. It was mid-morning. Yet inside the grey, box-shaped building on the edge of the estate with its grim tower blocks it could have been the dead of night. There were no windows, and the only entrance to the Jubilee Club was by a thick door with a sliding window through which the overweight black doorman could check for unwanted visitors before opening the door.

Despite the early hour, the Jubilee was in full swing to its regular members. The air was already thick with cigarette smoke, whilst the ancient juke-box blasted out vintage tunes that had been hits some thirty years before. A waitress with peroxide hair and heavy make-up squeezed into a short, tight-fitting black skirt more suited to a woman twenty years younger, traded wisecracks punctuated with four-letter words with two men playing pool. She was used to being the target for suggestive remarks, and openly encouraged their interest. Her raucous laughter at one such suggestion was interrupted by the ring of the telephone behind the bar.

The burly barman quickly answered it and then addressed the room.

'Is there a Naylor here? Mick Naylor? Telephone!'

A tall, lean, dark-haired figure in jeans and black leather jacket looked up from the pint glass he was staring into and walked over to the bar.

'Naylor here,' he whispered into the mouthpiece.

The orders were succinct. He was to take the 3.30 p.m. flight from Birmingham to Belfast International. A ticket would be waiting for him at the British Airways desk as usual. He should rendezvous with the others at the farm later in the evening. The rest of the details would be waiting for him there.

He acknowledged, and the telephone went dead. It was always like this – a brief call to the club on the designated day. Each time the message was short and to the point, but it had worked like a charm so far. No messing about – that was what he liked.

Without waiting to finish his beer, Naylor left the club and blinked for a moment in the brilliant sunshine. He had plenty of time to pack a small bag and drive to the airport from his flat. By the end of the week, he mused, someone else would be dead . . .

Chapter Three

She had not noticed the car that trailed her as her long legs strode down the deserted rows of red-brick terrace houses, many with their windows bricked up, that grimly stood as testament to the heyday of Britain's Empire. The heels of her thigh-length boots had echoed along the streets that made up the religious frontier of West Belfast, off the Falls Road — streets that bore such glorified names as Lucknow Street, Bombay Street and Cawnpore Street. Nearby were the twenty-foot wall and floodlit No Man's Land that divided the Falls from the Loyalist Shankill Road. Her shadows had danced in the street lighting and her silhouette had been cast on to the stone walls of the Church of the Redeemer with its statues of Christ and the saints in Clonard Gardens as she walked past, glancing at the gable wall with its larger-than-life depiction of the Virgin that had been the handiwork of a street artist.

The drizzle had eased as she turned the corner into Kashmir Road, and she had tossed her long blonde hair in a carefree manner as she walked on, considering who would be at the club that night. If the tall, black-haired guy she knew as Tim made a play for her tonight, she had decided she wasn't going to play hard to get. As a teenager she had dreamed of a life as a model; a life that would take her away from the drudgery that she had always known in Belfast; a life where she could make something of herself, relying on the only assets she could rely on — her body and almost angelic face. But the opportunities had never materialized and the dreams of a sixteen-year-old girl had faded to the resignation of a twenty-three-year-old woman trapped in her existence. Yet maybe life held new prospects because of the peace.

The car had pulled up by her side as she headed towards the Springfield Road. Kicking her long legs and attempting to scream, she had been bundled into the back of the Ford Sierra by two men.

After a drive lasting no more than ten terrifying minutes the men had dragged her into the derelict house on the corner of Ceylon Street, the house that had stood empty and shuttered since the firebomb had driven the family away three years earlier. She had been tied to a chair, too petrified even to scream. Then she had heard the three men recite her name, Sheena Maguire; they called her a 'Catholic slut' and tore open her blue denim shirt to reveal the body that she had prized as her passport to a new life. They had accused her of betraying one of their own, a man whom she had been with a year before. She had shouted her innocence; they had laughed again. She had only met one man whom she had later discovered was an IRA man; she had driven a car for him once, five years ago, that was all. She hadn't known he was IRA then.

The girl had pleaded with the men; begged, even offered her body if only they didn't hurt her. They had laughed and slapped her. She had seen the tall, lean man with dark, short cropped hair standing in the corner nodding with approval as her tormentors went about their work. Her bulging, terror-stricken eyes had settled on him, pleading for pity, as they had tied the gag around her mouth. She tried again to scream to release the pain as they stubbed out burning cigarettes on her breasts.

She had endured the humiliation of feeling her own water spread through her pants and jeans in panic as her eyes focused on the lean man with cropped hair moving towards her with the hypodermic in his hands. The girl had winced with pain as the syringe with its deadly cocktail had been plunged uncaringly into her arm. Her body had shivered, stiffened and shaken uncontrollably, then fallen limp as her head fell forward, covering her breasts and exposed body with her long, tumbling hair.

Two boys had found Sheena Maguire's body two days later as they kicked a football on the wasteland where the Springfield Road crossed the Forth River. The body that Sheena Maguire had once hoped would lead to fame and fortune had been discarded like a butcher throws out bad meat, and left for display on top of a council rubbish skip. The sight of the open, shocked, staring eyes of the once pretty face, and the half-clothed body with the sign denoting 'Catholic Whore and Tout' tied to her neck, had sent the two lads scurrying home in tears and fright.

The police officers, so used to dealing with violent death in that tragic city, were shocked at the torture. The savagery stunned the Catholic and Protestant communities alike. Yet a full forty-eight hours after the discovery of the body no party or group had claimed responsibility.

At first the RUC detectives heading the hunt had believed that the brutal death of Sheena Maguire signified nothing more than a settling of old scores. She had paid with her life for an act of betrayal she might have carried out months before – months before the ceasefire had ended the kind of tit-for-tat murder that was so familiar in this land. The killing made the front page of the *Belfast Telegraph* and was the lead story on the local television news. Fear and outrage gripped the communities on both sides of the 'Peace Wall'. The feelings of hate and mistrust which had barely been hidden beneath the surface since the ceasefire began to stir again.

Puzzled detectives, anxious over the method of death, began to issue statements that gave rise to the belief that Sheena Maguire had been the victim of a drugs feud and that the killing was not politically motivated. Never before had terrorists used such methods to claim the lives of their victims. Drugs had always been a dirty word in both communities.

But these statements failed to stem the bitter war of words between Loyalists and Catholics that erupted again. The talk was of taking up arms once more, of seeking revenge for an innocent life taken, and of people being forced to defend themselves. The police investigation had stalled. If this was another killing in a renewed war, it was a war that was using weapons so far unseen in this city of tragedy. But Sheena Maguire was not to be the last.

* * *

It took a lot to persuade David Matherson to leave the familiar surroundings of his office. It had to be something special, but he had decided that this was just such an occasion. This one would require the personal touch. He had set off for Hereford the afternoon before and had stayed the night at a comfortable country hotel at nearby Ledbury. There would be no point in surprising the man in the dead of night. It would take less than an hour to complete his journey to Hereford the following morning, and he would have had the benefit of a good respectable dinner, a reasonable bottle of wine and a good night's sleep under his belt. That was the civilized way to do it, he told himself.

It had not taken long for Matherson to be cleared by security on arrival at SAS headquarters, and to check with the commanding officer. Matherson told him only the minimum he was required to know: that he, Matherson, had been instructed by Whitehall to oversee this release and ensure that it happened as quickly and with as little fuss as possible considering the circumstances. In return, the visitor was given directions to the house in the married quarters where he would find his man.

Matherson's Rover pulled up outside the block. As he sat behind the steering wheel gathering his thoughts he caught sight of a figure dressed in a blue tracksuit playing with two children in the back garden. The man leaned on a stick and was attempting to push a little girl on a swing while a young boy dribbled a soccer ball. It had to be him.

Matherson took hold of his briefcase and walked down the path towards the garden.

'Seageant Scala? James Scala?'

Jim Scala looked up, startled, at the short man standing at the edge of the garden who looked as though he could be touting insurance. Scala's face assumed an expression of suspicion as he nodded. 'That's me.'

The stranger continued briskly, 'My name is Matherson. I've come from London . . . I wonder if we might be able to talk? I was advised to visit you by a former colleague of yours – Alex Carter.'

The name registered with Scala immediately. They had been friends, even worked together before Carter had left the regiment and disappeared off the face of the earth three years earlier.

'What do you want to talk about?'

'Well, ideally I would rather we went somewhere else to

talk, if that's convenient. It's somewhat personal, you see. It's nearly lunchtime – is there a local boozer around here or something . . .?'

Alarm bells sounded in Scala's mind. His subconscious had always alerted him to a possible threat and it had saved his life sometimes. But he had never been able to over-ride his curiosity on these occasions. He should play it cool . . . tell him that it wasn't convenient . . . that he was looking after the kids or something. But he knew he couldn't do that. If the man knew about Alex Carter, then he was worth listening to at least.

'Yes,' Scala replied, 'there's a place we can go if you say that we can't talk here. Come inside while I tell the wife . . .'

'I won't if it's all the same to you. Thank you, anyway. I'll just wait here,' insisted Matherson.

Scala ushered the children indoors and attempted to explain to Angie, busy packing, that he was going out to talk with this mystery guy. Angie left off wrapping ornaments in newspaper and placing them in tea chests to peep at the man outside. She attempted to protest, but knew that her objections were useless.

She watched from the window as her husband got into the stranger's car and they drove off together. Her heart was pounding. She had known these feelings before: these feelings of fear, apprehension and uncertainty that had now become a form of sixth sense that something bad was about to happen. It had been just ten days ago that Jim returned and promised a new life. In just two days' time they would be away from this place for good. Now she could not shed the feeling that her dreams were about to be shattered by the arrival of this man from London who carried a briefcase.

* * *

It took just ten minutes for Scala and Matherson to reach the whitewashed pub with its aged black beams, set back off the main road in a quiet lane. They would not be disturbed here. The two men sat in a far corner of the empty lounge, which stank of stale beer spilled on carpets and of the years of cigarette smoke that had turned the walls a dingy brown.

Scala sipped from his pint glass whilst his companion's vodka and tonic remained untouched on the table.

Small talk over, Matherson opened his case and took out a beige folder. As he opened it, Scala caught sight of a photograph of himself and saw the service file record underneath. It was headed with his name, and he turned his head to study some of the other entries: 'Age 34; Born Merthyr Tydfil; Parents Italian/Welsh; Service: Joined Royal Engineers aged 17, transferred Parachute Regiment; 12 years' service with the SAS; married with two children; served in South Armagh, Belfast, Iraq, Sri Lanka . . .' Scala quickly glimpsed the end of the service file and saw the word 'Bosnia' highlighted in yellow marker ink. Then there was a rubber stamp which stated: 'Discharged Due To Injury'.

'Don't tell me – you're from *This Is Your Life* and this is all going in the red book!' grinned Scala as he took another sip of beer.

Matherson turned. 'Well, in a way you're right. You see, I'm here to offer you a life – I want to offer you your life back!'

He saw he had Scala's attention. There was silence as Matherson turned to the psychological profile of the man before him. The shrinks had deemed Scala unsuitable for further duty due to his unstable emotions. There was no doubt that he was loyal – the army, and in particular the regiment, had been his life. They had agreed on that. He had taken rejection from the SAS badly. They had agreed on that too. He had been reliable, a man who could operate on his own initiative and who coped with the stress of undercover operations well. His intelligence-gathering had been second to none. His injuries were on the mend. But now it was his emotions that were suspect. The shrinks had questioned his capability to continue operating under such stress. Bosnia might have been the last straw.

'They seem to have turned me over good and proper,' Scala said resignedly as Matherson quoted the report. 'What bloody right have they got to tell me about my emotions? They weren't there, they didn't see . . .'

Matherson interrupted: 'I can understand your anger and disappointment. That's why I'm here. I understand that you are ... let's say reluctant to leave the service. Well, I can't do anything to overturn the decision, but I am in a position to offer you ... let's say another form of employment that I think would be well suited to your training.'

Scala was conscious of swallowing deeply. He had spent the last week resigning himself to the moment when he would have to leave his service life behind and attempt to adjust to an alien lifestyle, one which he feared would see his self-respect stripped from him. He was preparing to be a 'nobody' in civilian life. It had been hard, but he was prepared to give it a chance for the sake of Angie and the kids. Now this man from London seemed to be offering him something better.

'I am responsible for operating a certain department within the intelligence service,' continued Matherson in a matter-of-fact tone. 'It's not MI5 or anything like that ... we're not that posh. We're more a branch of military intelligence really. We tend to get lumbered with the grubbier kind of jobs – the ones that are a bit politically ticklish. No one really owns up to running us – but let me assure you, we do exist. Most of my lads are ex-service types, a bit like yourself, who for one reason or another have seen the end of their normal military service. But we find uses for them. We found a use for Alex Carter. Alex had thought that his career was over too – but he didn't like the idea of being put out to grass because he had reached a certain age. I found a use for him.

'The point is, I have been asked to go through the files and recruit someone who I think might be suited for a job we've got on at the moment – it's one the flash boys can't get involved with.' He took a gulp of his drink, then continued. 'I have made a selection of would-be contenders from the rank-and-file of the services, but by chance Alex was on hand to point you out as a man most likely to take the challenge.'

Scala interrupted: 'I thought Alex Carter was dead or had done a bunk with a rich widow!'

'That's what I prefer people to think about all my operatives,' smiled Matherson. 'Anyway, having studied your file, and taken account of this latest escapade of yours, I happen to think that you might be wholly suited to the job. Don't worry, it's hardly likely that you'll be asked to jump out of an aeroplane or anything like that. But I just hate to see all that money that Her Majesty's Government spends on training people like yourself go to waste. In a nutshell, I would like to offer you the chance of joining my mob. If you agree, then I am required to ask you to present yourself for briefing to me by the end of the week. Time is of the essence.'

Matherson had spoken quietly but confidently, and Scala detected a hint of menace and ruthlessness behind his narrow eyes.

'I don't expect an immediate answer,' he added. 'Sleep on it. But I must insist that you don't discuss anything I've mentioned here with your wife or anyone else. To all intents and purposes, we can arrange for her to be told that you are being transferred within the army after a rethink on your case – that you will be out of circulation for a while.'

Scala's mind was racing. What was this guy talking about? Was he joking? Could he be trusted? Had Carter really become involved in this outfit? Could Scala really be given this lifeline? Whatever the reason, one thing appeared certain: Scala was needed again! Someone wanted him for what he was good at, what he had spent years being trained for. He felt alive again.

Matherson saw the glint in Scala's eyes, and was certain that he had won his man. He had set the bait and the Welshman had accepted. The man from London laid it on thick now, relying on Scala's keen sense of loyalty to the regiment and service, and told him how highly qualified he would be for the job if he accepted. It could be a new start for him, said Matherson. He told him everything – except that the man who took the job would be totally expendable.

Chapter Four

Scala caught sight of his reflection in the train window. It was the first thing that he had been aware of since the train had left Guildford forty minutes earlier. The carriage had been empty, and it had been easy to lose himself in a maelstrom of thoughts.

He had made up his mind immediately. Certainly he had paced the floor of the house that night as his family slept, giving the illusion to anyone who might have witnessed him that his soul was being tormented by some nightmarish dilemma. But Scala had known it to be a facade. In his heart he knew what his decision would be, yet his conscience was putting up a valiant last-ditch defence.

Scala was still haunted by his final glimpse of Angie, standing at the window of her sister's house on the estate on the edge of Guildford where they had sought refuge after their hurried move from married quarters in Hereford. They had returned to the scene where they had first met, when he, as a paratrooper engineer stationed at nearby Aldershot, had made a play for the pretty, innocent-faced girl at the nightclub and swept her off her feet with his quick wit and devil-may-care attitude to life. How things could change in just ten years.

It should have been a new beginning. Instead she had watched emotionless as her man climbed into the taxi and headed for the station. There had been no farewell kiss, no fond goodbyes — just the frozen look of a betrayed woman. He had promised her a new life together: just himself and the kids. It was a promise he could not keep. Another, more powerful love was dragging him away.

He fought to dispel the image from his mind, and to concentrate on the potential 'offer' to hand. Was he acting like the blind fool they had expected him to be? The fool that would jump when they snapped their fingers because they had told him that Queen and Country relied upon him? Was he fooling himself that he was some form of indispensable super-hero and not some injured ex-SAS trooper who walked with a limp and who reacted like one of Pavlov's dogs when HM security forces demanded? Either way, it was a path that James Scala knew he had to follow. At least he would be true to himself, even if he could be true to no one else.

As the train rattled through Clapham Junction towards Waterloo Scala suddenly became aware of the grey high-rise tower blocks that dominated the skyline and his attention came back to the present. The image of Angie was quickly relegated as the silence of the carriage was shattered by the crackle of the guard's intercom, announcing their imminent arrival.

He stared at the view of the Houses of Parliament as the train slowed down for its entry to the station. The sight of the building brought a cynical smile to his face as he contemplated the idea that an unseen boss in that building might have directly sanctioned that he, a boy from the grim valleys of South Wales, should be chosen to represent his country in this dangerous game of life or death.

When the train stopped he stepped out carefully so as not to aggravate his leg. It seemed astonishing that, since being offered the prospect of new challenge, his leg had appeared to make a miraculous recovery. There was hardly any pain now, and sometimes he felt that he could walk without the aid of a stick whenever he wanted. To Scala it was a simple case of mind over matter.

Then he hurried from the platform, stick in his right hand and a suit carrier in his left. He headed under the giant clock to the taxi rank by the entrance and gave his driver directions to the office block in Docklands. The cab headed along Southwark Street and towards Tower Bridge, then disappeared in a maze of back-streets and grimy buildings before arriving outside the freshly built block with sparkling glass doors in the centre of a tanglework of iron bridges and yellow brick office towers.

He took the lift to the fifteenth floor, to the offices of the company named on the button panel as Delta Enterprises. When it stopped the doors slid open to reveal the figure of a uniformed security guard, who ushered Scala along a corridor. Matherson's secretary welcomed him and offered him a chair.

'Colonel Matherson won't keep you waiting long, sir, he's in with someone at the moment.'

Scala was shaken. He had never considered that the man who looked so like an insurance salesman could ever be a colonel in anyone's army. He was definitely not like the other 'Ruperts' – the name that SAS troopers gave to officers who were more the civil servant type.

He felt strangely nervous as he sat there, and concentrated his thoughts on the dark-haired, twenty-something secretary. Away from the office and out of her prim blue suit, there probably lay a positive wildcat waiting to spring out.

He was still lost in fantasy when the door to Matherson's office flew open and the short man who had journeyed to Hereford three days earlier stepped out to greet him like a long-lost son. Scala followed him into the office, his eyes immediately resting on the smartly dressed man in the leather swivel by the window. The man nodded to him, and Matherson offered a brief introduction.

'Sergeant Scala . . . or should we say *Mr* Scala . . . This is Mr Jacobson . . . shall we say a colleague!'

The two men nodded once more.

'Mr Scala, I appreciate your decision to come here today, from which I gather that we are in a position to proceed further. I apologise if my appearance at Hereford the other day was a little dramatic, but what I am about to lay before you is rather a dramatic scenario.'

Scala sensed a surge of blood through his veins. He could hear his heart beginning to pound louder and louder in his eardrums.

'As you know, our government and all the relevant parties involved in the search for peace in Northern Ireland have reached a crucial stage in the negotiations. God knows how, but the ceasefire between the various warring factions does appear on the surface to have held. Everyone is preparing to enter the next and probably most crucial stage. On the surface, everything seems to be going according to our timetable, doesn't it?'

Before Scala could nod agreement Matherson went on: 'The

problem is, Mr Scala, there appears to be a fly in the bloody ointment! We believe that someone out there is deliberately trying to bugger things up, and I'm not talking about the IRA or the Prods. According to our information someone else seems hell-bent on screwing things up for everyone! There have been incidents, you see – not that you'd know it from the newspapers, of course. At least that's one thing the bloody PR department have got right ... There have been killings – not nice ones, either – which have got the natives restless. They're about ready to have another go at each other, and there's bugger all we can do to prevent it. That's where *you* can come in ...'

Scala stiffened with surprise 'Me? Why me? What could I –'

Matherson interrupted: 'Please, Mr Scala, it will take a lot less time if I continue ... We believe that a member – or, to be more precise, a former member – of the security forces could be involved. If you could cast your mind back to the end of last year, you may recall an incident in which a helicopter "crashed" on take-off from Aldergrove Airport, killing a group of top-level security advisers. It was reported as an accident which occurred in poor weather conditions. I'm afraid I can tell you otherwise. You see, we believe that our man could have been behind it.'

Scala could restrain himself no more. 'Yes, but why would I come into this play?' he begged.

Matherson sat back. 'Well, Mr Scala ... or Jim, shall I call you? It might appear that our man is also a former member of the SAS – a wild card gone bad! After the chopper crash there was a full sweep of the area – a bit late, if you ask me, but there you go – and the guys on the ground found a few tell-tale signs. Apart from the 66mm rocket launcher used to bring the aircraft down, they found evidence to suggest that our boy had been living rough out in the fields nearby. But he knew how to cope – they found bags of human waste neatly bagged and partly buried, as well as other tracks. In short, it was all done regimental style – *your* regiment. We think we've got a rogue "player", possibly even some kind of mercenary!

'There have been other instances, too, all of which you can study later. True, most of the attacks do seem to have been targeted towards Catholics, but not all. The conclusion, I'm afraid, is the same. The result is that the warring factions are all beating their chests because they think the other side is up to something. My problem is that I have to find this sonofabitch before he and his pals can start up the whole bloody war again. And that, Mr Scala – sorry, Jim – is where you come in!'

The man in the corner stirred, taking the engrossed Scala by surprise.

'You see, Scala, we have a plan to put *our* man in the field over there – someone like yourself,' started Jacobson. 'MI6, the RUC and army intelligence are playing their usual silly games and refusing to pass on all the information. Consequently they don't appear to trust each other. That's why I want our man in there.'

Jacobson had got Scala's attention. Scala had no idea who he was, but his tone of voice and air of authority suggested that he was in a position to be listened to.

'According to your file, we understand that you have had considerable experience in covert operations against the drug trade. What was it, a year in Colombia with your squad training up the anti-narcotics police back in 1986? That was a pretty bloody affair, so I understand,' Jacobson continued. 'What was it now – your team took out that cocaine baron Ramirez, didn't they?'

Scala did not acknowledge the question. He knew that this man had done his homework and studied the files. Scala's memory drifted back to that Colombian operation, a year of working in steaming jungles training the locals how to fight the cartels that ran the cocaine trade that was ruining the governments of Latin America. It had been a war as ruthless as any other he had fought. He allowed Jacobson to go on.

'That was a good hit, taking out his bodyguards and lieutenants too! Pity about the others. That operation brought you into close contact with the drugs world, didn't it? And I see it came in handy with your attachment to the Drug Enforcement Agency in the States. You seem to be something of a specialist in the trade.'

Scala pondered. He supposed it was true, although he had never considered himself an expert. His thoughts were focused once again by Matherson's voice.

'It's that kind of knowledge that we're going to make use of in our plan,' he explained. 'It's an idea we've been working on for some time.'

* * *

The funeral procession had taken the best part of an hour to reach the giant cemetery at Milltown in the centre of the city. Crowds had lined the route as the hearse slowly made its way down the Falls Road towards the cemetery that had witnessed so many similar scenes. It appeared as if half the community of the Falls had turned out to pay their respects. In reality Sheena Maguire had been anonymous to them, yet the savagery of her death had placed a shroud of anger and revulsion over the entire community. There had been something else, too – fear; renewed fear that another form of death was now stalking the streets. It was the sign around the girl's neck accusing her of being a 'tout' that had made them feel this way. They were afraid that the unyielding mad fringe of the IRA, the ones who had refused to give up their guns, had taken to the war trail whilst the politicians spoke of peace. This time the victims would be a way to settle old scores. Sheena Maguire had been one of those victims.

The IRA leaders had tried to reassure them that their fears were unfounded. But there were still suspicions. Now, Sheena Maguire would prove to be more important in death than she had been in life.

As the mourners huddled around the open grave and the priest uttered his words of comfort to grieving relatives, few people acknowledged the small group of men in long black overcoats who gathered by the gates of the cemetery. They stood alone, and it seemed impossible that they could not be seen from the Andersonstown police station opposite.

Derek Macnamara was a slight figure of a man who looked even smaller in his giant overcoat. But when he spoke men listened – and obeyed. As commander of the 2nd Battalion of the Belfast Brigade of the Irish Republican Army he had the power of life and death. His two terms of imprisonment in Long Kesh had only fuelled his hatred of both the British and the Protestants. He was a committed man. He had argued against the ceasefire promoted by Sinn Fein. His solution to the problems could only be sought with Armalites and bombs. The Army Council had persuaded him to tow the line, for the time being at least. But he felt that the IRA would be seen to lose its influence now that the politicians were talking. The only way to make certain that people followed you was to rule by fear.

Now, as he witnessed Sheena Maguire's coffin being slowly lowered to its last resting place, he could almost taste the sense of outrage that existed amongst the people. The finger of suspicion had been pointed towards him. It was an untruth, but it might be something that could be used to his advantage. Fuck the RUC bastards who turned a blind eye to the death of a Catholic girl! This was an opportunity for the IRA to assert itself again.

As he spoke to his captains who surrounded him the bespectacled Macnamara felt himself in a renewed position of power. He was pleased that the people still feared him and the others like him, the ones committed to the cause. In a calm, clinical voice he ordered that the bastards who did this thing would be caught – not by the RUC, but by his men. They would be hunted, caught, bagged and executed in the old way. Then the people would know that the IRA had not betrayed its followers. The IRA would have the power of life and death once more. They would be the law, they would rule. Their own man-hunt was on!

*　　*　　*

The plan had seemed simple and convincing when outlined to him. At first he had been convinced. Matherson and Jacobson had been confident. But now, as he lay on top of the single bed in his cramped hotel room, he was filled with self-doubt and misgivings. For the first time in his service life he feared he was not up to the task. Never before had he felt this way; not when he had been separated from the other troopers of his squadron behind the Iraqi lines or during some covert operation in South Armagh. Worst of all was the fact that he was questioning the methods that he was to use.

His mind flashed back to the briefing; the briefing that had seemed endless and had left his head spinning with questions. No wonder they had said that his experience in the drugs trade would be invaluable. The only difference was that back in the eighties he had been one of the 'good guys'. Now they were actually asking him to become one of the bad guys. After all, the end would justify the means.

Scala was to assume the role of a high-powered drugs dealer. He would take his goods and peddle them in the Loyalist bars of the Shankhill Road and the nightclubs of central Belfast, which were now enjoying a renaissance thanks to the latest 'rave' craze which was sweeping the city. It seemed that the young people of Belfast today were eager to forget the misery of the years of killing, and if they had to rely on tablets to achieve it then so be it. The Church leaders from both sides had frowned on the use of drugs, no matter how mild, in their communities. Now they were powerless to prevent the culture from taking hold. The youth of the province were determined to live life to the full while they could.

Unable to thwart the growth of the use of drugs, the terror organizations who had originally condemned the practice were now prepared to use them to their advantage. Now, every doorman on every club door in Belfast belonged to either the IRA or one of the Loyalist organizations. They were not prepared to miss out on the opportunity. On the British mainland, one tablet of Ecstasy would be sold for £6. In Belfast it would fetch £25. The demand was growing. The tablets that would be sold in the Loyalist bars would raise money for the cause, to buy weapons for the urgent rearming process that was going on.

The use of drugs was not new to the terrorist organizations. In the mid-1980s the IRA had masterminded a worldwide chain of drugs operations in an attempt to fund its operations. It had also claimed that it would defeat the British authorities by undermining the economy with cheap drugs, which in turn would destroy society and cost millions of pounds to put right. The scheme had proved a dismal failure. But the use of drugs as a method of raising funds was here to stay.

The IRA alone needed £7 million a year in order to sustain itself. There were those who were already claiming that it had been fought to a standstill, that it had gone to the peace table because it had been starved of men and funds. Its cash lifeline from the historical supporters across the Atlantic had been slashed, and many of the IRA's front-line troops were now behind bars or in their graves. If they were to fight on, they would have to adapt to the new ways of raising funds. And if that meant peddling the misery that was drugs in order for the organization to live, then so be it.

Now, Scala had been told to peddle the very misery that he had fought hard against for years and detested. They had told him that it was a way in which he could appear in the city centre without arousing too much interest. He could use the Loyalist bars as a trading ground. Here eager dealers would be unlikely to question a self-confessed criminal with a bottomless supply of drugs to feed the growing habits of the city – and Matherson would see that the supply did not dry up.

He had been told that being a drug dealer would mean he would not have to fake an Ulster accent like the heroes in a string of television dramas about Northern Ireland. There would be no time for such coaching, anyway. They had told him that he would be in a better position to infiltrate the right sections of the still fiercely suspicious Loyalist terror groups, such as the Ulster Freedom Fighters and the Ulster Volunteer Force. They would come to him and approach him, he was told. If there was a British renegade at work, then someone in the bars would be talking about it.

They had made it sound easy. He had a perfect cover and a constant supply of material – supplied, ironically, from drugs raids on shipments from Europe that had been intercepted by customs officials at a string of British ports. As and when Scala required them they would be sent to him, courtesy of registered mail, wherever he was. Of course, no one in the authorities could be told of his activities, so he would also be fair game for any policeman on either side of the Irish Sea if he was caught. That went without saying. Even so, it was all made to sound so easy. Then they dropped the bombshell.

Part of the plan concerned the girl – an Ulster girl who had lived in London for the last seven years. When she was just twenty-one she had been forced into exile by the heavies of the UVF, because she refused to stash weapons in the family's home. It had only been out of reverence for her dead father and brother, both martyrs to the Loyalist cause, that the UVF had not ordered her to be crippled for life because of her disloyalty. Instead, like so many others from either side, she had been banished from Ulster. Most of those exiles, whether Catholic or Protestant, lived together in harmony in areas of London and other British cities, waiting for the time when they would be allowed by the terror organizations to return. She had been given just forty-eight hours to leave Belfast, and now lived in Shepherds Bush in west London. Her life in exile had been littered with disappointment and heartbreak. All she longed for was to be allowed to return and see her Mam. Now, Matherson and the rest were asking Scala to add to that misery: she would be a valuable pawn for him to use.

The peace process had brought her fresh hope. As the calls to release the political prisoners of both sides grew, so too had the pleas of families to the terror factions of both sides to allow their exiled loved ones to return home. For years, her mother had pleaded with the heads of the peace organization Families Against Intimidation and Terrorism to help negotiate for her daughter's return. Now Matherson's agents had told him that her efforts were soon to pay off. The UVF had relented.

She would be an easy target. Matherson had ordered Scala to befriend her, win her trust and maybe even her affection. When she returned, she would provide an ideal shield for their man. Scala would study her file, her photograph and every aspect of her vulnerable personality. She was one of life's victims, they told him. They would do whatever they could to smooth his path. She would be even more susceptible to his attentions by the time they had finished with her. They would start by cancelling her eligibility for unemployment benefit on some trumped up ground. Scala could become the proverbial knight in shining armour and then, if possible, he would return to Ulster with her.

'It's amazing what some women will do for a bit of affection and kindness,' Matherson had told Scala. 'Trust me, this young chicken is there for the plucking.'

They had made it sound so easy . . .

Scala stood looking at himself in the mirror in the hotel bathroom. He stared at his face and focused on the jagged line that the wound had left. It had healed well. But what he was searching for went deeper. He was looking deep into his own soul. He was searching to see the kind of man they were turning him into.

Chapter Five

The looped music tape of the Holiday Inn cocktail bar recycled 'Moon River' for the second time in half an hour. The monotonous sound had irritated him the first time around, and now it had got too much to bear. There were just a handful of customers in the bar now as he drained the last dregs of Famous Grouse from his glass. As he gestured for the waiter to bring him a refill he surveyed the other people in the room. There was the usual gathering of businessmen on expense accounts hoping for a quick shag on the firm's money. And there was a smattering of smartly dressed women seated around the tables in the bar, some alone, some lost in apparent deep conversation with a partner.

Naylor sneered at the whole array. God, he could not stomach people like these. To him they were the gutless, colourless people who relied on people like him for their security. They might want to hide behind men like himself, but could never bring themselves to acknowledge the likes of him. Where would they be without men like him? he wondered.

He looked out over the night lights of Birmingham's Bull Ring shopping centre from his window seat and pondered what his life would be like when he had left all this shit behind. He stopped quickly. It was bad for him to dream. He relied only on reality. Money and reality were the only things you could trust in this life.

He hated jacked up places like this. Why the hell had they got to meet there anyway? He had made a concession and worn a sports jacket and black slacks. But he had opted against a tie. Enough was enough!

He looked at his wristwatch again, and as he did so he caught sight of a tall, straight-backed man with thinning grey hair, in an immaculate blue pinstripe suit and carrying a briefcase, entering the bar. 'About fucking time too!' he muttered under his breath.

The tall man spotted Naylor immediately and walked towards his table, ordering a large whisky from the waiter who hovered.

'Sorry I'm late. I had a late surgery tonight – a lot of damn stupid queries from people who expect me to change the world for them!' he explained to an uninterested Naylor. The scotch arrived, and as it trickled down his throat it brought instant relief. 'That's better! I needed that.'

Naylor ignored the comment and demanded: 'Have you brought it?'

The man looked indignant. 'Of course I've bloody well brought it, as arranged. Don't I always bring it?'

He opened his briefcase, took out a large envelope and slid it across the table to Naylor. 'No need to count it, old boy, it's all there – a bloody great bundle of it, a full hundred thousand smackers as ordered, nothing bigger than a £20 note either ... From what I'm hearing, it looks like the last little episode with the girl stirred the bastards up somewhat. A job well done, I'd say!'

To any outsider, the two men made an odd combination. Just a glance would have told an unknowing party that they were from worlds apart.

At forty-five, Antony Hursley had been MP for one of the Birmingham constituencies for more than a decade; he had been one of the blue-eyed boys of the Thatcher era after several years as a popular county councillor. An architect by training, he had always had political ambitions, which had now been encouraged by his appointment as a junior minister in the Department of Trade and Industry. He was intelligent and wealthy, a personable and loving family man with every reason to believe that his ambitions would be realized.

An outsider would have been excused for thinking that the world looked a good place for Antony Hursley. But they would have reckoned without the burning sadness and hatred that had gnawed away at his very soul since that dreadful night in November 1974 when his world had been shattered. On that night twenty years earlier the carefree existence of his adored younger sister had been shattered for ever.

It had been the night when Claire had celebrated with her

friends the news that she had been accepted at Oxford to study law. It should have been the night that heralded the next phase of the exciting, joyful life of this charming, clever girl.

It had instead ended in the blood and fire and horror that had been the result of the IRA's bombing blitz on the Birmingham pubs. It had ended with Claire being trapped under the debris, her legs pinned and broken, her body ripped apart by a hundred deadly splinters. The doctors had said she was lucky – she would live, although she would never walk again. But there had been brain damage too – brain damage that had left the girl with everything to live for a mangled human shell who could now not even communicate her name. To her brother Antony it would have been better if she had died along with so many others on that night of horror.

Now Antony Hursley MP sat opposite Michael Naylor, a man who killed for a living and was good at it, at a table in a bar just yards from the horrors of twenty years before. Now it would be Hursley and his counterparts who would be in a position to turn the tables on the killers who had ruined the life of his sister and hundreds like her in twenty-five years of brutal murder. Naylor would help them: he would train the men who would kill and had already killed. He had needed little persuasion. The promise of the long-term contract would enable him to put his own special skills to good use. Now he took the envelope and buried it deep in his inside pocket. There was still no smile on his face.

Hursley leaned forward and whispered: 'I have had the word from the other side of the water. It seems that they believe it's time we moved on to Phase Three. They're already champing at the bit. Adams won't be able to hold them back for much longer, and once the next phase is under way then I think it's a safe bet that any idea he may have had of controlling the mad dogs will fly out the window. So I want you ready to start the next phase within three weeks. Dublin is hell-bent on setting loose their prisoners, and it seems that a timetable has been agreed for a big meeting later this summer – which means that time is of the essence.'

He finished his drink, snapped his briefcase together and stood up. 'You'll get your travelling instructions in the usual manner. Good hunting!' he said as his politician's ever-ready smile spread across his face for public consumption. He turned and left.

Naylor felt good. He had the money, he was working towards his future and he had a job to do – a job he was good at.

* * *

He was as ready as they could make him. The last three days had been spent hidden away in a stifling office, surrounded by files and mug shots of the senior players whom he should know about.

Matherson had made certain that he had everything he wanted. Scala had been given a 'company' Gold American Express card, a sleek metallic British racing green BMW 3.25i car, a Rolex wristwatch and a generous allowance for wardrobe – the Hugo Boss and Jaeger outfits that were the trappings of the successful businessman. They would make him appear smart but not too flash. The use of an elegantly furnished three-bedroomed apartment off Sloane Square also went with the job, and in case of emergencies he was given a special Freephone number that would be answered twenty-four hours a day.

The supply of Ecstasy that would provide his passport to the dealers had also been dealt with. It would come courtesy of a recent drugs bust at Harwich of thousands of tablets which had been smuggled in from Holland disguised in sacks of cat litter, a popular method because the drugs could not be detected by sniffer dogs. It had therefore been a lucky find, but one which the authorities had been happy to boast about. The value of the haul was estimated at £500,000. In PR terms it proved that the fight against drug imports was still being waged. Now, through a twist of irony, the drugs would still be used as they had originally been intended; the only difference was that the 'good guys' would be using them, in an attempt to catch bigger fish.

Matherson had also said that he would supply Scala with crack cocaine should it be necessary to enhance his credentials. Scala had not asked about the origins of the drug; he preferred to remain ignorant.

The days had gone quickly. There had been study, weapons training, physical fitness, a chance to dust off his unarmed combat techniques, and even physiotherapy for his injured leg. He had not required his stick for days and his formerly pronounced limp was improving rapidly. There had, in fact, been plenty to occupy his mind. The one thing that he had cast out of his brain was Angie and the kids. The job was all that counted now. And for that, he told himself, he was as prepared as he could be.

* * *

The sound of the lead guitar blasted through the giant speakers as the band began the first session of the gig. The familiar strains of the old Dire Straits hit echoed throughout the pub, just as they did at this time every Tuesday and Thursday night. The aging lead guitarist, clad in tight black leather trousers, tee-shirt and headband, began to gyrate on stage almost as a symbol of his virility to the groups of giggling girls in the front row of tables around the makeshift stage. The grey-bearded drummer switched to overdrive to compensate for the noise that originated from the bar and threatened to smother the performance. The punters in the half-filled bar listened and instantly turned their back to their conversation and their drinks.

Little passing trade stopped at the pub during the week, even in this highly regarded part of Notting Hill Gate. If it was to stay like this all night, then it was going to be a very long and dreary Tuesday for the two girls who served behind the bar.

One of them ran her fingers over her forehead to push back the unruly lock of hair that had fallen over her face. She had always fought a losing battle to keep her mop of gypsy-like black curls tied back. She knew the band's routine by heart, even though she had worked in the pub for less than two weeks. What she was being paid was tantamount to slave labour, but she was in no position to complain. It was money. And money was something that she had never known much of.

She was indifferent to most of the customers, yet she always managed a cheering smile which seemed to light up her bright green eyes. It had not taken long for her to become a favourite amongst the regulars. One look into those smiling eyes and the troubles of the day had faded for many a businessman. She made each one feel special.

She wore little make-up – just a little mascara occasionally that highlighted those eyes even more. Her skin was silky-smooth and unlined, despite the trauma that she had silently endured.

The music was deafening, but she still heard the crash of the glass as it fell from the table and smashed on the scrubbed wooden floor. The sound made her start and she jerked her head upwards from the task of washing the dirty glasses. Her eyes focused on the stranger at the table nearest the bar who was bending down to pick up the shattered remains. He looked up and stared pleadingly into her eyes, shrugging his shoulders and miming the words 'Oops . . . sorry!' Then he deliberately raised his eyebrows apologetically before giving her a beaming smile that spread effortlessly across his face. The effect was disarming.

It took a great deal for Noreen Dillon to notice a man. She had learned to distrust so many of them for most of her life. It had seemed that every man she had ever cared for had deserted her. When she was just twelve years old her father had died, and her brother had died senselessly trying to prove himself a man when he was no more than a boy. In the seven years that she had been in England, away from her home, she could claim to have cared for just two men. Both had let her down, leaving her feeling betrayed and empty. She had feared she would never trust a man in her life again. She would guard against that. Yet she liked what she saw as she gazed at the man in front of her. He had the look of a naughty boy who had been caught and reprimanded. She could not stifle the smile that came to her mouth so easily.

The man was smart, in an expensive suit and smart silk shirt buttoned at the collar. Her eyes landed on the scar on his right cheek. On most men it would have been ugly. On this man it seemed to put the finishing touches to the finely chiselled features of his face, giving him the dashing appearance that, as a small girl back in Belfast, she had imagined would belong to the man who would sweep her off her feet and protect her from the pains of life.

She hurried from the bar with a dustpan and brush and knelt at the side of the table, by the customer's feet, ready to sweep up the jagged pieces of broken glass. She felt her heart leap as the man leaned forward to touch her hand and take the brush from her. It was a soft, gentle hand, yet she could feel the strength that was there too.

James Scala took the dustpan and insisted, 'Leave it – I broke it, I'll clean it up. I don't want you cutting yourself because of my clumsiness.' It took just a few moments to clear up, but he was aware that the girl had watched his every move. Kneeling, he looked up into her face and stared directly into those huge green eyes that sparkled with an almost childlike innocence.

'I suppose I have no option but to ask you for another drink!' He stood up and walked across to the bar, ordered a fresh bottle of Beck's Pilsner and insisted that she took the money for a drink for herself too. He watched as she accepted the money, yet put it immediately into a small glass by the side of the cash register.

'I'll have it later,' she said quietly. 'Thank you very much.' There were not many men who would take the time or trouble to offer to buy her a drink in this place.

Scala was mentally rehearsing the script that he had prepared back at the flat an hour earlier. He had never had many problems with women. He could be charming, witty and totally disarming for most of them, and had never had much difficulty in getting them to bed if he wanted. This one, however, was going to be different. He had been ordered to win this woman because it was part of the job.

But it was a job he was going to enjoy. He was aware that he was smiling at the girl without even thinking about it. He actually wanted to. Scala had made contact with his own Trojan horse.

Chapter Six

The youth with the acne-ridden face and spiked greasy hair ran his hands up and down the girl's body as they pressed themselves into the darkened corner of the room. She responded by pushing her own body deep into the youth's groin as the pair ground together in rhythm to the loud music that echoed throughout the club. Scala's eyes alighted on the groping bodies as he sat pondering his drink at the bar in the smoke-filled basement rooms. He watched, fascinated, as the youth's hand rested on the girl's breast and slowly squeezed. She did not resist. Scala grinned – neither of them could have been more than seventeen. He caught sight of the girl's face – pretty and purposely made pale by the fashionable make-up of the day. She swept her tumbling hair from her face, and Scala's expectations faded as he noticed the girl's pierced nose.

How the hell could anyone go out with a ring through their nose? How the hell could anyone fancy something that looked like it belonged on a Swish curtain track rather than between the sheets? he thought. He had never understood the present-day trend. It was a pity – with a bit of care and attention the girl would certainly be passable. A good bath for the pair of them might help, he mused.

God, he felt old! The way he was looking at the couple, he wondered if others watching him might think of him as the proverbial 'dirty old man'. It had been different in his day, back in the pubs and clubs of the valleys. At least the girls that he and the boys had gone after on their Friday and Saturday nights out had been clean; get a few drinks down them and they would shag for Wales, but at least they were clean. Even in those early days in the army, when the lads were not too choosy, they would have thought twice about poking a bird with a curtain ring through her nose. It all seemed so long ago now.

A sharp dig in the back from a passing reveller brought Scala back to reality. He looked around him at the dark surroundings. He could not abide places like this. The whole place was heaving with drunk and sweaty teenagers, most of whom, he estimated, were probably not old enough to drink legally in the first place. But this was supposed to be an 'in place'. Matherson had told him so. He had supplied him with the identity of the man he should contact and target. If Scala was to enhance his cover as a dealer, then this club, known as the Cellar, was the place to be.

The loud music to which the heaving bodies bounced up and down on the crowded dance floor was beginning to grate on Scala's nerves when he noticed the blonde-haired barman with the name tag on his shirt which identified him as 'Gerry'. He waited until the man was free and then demanded a fresh beer. As the barman poured, Scala asked in a low voice: 'Would you be the man they call Gerard . . . Gerard Connor?'

The man's eyes looked up cautiously and stared unblinking into Scala's face.

'I could be. Who wants to know?' came the reply in a strong East End accent.

Scala shrugged. 'It's just that I believe we may have a common interest – that's what I was told. I was told that you might be the man who would be interested.'

'And who would tell you something like that? Who do you know that I might know? I've never even seen you in here before,' replied Connor.

Scala recalled the name that Matherson had drilled into him, the man they knew as Big Andy Pierce, the man who had been behind a string of major drug imports from the Continent over the last two years and who touted his wares in the London clubs like the Cellar, but who, Scala reckoned, would now be languishing in a police cell somewhere – if everything had gone according to plan. Scala knew that Connor could not be aware of Pierce's arrest. He noticed the flicker of recognition in Connor's eyes as he mentioned Pierce's name.

'How do you know the Big Man?' fished Connor. He was still cautious with the stranger.

Scala spun the yarn of how they had met in the clubs in south London; of how Pierce had supplied him with the tabs that had started him off in business; of how Scala was now spreading his wings and wanted to expand his own business; of how Pierce had recommended Connor and the Cellar.

Connor beckoned Scala to a table where two glazed-eyed teenagers sat motionless over bottles of beer, their opaque eyes seemingly looking straight through the tall dark man. 'I can supply you with all you might want to keep our children here happy!' promised Scala, smirking. 'I'm looking to grow, and I need a new outlet. I have friends in Holland who will keep the stuff coming – all you want. And as a sign of good faith, I'm happy to offer up a sample free and gratis to you. I can't be fairer than that now, can I?'

Scala reached into the inside pocket of his leather jacket, produced a folded manilla envelope and slid it to Connor. 'There's a sheet of tabs in there, with a hundred tabs on it. It's worth a few bob. And by the look of things here, I would say you'll have no problem finding the necessary customers. There's a lot more to come from where they did . . .'

Connor registered the idea of having a fresh and ready supply of thousands of Ecstasy tablets, the drug that the police classed as 'kids' stuff', the drug that turned quiet youngsters into gyrating extroverts and cooked their bodies from the inside at the same time. There would be a healthy profit from the eager customers.

'And it doesn't have to stop with tabs,' continued Scala. 'I can get whatever you want – I mean the big stuff, the big money stuff.' He knew he had his man.

'I might be interested!' retorted Connor, attempting to disguise the eagerness in his voice. 'If I *was* interested, when could I see some more merchandise?'

'Just as soon as you want,' replied Scala. 'I'll be back tomorrow night with a lot more of this stuff . . . just in case you might be interested.'

He sat back, measuring Connor, who he judged to be a greedy, get-rich-quick opportunist. He knew the barman would never be able to resist the opportunity he was offering. Without further hesitation Scala rose and left.

As he stepped from the club he breathed deeply, gulping in the clean air. It took just twenty minutes to drive back through the near deserted night-time streets to his flat. Although it was so late he had to shower and wash the smell of the place from his body. As he stood beneath the jet of water he wondered if he was also attempting to wash away his own part in this sordid game. For years he had despised people like Connor; now here he was trying to be one of them.

* * *

St Patrick Day's had always increased Noreen's feelings of home-sickness. Each year she thought with longing of the get-togethers in the community centres and pubs back home. It was always an excuse for a knees-up with drink and laughter, topped off by her Mam's Irish stew.

These days she hated the sound of mail arriving through the letter box. It generally spelled bad news, and today was no exception. The letter from the Department of Social Security had left her gutted. She found it difficult to understand how they could stop her benefits just because she had been unable to find a suitable job. She had always thought that the state was there to help cases like her. Christ, she was already behind with the rent – how could she afford to survive on what she earned from the bar? She would go under, and there was nothing she could do about it.

Thank God for her Mam! At least there had been some cheering news there. Noreen reflected on how she always looked forward to her twice-weekly stroll to the corner phonebox to speak to her mother. It was her only contact with home – the only real home she had ever known. Her Mam was still battling away. She had chiselled away at the faceless men who ran the UVF – the men who had sent her away all those years before. Now it looked as if they might relent – the peace had done that much, anyhow. Now, with so many of those who had been exiled daring to return, they were looking hard at her case. After all, her Da had been a victim and her brother had died a hero. Now, after seven years, she had seen the error of her ways – her Mam had said so – and maybe they should give her a chance. Within a few days she would know for certain. Then she would be away, back to her Mam's side to begin her life again.

But there was something else, too, that was cheering Noreen.

As she looked in the scratched mirror that clung to the faded floral wallpaper of her tiny bedsit, she recalled the handsome features of the man from the bar who called himself Jim. She fought to recall what he had given as his second name: Scala – that was it, Jim Scala. He had said he would be in the bar again tonight, that he would come and see her. For an incomprehensible reason she found the thought warming.

Then she tried to shrug off his memory – maybe he had just been joking. She told herself that she was acting like a stupid schoolgirl who hoped to be spotted by the classroom stud. She knew it was pathetic, yet she also knew that she had found his attentions welcome. He had not been over-familiar . . . he had been charming.

As she looked in the mirror, scrutinizing her smooth skin for signs of wrinkles, she found her heart thumping with anticipation. She stepped back and took a sideways glance at herself in the mirror, using her hands to straighten out the tight black skirt which showed off the contours of her body. She found herself breathing in to enhance the outline of her breasts. She laughed aloud. They were the actions of a schoolgirl, sure enough. But if Jim Scala was to come to the bar tonight she would do her best to make sure that he was not disappointed in what he saw.

* * *

He could hear the sound of his own blood pounding through his brain. He struggled to catch his breath, but each time he attempted to get some air all he managed was to inhale the material of the filthy hood that covered his head. Worst of all was the darkness. He could hear movement, he could hear whispers, and he could hear muffled sobs coming from his right. But the constant darkness made him a prisoner of his fear. The cord that bound his wrists to the chair was biting into his flesh, and he could taste the blood in his mouth from where he had bitten his lip in terror.

It seemed as if he had been there for an eternity, but as he attempted to think logically he figured it could only have been an hour at most. He tried to guess where they could be. They had been standing at the junction of Divismore Park and the

Springfield Road when they had been grabbed and thrown into the back of the van. He and Billy had been on their way to the club. Tonight would be a busy night, so the boss would be going ape-shit. They couldn't be far from where they had been taken.

He could smell the dampness from the walls of a building long unused; the slightest noise echoed throughout the room. He fought again to think clearly. They could be in one of the warehouses by the works at the back of Springhill Avenue – that would only have been minutes away from where he and Billy had been standing.

'I'll ask you one more time,' came the deep thundering voice from the other side of the hood, 'and for Billy's sake here, you'd better be coming up with the right fuckin' answer, Sean me boy!'

The hood was yanked from his head. He blinked uncontrollably and tried to regain his composure. The paraffin lamp on the wooden tea chest cast shadows around the walls. He caught sight of his inquisitor, a bear of a man in a washed out green combat jacket and a balaclava helmet. A man behind his chair seized him roughly by the hair and dragged his head back. His terrified eyes caught sight of Billy, his eyes reduced to angry red slits from where they had been punched. He could not stifle his sobs.

'Who the fuck was responsible for the girl? Which of your miserable cock-sucking drug-peddling bastards saw to her? Who's trying to pull something off? What the fuck's goin' on, Sean me old son?'

The questions were spat at the terrified youth and his mind raced to comprehend. They had said a name . . . the girl they called Sheena . . . they had cursed him about a needle, about drugs. They had said that all that drugs shit started in the clubs – that he was involved in it and had peddled the drugs to ease the cravings of the kids.

'I tell yer, Mister, I haven't a fuckin' clue what yer on about! Neither's Billy here. We only work at the fuckin' place. Oh, for Jesus' sake I swear it. . . . I know nothing about the girl . . . I know nothin' about the fuckin' drugs . . . I – '

But before he could finish his plea the man with the balaclava raced towards Billy and raised the long metal bar high above his head. Sean saw it fall and heard the sickening crack of bone as it landed on his friend's leg, and then the cry of agony.

'I'm tellin' yer, Sean me boy, there's more of this to go round. See here now, our Billy, wouldn't it be better for yer if your man Sean was to tell us what we want to know?'

Sean Brady had been a good boy all his life. He had kept out of trouble, he had gone to Mass with his Ma and Da. He had never touted on anyone and he had never been asked to. All he had done was to work at the club; him and Billy. It was a club where the raves were and the drug they called Ecstasy was passed for a score a time among the new generation of Belfast. They had worked on the door of the place where the kids came to forget about the soldiers and the police and the gunmen. That was all Sean Brady had done. His tears rolled down his face uncontrollably as the iron bar slammed down on Billy's other leg. Once again there was a crack of bone.

'Don't worry there now, Seany. Our boy here still has a pair of arms to go! Then it'll be your turn . . .'

'I can't tell yer, for God's sake,' blurted the youth. 'I tell yer, man, I don't know a thing,' he cried in despair. Then, as if he had been struck by lightning, a memory, a rumour, a garbled conversation in the men's toilet at the club sprang to his mind.

'All I know is there's talk,' he gasped.

'What fuckin' talk, Sean me boy? Tell me now, what fuckin' talk could you have heard?' The bar was raised again.

'They say it might have been a fella from away! An outsider who the girl was mixed with . . . a fella from England . . . that's what they say . . .'

'That's what who say, Seany? Who's sayin' it?'

'It's the talk in the club, that's all I know.' Sean Brady felt a lifeline. 'They say that some English bastard has come here and is mixing it . . . that the girl had crossed him . . . that it was a man with drugs . . . that he was fixing an old score. But Jesus, mister I don't know any more! On me Ma's life, I swear I know nothin' else!'

It wasn't much. It was rumour, but it appeared to be enough for the men to stop the beating. Sean Brady didn't know if he had spoken the truth. He wanted the beating to stop. It had worked – for the time being anyway. He was left to see to his friend.

The two men had disappeared into the night, to the back room bar of the pub in Turf Lodge where Macnamara was waiting. He had only begun to make his point. The news of his justice, to the little shits who worked where the sale of drugs was the fastest-growing business in the city, would spread like a prairie fire among the rows of terraced homes that made up the Ballymurphy area, and it would spread far beyond by the time he had finished. He had a rumour to work on – a story about an English bastard who had come to his country to peddle the shit, who had known Sheena Maguire and who might have helped kill her. Sheena's death meant nothing to Macnamara, but the idea of her being mixed up with a Brit who had come here to kill her was too much. He would find the bastard and administer his own punishment.

* * *

St Patrick's Day had brought its usual rush at the bar. Noreen and the other two staff had had barely a moment to themselves. The same band, playing the same songs with the addition of a few Irish classics given an upbeat treatment, still rocked the place. Noreen had watched for the stranger who had promised he would be there to see her. There had been no sign. She should have known better than to think otherwise. He had made her feel good, but now she made herself believe that he had not meant his interest.

Despite the noise in the bar, she allowed her thoughts to drift momentarily to Belfast. What would her Mam and the others be doing tonight? She conjured up a vision of her friends and her Mam gathered around a table in the city centre, whooping and clapping to one of the countless country and western bands that flooded the bars. She found herself smiling. As her thoughts faded and reality returned she found herself focusing on the beaming smile of the handsome face before her – the scarred face of the stranger with the penetrating blue eyes.

'I think I'd need to pay more than a penny for those thoughts,' said Scala, grinning. 'Don't tell me, now! You were dreaming you were on an empty beach, dreaming of a hunky great Bounty hunter who fed you chocolate bars and went skinny-dipping with you . . .'

'Actually,' replied Noreen, 'it was more of dirty streets and drunken middle-aged men making fools of themselves through drink. It's called Shankill. But I tell yer, I'd rather be there than on some deserted beach any day.'

Scala noticed how the very mention of her home had prompted her to slip into a more prominent Belfast dialect. He guessed it was on purpose. Noreen served him with a beer and they chatted easily. Her heart felt lifted in a way which she still could not understand.

No one really knew how the fight started. It was the usual kind of affair. Two men in drink, arguing over a tarty girl or a spilt beer. It didn't matter who threw the first punch, the result was the same: lots of screaming, lots of men rolling around on the floor on broken glass, and lots of other jeering drinkers to encourage the combatants. Noreen looked horrified. She hated violence. Scala saw the look of pain on her face and the way her hands trembled. The manager attempted to separate the fighters, who left in a hail of abuse and aimless punches. The other customers began to drift away, too. St Patrick's Day at the bar had reached its climax

Noreen was still trembling and did not hear Scala's attempts at a joke to ease her anguish. He considered that she must have known a lot of violence in her life. But there were some people, unlike himself, who would never adjust to it. He guessed that this was the moment to strike. As she fought to regain her composure and the smile gradually returned to her face he suggested a date – a late meal, if she would do him the honour of accepting. He was at a loose end and would like the company, and he guessed she might like a change too. He had calculated right. She had half hoped that he would ask her out – it had been a long time since she had been with a man on a real date. She asked herself what harm it could do, and accepted.

'Good. Well, there's no time like the present – we'll go as soon as you finish work,' laughed Scala with a flash of his white teeth.

It was against everything that Noreen had known about herself. But possibly now was the time for her to change.

* * *

Declan Holmes could hardly contain his fury as he glared at the television screen. They had laughed, jeered and snarled at him as he tried to warm the bloody fools of their errors of judgement. He should know – he had been shot twice by the IRA bastards. He, for one, would never trust them and neither should anyone else.

But the bloody fools who sat on the benches of the House of Commons had told him he was a warmonger; that his judgement had been impaired; that he should give peace a chance; that the killing was all behind them now. Against all the odds the ceasefire had held. Even his own Unionist MPs had started to see the light of hope. There was no room left for mistrust; the government would have to press on with the process; too much effort and hope had already been heaped on to the peace process to let it be jeopardized now by the likes of a fat old troublemaker like Declan Holmes, despite his thirty years in the House.

Now he sat in his Bayswater flat squirming at the scenes on the late night news which showed him being ordered out of the House while other MPs flung their order papers at him. Who were they to say that his outbursts could no longer be tolerated? Who were they to ban him from the House for speaking the truth? Who were they to demand his apology for what he had said about those Sinn Fein killers? He knew the truth of the matter regardless of what any wet-behind-the-ears prime minister or self-centred MP might claim. There could be no peace in Northern Ireland for as long as the Provos were allowed to exist or their Sinn Fein puppets with their murdering leaders were offered places at a peace table. To Holmes the only way ahead for Ulster relied on the total destruction of the IRA and all it stood for. One day, when he had proved the others wrong, it would be his voice, the voice of truth over the decades, that would shine through and he would be able to lead the Unionist cause. One day they would listen to him. And that day was fast approaching. He knew that the killing had far from stopped.

He barely heard the telephone ring as he hurled abuse at the television set. It was left to his long-suffering wife of forty years, Jean, to shake him from his mood to tell him that the call was for him. Still shaking with anger, he grabbed the handset to hear Hursley's matter-of-fact tones at the other end.

'Saw the show on telly, old boy!' came the quip. 'Thought you might need some consolation. You know we're behind you, at least. I just wanted to make certain that, with all the fuss, you'd remembered our little meeting tomorrow. I think we should just go over the ideas again to bring ourselves up to speed.'

Holmes grunted his approval. That was all that was required. The meeting would go ahead as planned.

*   *   *

To her recollection, Noreen had never been in a Thai restaurant before. In her world, when a man said how about a meal he was only planning a fish supper in paper while walking home from the pub.

Scala had put her at her ease. He had wanted to impress, but not scare her off. This venue seemed ideal. He could really break the ice here. It would be novel for a small-minded innocent from the streets of the Shankill, he thought.

Noreen giggled like a small girl when she was told that she would have to eat sitting on a cushion on the floor, and would have to remove her shoes while doing so. She looked across the table as Scala took command and ordered the food, suggesting that they should begin with two bottles of Tiger beer; he assured Noreen that she would enjoy it, and then they would have wine with their food.

It was easy. As Scala chatted and made jokes charm seemed to ooze from every pore of his body. She questioned him about his limp, his scar and his work. He fobbed her off with tales of a recent car accident after which he was lucky to be alive, and told how he was improving daily. She digested his stories about working for himself in the 'leisure industry'.

In turn, he subtly brought the questioning about face and began asking about Noreen. For the first time in years she found herself able to talk about herself. She told him how her father had died when she was just twelve years old and the IRA gunmen opened fire on the bookmaker's shop. She told him how her Mam had tried to stop her brother Noel from joining the Ulster Volunteer Force and taking up the gun to seek revenge for the death of their Da. Her eyes welled with tears as she recalled how at the age of nineteen Noel had gone out one night to be a hero; how he had gone with a gun and another 'patriot' to seek justice against some Sinn Fein councillor; and how the two boys had panicked when they had driven headlong into a British army checkpoint. The three nervous British soldiers had opened fire on the car as it burst through, killing Noel and his accomplice. It had been an accident, but the boys should have stopped when challenged. She told how the UVF had called her Noel a 'hero', but she had called him a 'fool' – a 'fool' who threw his life away for a cause that he did not understand anyway. But now the killing had stopped at least.

Scala listened in silence as she explained how she had been driven out of her home with her Ma by the UVF men, who called her a traitor because she refused to hide their weapons in her house. That had been seven years ago. Since then she had lived from hand to mouth, scratching a living amongst the other exiles from Northern Ireland who lived around the Bush. Certainly she'd had boyfriends, but few had mattered . . . none had taken the time to get to know her. There had been a relationship that she had hoped would lead to love, but it had ended with her tears and pain when the man had refused to take no for an answer. Fear of attempted rape had put her off men.

'So what I'm doing here, sitting on the floor in a strange restaurant on St Patrick's Day, pouring out my life to a strange man, I haven't the Jesus of an idea!' she laughed. Her face lit up again. 'You make it easy for someone to talk. It's been a long time since I've talked about me to anyone but me Mam, and even then I only tell her what I think she wants to hear.'

He reached for her hand, and gently stroked it as he stared into her face. He thought how she must have suffered in her life, and gazed into the wide green innocent eyes that shone in the candlelight. Then, in his mind, he rebuffed himself. He was not going to care a damn about this girl. She was a tool of the trade, and that was all she was ever going to be.

He insisted on escorting her home, despite her protests. She had no choice in the matter. Home was a first-floor bedsit in the No Man's Land between Shepherd's Bush and Chiswick. As their taxi pulled to a halt outside the grim turn-of-the-century terrace Noreen's heart plummeted. To her, the evening had been a fairy-tale that she would now have to wake from, unless she made a shameless offer for her man to come upstairs. Her mind was spinning with expectation and the effects of the wine. How would he react? She did not want him to think that she made a habit of offering invitations like this to every man she met, yet she felt that she could not let this one slip through her fingers like so many before.

As Scala opened the door of the cab Noreen found herself leaning towards him, and placed a hand on his thigh before planting a kiss on his scarred cheek. To her, it was a clear indication of her intentions towards him. She hoped he would realize that and take the advantage.

Scala understood the signals, but merely gripped her hand tightly with his own. He knew he mustn't rush this. He didn't want her to think he was too eager to get her into bed. He had to win her confidence, not just bed her.

'I'd better be off and let you get some sleep,' he whispered. He noticed her expectant face fall instantly.

She became flustered, feeling that she had gone too far. She felt a fool – he would think of her as nothing more than an easy lay! If only the earth would open and swallow her up. Quickly she made a dash for her front door. As she fumbled for her keys, she felt Scala's arms grip her waist and gently spin her round to face him.

'I'll be here at ten in the morning to pick you up. So get your glad rags on – we're off out for the day, Noreen Dillon. And I'll want to see more of those smiles that we had tonight,' he beamed.

Before she could reply, he had turned back to the cab and closed the door. She could only nod and wave to him. The rest was taken for granted. They would spend tomorrow together.

Scala's cab pulled away, and he felt a deep, warm flush of success. It was the first time he had ever turned down a sure-fire offer of a tumble between the sheets. Angie would be proud of him, he grinned.

Chapter Seven

The crack of thunder seemed to shake the fragile brick walls of the old boatyard. Seconds later, a brilliant flash of lightning rebounded off the shimmering water in the tiny bay. As the water tossed high into the air some of the ancient wooden craft that were moored against the battered old jetty, the waves began to creep their way up the shallow bank towards the main building.

Naylor stared through the cracked glass of the rotting window to watch the fork lightning streak through the angry skies on the distant horizon. The flashes from the storm illuminated the bleak interior of the cramped room which had once been the main office for the yard, and lit up the faces of the five men huddled around the floor. Three sat on wooden crates stacked in a corner, while the remainder squatted against the whitewashed walls. All eyes were fixed on the small television screen perched on a rickety table in the corner.

Naylor turned to face the group and stabbed at the button on the remote control handset to rewind the videotape.

'Just one more time ought to do it.' He waited for the moans of dissatisfaction from the men to fade away before continuing. 'Yes, you *will* see it one more time. I know you think you've all got bloody photographic memories, but take it from me, there's no such thing when it comes down to it. You *will* see this tape one more time, you *will* study these people, you *will* memorize every last detail – even how these people fart! *I will not tolerate failure.*'

The videotape crackled into life again and each man turned his eyes to study it. Naylor in turn eyed the men in the group. He tried to compare them with the men he had served with before. They had been real soldiers, he thought, not simply the shit off the shoes of the world. The men he had soldiered with before he would have trusted with his life – he *had* trusted with his life way back in the days of the Falklands, on that night in May 1982 when he and his team had helped take out the Argentinian Pucara ground support aircraft on Pebble Island. That had been what Naylor considered a real war.

But as his eyes darted from one huddled figure to another he congratulated himself on what he had managed to achieve with them in such a short time. They had been given to him as volunteers, committed to what they believed to be a just cause. The blind fools probably thought of themselves as true patriots, he had thought. They had been united in hatred. They were killers – men who would snuff out a life without hesitation because they believed in the cause, When others around them had hung up their weapons while the politicians had talked, they had proved their commitment to their cause.

Like him, they had not been difficult to find and recruit: it was just a matter of knowing where to look. There were probably hundreds like them. Each one could justify his actions to himself and to anyone who questioned him. But it had been Naylor himself who had boasted that just 'six good men' could engulf Ulster in flames and blood once more.

He had trained them and moulded them into a fighting force, using the same rigorous routines that he had drilled into his old-time squaddies. Now his renegades were a team, instead of a group of individuals whose only common denominator was that they enjoyed killing Catholics. In reality his renegades now belonged to neither side, because they were pledged to fight on, despite what the politicians of any side said. Yet in their own way they would die for the Crown like countless natives of Ulster who felt themselves more closely linked to the Queen and Britain than most people living in Liverpool or Manchester or Birmingham. They would rather die fighting the notion of republicanism and nationalism than surrender their ideals. They believed in Ulster. There could be no surrender. Now, they had been given the opportunity to strike a death blow for any process that meant dealing with the IRA scum, or which smacked of a sell-out.

Naylor grinned. These days, the only thing that he believed in was himself and the huge pay cheques that would buy him a new life in Rio when all this was over. But Brazil seemed a long way away at present. Home for the last two weeks had been a disused boatyard on the windswept Ards Peninsula south of the picturesque resort of Donaghadee, less than half an hour from Belfast by car. Few people had taken notice of the group of men who had arrived at the yard by Transit van and begun unloading boxes, even though the premises had ceased to be used as a fully fledged boatyard at least five years earlier. The actual ownership of the place had always been a cause of confusion. Old man Hoy had sold the lease to one of the big firms from Belfast when he had gone bust years before, but no one had ever figured out what use a clapped out old boatyard and jetty could be to anyone from the city. But more to the point, in this neck of the woods no one took the time to care either.

As the tape reached its conclusion once again, Naylor turned to the thick-set man with fashionably short-cropped red hair at the edge of the group and ordered him to switch on the light. As he watched him, Naylor thought how he had always seen Lorcan Moore as the best of the bunch. Possibly it was his three years in the Ulster Defence Regiment that had given him the edge. He was calm in tense situations, he obeyed without question and he was loyal. He had mastered the art of bomb-making – even from the rawest of material – and was a superb marksman. In his own mind, Naylor had unofficially thought of him as the obvious second-in-command.

'So there you have it. This is the bastard who should have still been serving twenty years,' grunted Naylor, pointing to an aging passport-style photograph of the man whom the group had been studying on the video. 'Instead, he's served three paltry years for blowing your people into a million fuckin' pieces. He's back on the streets now, as we're sitting here talking.'

The men glanced back at the freeze-frame image on the screen to study the differences. In the three years that the man known as Paul Kean had been behind the walls of the Kesh his hair had turned grey, making him appear older than his thirty-two years. The video had followed Kean as he appeared from the gates of the prison, to be hugged and cheered by the group that had waited so patiently. They had hailed him as a hero. The woman with the white tee-shirt and blonde curled hair had flung her arms around his neck and cried. The photographers had clicked away. The man had beamed with happiness as he punched the air in triumph with his fist. He had once been the most notorious bomb-maker within the IRA's ranks. Now he was a returning hero.

'Take a close look and inwardly digest the differences in our boy,' commanded Naylor. 'Never forget that face.'

He took the old photograph and placed it on the wall alongside a rogues' gallery of other snapshots. Kean's photograph was given prominence next to that of a pretty girl with long blonde hair – her picture had a cross scratched across it in red ink.

Naylor turned to the group and grinned. 'And the Lord said: "Let justice be mine . . ." And that, my fine friends, is just what it's going to be. Mr Kean will be the next to feel that justice.'

As one, the group of men before him nodded in approval.

'And you, my avenging angels, will make sure that he's not the only one. You each know what you have to do, and the timescale.'

Vengeance was heading on to the streets of Belfast.

*   *   *

She slipped her fingers through his and clutched his hand tightly. Her bare head barely reached his shoulder as she attempted to rest it on him. Noreen could hardly resist the temptation to skip with happiness. As they strolled along the footpaths in the brilliant sunshine of an early spring day Scala looked down to see her looking directly up into his face. Her nose crinkled in a smile. He could not resist returning it. Neither could he resist the feeling of male pride in having a girl with such innocent and obvious beauty on his arm. He enjoyed the envious glances from other men as they went by.

It had been a long time since he had visited London Zoo. He felt a twinge of guilt when he thought how often he had promised to take his children there but had never done so. There had always been something else to prevent him. His previous visit had been with other young soldiers when they had been stationed in London.

Noreen felt good. Scala had arrived, as promised, at ten o'clock on the dot. He had always prided himself on his punctuality. They had driven across London in the BMW to the park. Then they had laughed at the apes, cringed at the snakes and stood in silent admiration at the power and beauty of the tigers. He had made a fuss of her, bought her chocolates and popcorn. She had giggled.

As they sat quietly over coffee, Scala had handed her a brown envelope. Her eyes had glistened as she peeked inside and saw the wad of £20 notes. He had insisted she took the £500. It was for her: rent money. It was a drop in the ocean to him. He knew she needed it. A gift from him to her: she had to take it.

Scala felt a strange sense of peace within himself. Business had been good, and Connor had taken the bait. There had been an increasing demand from him during the few days that the pair of them had dealt together. But at least some good would now come from the money that he was making from his drug-peddling.

Noreen had flushed, unable to speak at this gift from the man whom she admitted she barely knew, but strangely felt she had been waiting for most of her life. He had been a handsome stranger, then a friend to whom she could talk; now she felt confident that he would be the lover that she had unknowingly yearned for in her dreams for so long.

* * *

Hursley tucked into the goose and red cabbage that was claimed to be a speciality of the restaurant. By contrast, his lunch guest Declan Holmes appeared more satisfied with the deep red Hungarian wine that slipped down his gullet so easily – too easily, to Hursley's way of thinking. This was one of his favourite eateries in the centre of London. He felt comfortable amid the red leather seats and dark wood-panelled walls. He was never out of place, surrounded by the smart businessmen and women who frequented the place or couples indulging in discreet extra-marital affairs.

Holmes was feeling decidedly more cheered than he had been the night before. The news from the United States had done that for him. The Sinn Fein bastards had gone there to raise money for their party. But the carefully 'leaked' document in the press had given credence to the Unionists' claims that the IRA were still busy raising millions for their cause through common-or-garden Mafia-style crime such as extortion and fraud. The American visit had already caused controversy, as the TV cameras had focused sharply on the queues of Sinn Fein and IRA supporters across the Atlantic waiting to chip in with their dollars for the cause. Many Tory rebels were already in open revolt against government policy, which was to push along the peace process. The newspaper 'leak' had achieved maximum impact – especially when it claimed that the IRA were restocking their arms. Hursley had seen to that. It was obvious to Holmes and his 'supporters' that the IRA were planning a new onslaught. Hursley had told the Commons that, and he had warned the do gooders. But they had not listened. Maybe now they would begin.

'I have to say, the timing really couldn't have been better,' smiled Hursley as he washed down a mouthful of his excellent goose. 'It will certainly make people think twice about the intentions of our Sinn Fein brothers. I don't suppose the idea of having our boys in green going over to the States cap in hand to add to the coffers – and succeeding – will do much to strengthen the so-called "special relationship" between ourselves and the Yanks. So at present we might have fallen behind in the PR battle a bit. But I think things will take a decidedly dodgy turn for the worse by the time we've finished,' he added, taking another sip of wine.

'What the hell do the bloody Americans know about the bloody thing?' retorted Holmes. 'They sit there on their fat arses in safety . . . and console themselves with the fact they are doing their bit for the "old country" by reaching into their fat bloody wallets. They've never known the pain of being bombed or seeing someone you know end up in pieces because of the bastards. They think it's like some bloody John Wayne film.'

Hursley saw Holmes' fingers tightening around his glass. 'Yes, I know that – we all know that. It's what most people in the street say every day,' he said. 'But if we time our next little bombshell to go off at the right time, I think we can safely say that a lot more people will sit up and take notice. I want you ready to go public in two weeks. I've been in touch with our chaps across the water, and they expect to begin moving into the next phase by then. They've already got the stuff. What I can tell you, if it makes you feel better, is that your IRA chums will be getting a bit of a shock within the next few days. I think you know what

I mean. It should really start them rattling their sabres all right. But at least some of the scum will be off the street.'

Holmes grinned. He was finding his appetite again. 'I'll be ready to go public in a couple of weeks as planned. You just tell me when. Then we'll see who are seen as the saints around here,' he replied. 'Suffer little children, eh? Well, suffer you little bastards . . .'

Hursley looked anxiously around the restaurant. 'Declan, I really do wish you'd learn to control your mouth sometimes. There's a time and a place for everything, you know!' he said quietly in a faint-hearted attempt to admonish Holmes. 'Anyway, I need to know straightaway the moment you hear if your esteemed Unionist friends are going to agree to attend the talks. It's only a matter of time before some of my more senior chaps decide to give the go-ahead to the other side and agree to a meet. I want to be ready with a time and a place.'

Holmes, his mouth filled with food, could only nod his agreement.

* * *

Scala slipped the coat from her shoulders as she stood to take stock of his Chelsea apartment. He had called it a flat, but to Noreen it was as big as any house that she had ever been in. From the huge square sitting room with its giant leather armchairs she was able to look along the corridor off which were the three bedrooms. The walls were dotted with photographs and antique maps. The furniture was sparse, but expensive; the lighting intimate and welcoming. Scala pointed out the bathroom at the end of the corridor and the small kitchen. She began to feel nervous once more, but Scala noticed the signs and quickly moved to calm her. He poured her a glass of wine and urged her to relax.

It was almost 7.30 p.m. and had been a long day. He told her that he would have to go out for a short while, but she was welcome to stay. She should relax, have a bath. He would not be long. Perhaps they could do something when he returned. They could go to the new burger restaurant for supper when he returned.

'But where are you going?' Noreen questioned nervously. 'I thought we were going to be together.' She stared into her glass. 'It's been a smashin' day, Jim. It'd be great if it could just go on.'

'And on it will go,' laughed Scala. 'I've just got some business that I have to attend to. It's the only time I can see this bloke. I have to earn a crust, you know!'

Noreen looked around the room. 'It's not exactly a crust you need to keep this lot going. What does this fella do anyway?'

'I've told you – he's in the leisure business with me . . . It's like supply and demand. He wants things for his leisure industry, and I supply him. It's as simple as that.'

'It sounds shady.'

'Well, it's not, I tell you,' said Scala more firmly than he liked. 'Now make yourself at home. I'll be back later. Telephone your Mam if you want.'

She felt it was futile to argue further. Besides, she wasn't about to let the day end so early and on a sour note.

*   *   *

Scala had become a regular face at the Cellar. The two overweight ex-boxers on the door now greeted him as old friends when he appeared. The sight of those ghostly white-faced girls desperately attempting to look older than their teenage years, and their sweating macho suitors who mauled their young bodies, no longer bothered him. In a strange way, he felt he was beginning to belong.

He felt confident. He knew he'd had a good day with Noreen. She was coming along nicely now, he thought. Matherson would be satisfied. She was ready for the plucking. He caught sight of himself in the mirror behind the bar, and adjusted the jacket of his green Hugo Boss suit. Connor came towards him, smiling now.

He had confidence in Scala. Certainly Pierce had been lifted. But that was his tough shit. It was fortunate that Scala had been able to step in. Certainly, it had been a coincidence of timing that Scala had arrived when he did – but he *had* to be okay! Connor had persuaded himself that Scala was okay – after all, no copper would actively sell the drugs the way Scala was doing. That had always been the ultimate test for spotting coppers – they would never sell anything. They stood out a mile.

As far as Connor was concerned, the stuff was selling well. They'd handled ten grand's worth of business in a week. Now was the time to move on to other stuff. He had been thinking about this for some time, and Scala had promised him that he could get whatever he wanted, hadn't he?

Scala drank and Connor talked. Scala was in agreement. But Connor would have to wait a minute – Scala needed a leak.

He was just finishing rinsing his hands when he saw the two men enter the wash room. He watched them purposefully in the mirror as they took up positions behind him. Without exchanging a word the taller one, a bear of a black man wearing a creased black suit, with tell-tale eyes that had spent years being hammered senseless in the boxing ring, took up position by the door.

The second man, white and shorter in a brown leather jacket and tee-shirt, but with the thick, solid frame of a bodybuilder, stood by Scala's side.

There was no one else in the toilet. He had never seen them before, but his instincts told him they meant trouble.

'Wotcha, Taff!'

Scala turned to meet the gaze of the second man, who spoke in a thick East End accent.

'Me and my mate Ade 'ere 'ear you've been setting up a bit of business round – 'ere a good little business an' all!'

Scala fixed a steely stare on the man. 'And what might that have to do with the likes of you, then? Even supposing that I had done as you reckon?' he brazened.

'Well, you see, mate, Ade and meself and some other geezers who we work with might reckon that you could be trampling on our patch. We've had this little number fixed up for months, before some crippled bleedin' Welsh twat came in spreading his stuff around like Smarties! No one asked us if they could work 'ere, did they? We might not want 'em working 'ere. We might have to send them to fuck with their balls in their pockets if they were to try that. We might not like that kind of thing, yer see – do we, Ade?'

The black man stood motionless. Scala watched him in the

mirror through the corner of his eye, then squared nearer to the white man by his side.

'Firstly, let me tell you no one's called me Taff for years – you see, I don't like it. Secondly, I doubt if little pieces of shit like yourselves could ever be a "mate" of mine, so I don't like being called that either. Thirdly, and perhaps more important than the other two, no one ever tells me where I'm going to carry out my business – and anyone who does can stay the fuck out of my way! No one here has told me about any streaks of piss like you two or anyone associated with you. So stay the hell out of my way!'

Scala had hardly finished when he saw the black bear begin to move towards him. In a split second the ex-SAS soldier brought his knee up to catch the short white man squarely in the groin. The man's legs buckled with the impact, sending his face forward. In the same instant Scala followed through with a blow from the base of his hand which smashed into his victim's nose, shattering it with a deafening crack and sending splinters of bone shooting into the man's head and eyes. He fell to the floor, clutching his blood-spattered face.

As the black figure pounced, Scala nimbly dodged to the side before letting fly with his right leg to crash directly under both of the man's kneecaps. The pain of the impact shot through Scala's injured leg as the giant sank to his knees.

As Scala caught his breath he put his full weight behind a right-handed punch which caught the groaning hulk plum on the wide, flattened nose. Then he pulled his hand back, lurching forward and stabbing the screaming man directly into his boxing-battered eyes with two straight fingers from his right hand. He thought he felt at least one of his fingers pierce an eyeball. The bear dropped squealing, holding his hands to his eyes in agony.

The second man was still groped around the floor sobbing as blood spurted from his wound.

The entire incident had taken less than ten seconds. Scala had combined his street fighting ability and his training to deal with the thugs, whom he only rated as bullies. His leg was still painful from where he had made contact with the bear's kneecaps. He hoped he hadn't injured it seriously again. That would screw everything up.

Suddenly the door burst open. A teenage youth who had come to use the toilet stood wide-eyed at the scene of carnage in front of him. His petrified reaction meant that he would not now require the use of the toilet.

Scala adjusted himself and pushed past the youth. Back in the bar he sought out Connor and pulled him to one side.

'So tell me, Gerry boy, what the fuck would two guys – one looking like a friggin' black gorilla and called Ade and the other a piece of East End shit who fancied himself in the mouth stakes – be doing asking about me and trying to muscle in on my stall?'

Connor fought for breath and attempted to regain his composure. 'Honest, I don't know them. I think they belong to a mob who operate some of the clubs on the other side of the river. They want to branch out, kinda thing . . . but I told 'em that I was 'appy with the arrangement I 'ad with you! Honest, that's what I told 'em, Jim. The trouble is, they belong to a big mob. They could be real trouble – I mean real trouble! What the shit did you do to 'em?' begged Connor.

'Absolutely bloody nothing compared to what I'd do to you if you tried to cross me, me old mucker!'

The two heavies from the door had come to the bar after hearing about the commotion in the toilets. They spied Scala in a dark corner with Connor. As they approached, Scala released the barman and turned to smile at his two 'new-found friends'.

'All right lads, I'll be on my way now. Look after my old chum Gerry here, will you? I think he might need looking after!' he said in an exaggerated Welsh accent.

*   *   *

The smell of cooking wafted through the flat and greeted Scala as he walked through the door. It was something he had grown unused to. Even in his latter days at Hereford, Angie had only managed to serve up a variety of instant foods from the microwave or the take-away.

His leg was throbbing and his knuckles were grazed and swollen from where they had connected with the black man's face. He stepped into the sitting room, where a single candle burned brightly in the centre of the dining table that was squeezed into the corner of the room. He was later than he had said he would be, and there was no sign of Noreen.

He went to hang his jacket over the back of the sofa. As he did so he caught sight of the angelic face caught in sleep as she lay sprawled full-length along the cushions. Slowly she opened her eyes to look him straight in the face. The reflection from the candle danced in her eyes as she smiled.

She was wearing nothing but one of Scala's shirts, which stretched to just below the beautifully rounded cheeks of her buttocks.

'I'm sorry I'm later than I said I would be – we ended up having a lot to talk about . . .'

Noreen stretched forward to place her finger over his lips to silence him. 'It doesn't matter, darlin'. You're here now – that's what counts!'

'What about dinner? I guess you've been cooking – I'm bloody starv . . .'

Noreen stopped him again. 'That doesn't matter either!' She leaned forward and kissed him on his scarred cheek again and again.

Scala could smell the scented bath salts on her body.

She rose completely from the sofa to stand before him. She had never known herself behave quite like this before. But she knew she wanted this man, she wanted to know what it was like to be loved by this man. As she stood, the light from the hallway silhouetted the beautifully rounded outline of her body within Scala's shirt.

She took his right hand. Scala winced with pain. She noticed the grazing and angry red swelling. She was startled. What kind of work would result in this? she thought; but quickly pushed the thought to the crevices of her mind. She kissed the fingers of his injured hand and gently stroked them, before placing his hand on her breast.

'Oh, darlin' Jim . . . it's been so long . . . it's been a lifetime . . . I need to be loved . . . for God's sake I need to be loved . . . love me, Jim . . . love me please!' she whispered time and time again.

Scala stepped forward and gently took hold of her tiny waist. She threw back the mass of curls from her face and dragged his mouth to hers. With the expertise of years he searched for the buttons of the shirt and slowly began undoing them, one after the other, as the couple slowly sank to the floor, gently and deliberately stroking each other's bodies as they entwined.

Chapter Eight

The sound of distant, muffled voices stirred her. She turned from her deep, delicious sleep and fought to focus her thoughts. The rays of sunlight pierced the gaps in the drawn curtains and spotlighted her naked body on the rumpled bed. Desperately she recalled the events of the hours before, the warm sensations of gentle lovemaking with a man who made her feel wanted and knew how to please, who took control of her emotions in a way that she could not recollect ever feeling in her life before. She stretched, then strained to listen to the faint noise of talking that came from another room.

Now, strangely shameless and confident in her nakedness, she rose from the bed and gently tiptoed down the corridor towards the sound.

Scala was sitting cross-legged on the sofa, comfortable in jeans and sweatshirt. He had the telephone handset under his chin and was speaking in a virtual whisper. Noreen watched in silence from the darkness of the corridor, watching the man who had brought a new sense of purpose to her life. Scala could not see her.

In a slow, deliberate tone he related the previous night's events at the cellar to Matherson. He was not 100 per cent certain who 'Ade' and his partner were, who they belonged to, or if they posed a threat. But his instinct told him that they would be back, that there would be trouble and his position would be threatened. Although he was confident in his ability to handle trouble, he felt he was treading new territory here and that he was caught in a No Man's Land which he would not be able to control. He told Matherson that he felt he had done enough to assure the right people of his credentials. It was time to move on.

There was silence at the other end of the line.

Barely able to control his temper, Scala hissed: 'Are you still there, sir? Are you listening to what I'm telling you? I believe there is a real danger of me being compromised by these outsiders! I'm requesting some back-up – otherwise I can't be responsible for what happens!'

His tone prompted a reply from a pensive Matherson. 'All right, James, that's enough!' Although he had done so at the briefing, it did not seem right to Matherson to use the Christian name of a man who worked for him. It smacked of familiarity, and that was something that he always fought against with his people. He refused to become close to them – he didn't know how long he would have them. 'I'll see what can be done. I agree that you seem to have made the right impression. Maybe it *is* time to move . . .'

Before he could hear the end of Matherson's sentence, Noreen entered the room and slowly walked towards Scala. His mind blanked as his eyes ran the full length of her nakedness, her wild hair cascading over her shoulders. He had not prepared himself for this vision. Swallowing hard, he fought to regain his composure as she sat down beside him. He was aware of Matherson bellowing down the line, and his apparent flush prompted Noreen to burst into a fit of childlike giggles.

Matherson was aware of the background noise and realized that his man was not alone. 'What the hell's going on there, Scala? It wouldn't be our little angel, would it? Are things progressing? Talk to me, dammit, man! I want to – '

Scala gathered his composure and, as Noreen nestled under his arm, sharply cut short Matherson's tirade.

'Spot on! I suppose you could say everything is in hand,' he grinned. 'But I would be grateful if you could look into the other matter as soon as possible, though. So I'll look forward to hearing from you . . .' He slammed down the telephone.

'Who was that?' begged Noreen. 'It's early for secret squirrel phone calls, isn't it?'

'It's never too early for business!' insisted Scala. 'He's just someone who supplies me with goods. There's no rest for the wicked, you know!'

She felt too good to enquire more. The way she felt this morning, even if he had been one of the hated UVF men who had brainwashed her brother and got him killed she could have forgiven him.

*   *   *

The massive stone bulk of the Corpus Christi church afforded enough protection for the car parked alongside it to go unnoticed for a long time. From here the two pairs of eyes could keep a close watch on the drab house in the dull rows of terraces that fill the Ballymurphy Road, the central stronghold of Belfast's IRA territory. It had been a long night and they had taken it in turns to watch the comings and goings at the house. The well-wishers had arrived with their bottles and the lights of the house had burned well into the early hours of the new day.

The eyes had watched Paul Kean welcome his visitors. They had paid tribute to a hero home from the struggle, a martyr who had suffered at the hands of the Brit bastards. They came to congratulate him on his struggle – the struggle he had won, because the politicians had said he should go free. They had drunk into the night, and they had danced and laughed. Now, as the sun rose over the grimy estate, Naylor and Moore watched and waited. Elsewhere in the city, others were keeping similar vigils.

*   *   *

The chief inspector in charge of the Drugs Squad had not wanted to know about the telephone call that threatened to ruin his day off. The golf foursome had been planned a fortnight ago. Indeed he would have ignored the call, if the young detective sergeant from the office had not subsequently rung him at home and told him that the superintendent had been on: someone from on high had been pestering him, he had said, and he wanted something done immediately to get them off his back. The superintendent had demanded immediate action.

The chief inspector had thought it could wait. A raid on some god-forsaken slimy club was not going to make the headlines for the tabloids, no matter how much shit was changing hands or no matter what kind of scumbag characters were involved. But orders were orders, especially if they came down from on high. Something would be done – even if it did balls up his day off.

*   *   *

The two men sat in silence. Neither Naylor nor Moore felt the need for talk. They were old soldiers, used to spending hours in silence on observation missions. The interior of the Peugeot 205 was cramped. The car was built for speed, not comfort. It had been hours since they had stretched their legs. It was not really necessary for them to remain, but Naylor demanded that nothing be left to chance: he wanted to witness the event for himself. Moore understood; besides, he too had been drilled in the art of obeying without question when ordered by someone you respected.

The bright early morning sunshine had given way to grey cloud before the front door of the house opened. Two red-haired little girls no more than five years old, dressed in identical party frocks and carrying identical dolls, sprang from the house and ran to the Volvo parked at the roadside. They laughed and giggled as the woman with blonde hair, whom Moore and the rest had seen in the video, shouted at them to come back. The woman, dressed in a scarlet trouser suit, shrugged as her daughters ignored her and then laughed as she gave way to their excitement and happiness. They were happy because their Daddy was home. He had been away at work for a long time. Daddy was a good man, they had been told – they were very lucky little girls to have a Daddy like him. Now he was back they would always be together.

Naylor sat up as he saw the grey-haired figure of Kean step from the house. The years in prison seemed to have suited him and he looked smart and relaxed in his sports jacket and slacks. He would have had his 'welcome back' cheque from the boys in the brigade to tide him over until he could get back on his feet, thought Naylor. He saw the knuckles on Moore's hands turning white from the tension of gripping the steering wheel, and secretly smiled.

Naylor watched the small girls dance impatiently as they waited for their father to open the car door. He watched as their mother strapped them into the two child seats in the rear and saw Kean get into the passenger seat as the woman positioned herself behind the steering wheel and slotted the key into the ignition.

Then both Naylor and Moore narrowed their eyes as the glare from the flames and explosion momentarily blinded them. In that split second the Volvo had erupted in a wall of fire and vivid colours from the device planted as the estate slept in the dead of night.

The two men watched from their far-off viewpoint two hundred yards down the road, scrutinizing the scene from their binoculars. The body of a burning doll lay on the road not far from them. It was Naylor who broke the silence.

'Let justice be mine!' he quoted. 'A good morning's work, I think. And the day's not over yet. Home for a brew.'

He signalled for Moore to drive. The red Peugeot moved slowly and deliberately away from the scene towards the Whiterock Road, as the people gathered in the road by the burning debris to witness the end of the man who hours before had been their hero.

* * *

The two gypsy boys carefully skirted around the golf driving range near their site. There were always arguments between the gypsies and the enthusiasts who swiped their balls down the purpose-made greens in an attempt to improve their game. The children who lived on the near permanent site on the western outskirts of Belfast were often being accused of mischievously taking the unseen balls that showered down like hailstones. This time the boys were determined not to be the target for argument. This time they were more interested in retrieving their wayward mongrel than the stupid bloody golfballs of the rich people who played there.

It wasn't the first time that the cursed dog had run off like this. As they sank into the mud of the tiny plain of reclaimed land they shouted for the missing beast. This time, they would beat it to within an inch of its life. As they neared the disused quarry they could hear the barking of the dog, and as they drew nearer the bark became more of a frantic yelp. They caught sight of the excited animal determinedly pulling and scratching the muddy wastes at the bottom of the quarry.

The boys cursed, then froze in terror as they glimpsed what the animal held in its jaws. The limp hand flapped wildly in the dog's mouth as it shook the arm and attempted to pull the rest of the torso from the muddy hole. The two pale-faced, wide-eyed youngsters edged forward. As the dog continued trying to shake the corpse free the colourless eyes in the man's head turned towards the boys. They recoiled, petrified.

Another pull from the dog shook the body sufficiently for the gaping wound in the back of the head to be revealed. It was enough. The boys turned and ran shouting towards the massed players on the driving range, followed by their yelping dog.

Naylor's other teams had not been idle. An hour before Kean had met his maker, so too had Thomas Gallagher. The day before, like Kean he had celebrated and been called an IRA hero after his five years behind bars of the twenty to which he had been sentenced. Now the man who had lived by the gun had died by the gun. Drink had made him careless as he stepped from the bar. He had not noticed the two men by the alley who came with guns, like he had done in a previous existence. Five years earlier he would have seen them, but prison and the notion of a ceasefire had blunted his instincts. He had paid the price.

*   *   *

Jacobson was in no mood for excuses. He was having his balls chewed and he was determined to pass on the bollocking.

'The shit is well and truly all over the bloody place,' he heard himself repeating down the telephone. 'What the hell is your man up to? I agreed to your plan because it seemed sensible – but I want results *quick*!'

Matherson shuffled uneasily at the other end of the line. 'All I can tell you is that we're making progress. Things are moving along, I'm sure . . .'

'Progress?' blurted Jacobson. 'You call this progress? I've got one IRA ex-bomber blown up, there's one of their shooters, this Gallagher fellow, with the back of his head blown out, and a third with enough bullet holes in his head to pass as a sponge – and all targeted on the same day, within a week of coming out of jail! Yes, I suppose you could call that progress if you've got a warped mind!' he shouted. 'And to make things slightly more confused we've got the UDA saying they know bugger all about it – while Sinn Fein and the IRA are baying for blood and calling them all the bloody liars that God made. Yes, that's progress!'

Matherson rallied. 'I tell you, sir, we're on the move. I expect results quickly. Scala has passed the first phase. But, for what it's worth, I'll give him a gentle nudge up the backside.'

* * *

It had been so long coming. She had thought it was the only thing in her life that she had wanted. But now that the time had come, she felt torn. Why did it have to happen now?

Noreen had heard the joy in her Mam's voice as she told her the news. All the people that her mother knew were talking about it too. All Noreen's old friends from the years before had thanked God. The committee from the UVF had felt like gods themselves when they had told her Mam. They had hugged her in friendship when they told her that her daughter could return in safety. They had given permission.

Now Noreen was not sure she wanted that permission. She felt that at last she had something else in her life – someone else! She had waited all her life to feel as complete a woman as she did now. She would never have believed that a few days could have changed that. But a few days *had* changed her, and she would not give up this new opportunity easily.

She knew she would have to tell Scala. But how? He had given her money to ease her life. In return, she felt as though she had given her whole being. But for the first time in years she felt a purpose in life because of this man. She would tell him of the chance to return just as soon as he got back to the apartment that night. She would wait for his reaction. Then she would know what to do.

* * *

The news bulletins talked of nothing else but the killings. Every channel on the mainland and in Ulster tripped out the usual string of dignitaries and rent-a-quote spokespeople to add their ten cents' worth to the furious debate. The sweating form in the corner of the rest room sat on the bright floral sofa impassively watching the endless string of puppets whom the TV newsmen were attempting to interview. Clad only in a white towelling robe, Justice Niall Hennessey impatiently flicked the channel switches on the remote control in an attempt to monitor the varying reports.

He watched intently as the news presenters read statements from the various Loyalist factions and quoted a spokesman from the Ulster Democratic Party, who denied any UDC involvement in the killings of Paul Kean and Thomas Gallagher and the near fatal shooting of Gerry O'Connell within days of their release from prison. Then he flared his nostrils in disgust as the cameras focused on another man. To Hennessey, Eamon Clancy was still nothing more than a Provo killer whom he would have jailed years ago if there had been sufficient proof. Now the judge watched with mounting fury as the man he knew to be a killer spoke as the leading representative of Sinn Fein – a would-be politician who now ranted about the outrage to peace-loving Catholics.

Hennessy reddened with anger as Clancy told the interviewers how his party wanted peace, but how the killings of Kean and Gallagher and the attempted murder of O'Connell proved that the IRA were right to refuse to give up their weapons. How difficult, he asserted, it would be to control the sense of outrage and the demands for revenge that would now certainly follow the betrayal of the ceasefire by men who would almost certainly be identified as Loyalists at the end of the day.

The judge sat upright during a segment of the report that showed the Assistant Chief Constable of the RUC, Philip McGann, visiting the scene of the car bomb in Ballymurphy Road. He considered that McGann showed the right amount of concern at the grave situation as he warned that, as feared in many sectors of the community, the spectre of sectarian killings had returned. But he laughed aloud when he heard McGann call for restraint.

'I take this as a grim reminder of what has gone on before,' said the Assistant Chief Constable. 'Let us nip this violence in the bud before it blooms from isolated incidents into a full-grown tree of death and destruction.'

Hennessey whispered to himself, 'Quite the little performer, aren't we, Philip? You should think about politics in the next life . . .'

The reporter had pressed McGann to name who he thought was responsible. But the policeman had hedged his bets and refused to be drawn.

'I think the community will draw obvious conclusions from today's atrocities, but let us not react in haste – we should guard against assumption.' It was a good performance.

The faces of the victims continually flicked on to the screens. Hennessey shuffled with satisfaction. These men had escaped the justice that he had meted out in court – despite his outcries, they had been released. But now they had had justice thrust upon them. He felt good.

Half an hour after his steam and massage, Hennessey was still oozing sweat. He kidded himself that he loved coming to the club for his health and for the soft and relaxing surroundings. But the real attraction was the 'extra services' offered to members by the willing female staff, eager to boost their salaries with their own personal skills. God knows, there was nothing like that on offer at home.

One afternoon a week was enough. The driver would leave him at the luxurious house with the huge white columns which stood in its own grounds surrounded by the exclusive properties of the Malone Road. The two guards would wait patiently outside as the judge enjoyed being pandered to. God knows, he had worked hard all his life to achieve the trappings of success that membership of a club like this brought. And God knows how long he would be allowed to continue enjoying such perks.

His career was stagnant – thanks to the peace, there were no brighter prospects in sight for him. There would soon be no need for people like him – people who had believed in the law, lived according to its precepts and given their lives to it. His stagnation would eventually lead to him being stripped of the cars, the assistants, even the security systems that surrounded his home. He would be left only with an over-ambitious wife and a yearning for the power that he felt should be his reward after twenty-five years as a slave to the law.

Still, he cheered himself in the knowledge that he had seen to the likes of Kean and Gallagher at least. And there were many more on his casebooks to face the wrath of his Judgement Day.

The husky voice of the buxom girl attendant who was

Hennessey's favourite shattered his concentration on the television screen. She strode into the lounge carrying a glass of freshly squeezed orange juice and, as she bent to place it on the table, made no attempt to disguise the view of her ample breasts.

'Will there be anything else today, sir?'

Hennessey looked at the knowing smirk on the raven-haired girl's face. He could not resist – he knew he should enjoy the perks while he could. 'I feel I am in need of a little extra treatment today, my dear,' he replied in his croaking, clipped, public school voice. Justice could wait for thirty minutes.

*　　*　　*

Matherson's telephone call had worked. There was nothing that brought about such quick response from an old police chum as a little blackmail.

As Scala turned the BMW into the normally quiet and grim street that housed the Cellar he was stopped in his tracks by the mass of police activity before him. The flashing blue lights from three police mini-coaches greeted him, as well as an array of squad cars. What seemed like scores of uniformed officers were scurrying in and out of the club. Dozens of young clientele filed out into the street to be herded into the waiting vans. Some scuffled, others contented themselves with hurling abuse.

Scouring the scene for a glimpse of anyone he recognized, Scala glanced through the open rear doors of one of the police vans and saw a sight which pleased him. He had guessed right: Ade and his mouthy accomplice had returned, but not alone. The white flash of bandage over Ade's left eye shone out against the black face like a beacon. Alongside him sat another five muscle-bound black thugs. Scala took them to be Ade's sidekicks who had walked into the trap that he had hoped Matherson would spring in order to protect his man.

Scala wondered what had happened to Ade's shorter, stockier white accomplice from their encounter in the toilet. As he recalled the sound of the man's nose splintering he presumed that he might now be residing in one of London's overstretched hospitals. Scala felt a smug satisfaction.

Then his eyes flicked to the open door of the club, to watch the struggling shape of Connor being bundled out and into the back of the waiting police vehicle. It would surely not be long before Connor was squealing like a pig for his own protection. And not very long after that, Scala considered, he himself would be a wanted man. The plan was working.

*　　*　　*

She looked deep into his blue eyes. There was going to be no easy way for her to say this. Maybe he wouldn't care anyway . . . but she hoped against hope that her fears were wrong.

'I called her, like you said I could . . .'

'Yeah! Don't worry – that's okay. How are things?' Scala sounded genuinely interested.

'Me Mam says that things are fine, just fine over there. She had some news for me . . . it seems that the men in the know have been in touch with her. It seems they've said I can go back . . . Lots of people are going back these days . . . and they've said I can go back,' she muttered.

There was silence, then: 'That's nice for you,' murmured Scala, in a manner which purposely indicated pain. 'Looks like I found you just at the right time then, doesn't it? I find you, and the next thing you're off to foreign parts!'

He thought he heard the sound of a muffled sob.

'But Jim, that's what I'm thinking about . . . you see, I don't know if I want to go back. I mean, these last few days have been some of the best of my life . . . I feel as though I've started to live all over again.'

Scala smiled to himself. Play hard to get, old son, play hard to get, he thought.

'Jim, despite what you think – if you think about me at all, that is – I don't go around doing this. I don't jump into bed with just anyone I meet – Jesus Christ strike me down if I do! You've treated me like a queen, sure you have. No one has ever treated me better . . . no one has loved me like you have . . . no one – '

'All right,' interrupted Scala, 'I get the picture. I'm a real knight in shining armour. But it doesn't seem to be doing me any good, does it? I don't mind what I give you and I don't mind what I do for you – that's the truth. You're a beautiful lass God help me. But from what you tell me, you've wanted to go back for years.'

'It's true!' Now she was crying openly. 'But sweet Jesus, I don't want to lose you either. I've waited years for someone like you too . . .'

It was as if she had been struck by lightening – simply saying her idea seemed to bring relief. Suddenly she sat bolt upright in bed.

'Jim, I know it's mad, but would you think about coming with me? For a while at least, until I get to know the lie of the land. And then we can take it from there. I know me Mam won't mind you coming. Sure, it'll be great to have a man around the house again . . . Oh, please, Jim – I can't explain to myself how I feel, never mind to you, but tell me you'll at least think about it?'

He had played her and won her! Now he would go on to the next stage of the game.

'But I've got business to attend to,' he protested. 'I mean, you're asking me to drop everything here and go trolling off like a bloody lovelorn schoolboy!'

Her heart sank and fresh tears welled in her eyes. She pulled the sheet to her face to dry them. She was about to lose him and she knew it.

'Yeah, okay!' he said, as if her tears had moved him. 'I'll come with you for a bit. I think I owe myself some holiday anyway. I'd be lying to you and myself if I said that I didn't think we had something going here. So, being the romantic bloody fool that I am, I'm willing to give it a go. What's to lose? At least they've stopped blowing themselves to pieces over there!' She could not believe her ears. She hugged his face to her breast and kissed him on the top of his head.

'When do you want to leave?' asked Scala, trying to control Noreen. 'If we're going to behave like fools, then we might as well do it as soon as possible. I can leave straightaway.'

Noreen gushed with ideas, and garbled plans were made. In his mind, Scala wanted to leave as soon as possible. He thought of Connor being questioned: he didn't want any smart-arse boy in blue wrecking his chances now, if Connor was going to make a deal with the police. Quickly he and Noreen agreed that they would leave London in a couple of days' time. She had nothing holding her to her miserable bedsit. She would simply pay the rent and say goodbye to her friends at the bar. They could drive to the coast and take the ferry to Belfast. To Noreen it was like eloping. To Matherson it would be confirmation that his plan was working. For Scala it was a step into an unknown world of danger.

Chapter Nine

The wind from the bay whistled through the broken pane of glass, making a low moaning sound in the room. It brought with it the stench of decaying sea life that had been washed to the shore. Naylor sat brooding behind the bare table in the corner of the room that had been the office of the old boat yard. Anxiously he fiddled with the custom-made gold ring engraved with a death's-head motif that he wore on the third finger of his right hand.

Forged from a gold nail, it had been specially made for him by a back-street jeweller in Bogota eight years earlier. He cared not that it accentuated the fact that the top joint of the finger had been severed at the knuckle – lost when an ignorant rookie hadn't paid sufficient attention when moving ammunition boxes. The amputation had not affected his use of the hand. But Naylor's insistence on wearing the ring – which he called his identity tag – never failed to focus attention on it.

The silence hung over the room like a shroud. The two men stood before the table, watching Naylor's eyes narrow as they darted between the ring on his hand and the line of photographs on the wall. Now three of the pictures bore red crosses.

Naylor stared at the photograph of Gerry O'Connell, then flicked his piercing gaze at the two men in front of him. They shuffled uneasily like schoolboys awaiting punishment from a headmaster. Finally Naylor could countain his venom no longer and slammed his ringed hand on to the table in rage. 'A pair of pig's arses you turn out to be!' he bellowed. 'How the fuck do you manage to put three bullets into a man's head and yet still leave him alive? You're supposed to be some of the best that money can buy – I wouldn't wipe my arse with you!'

To Naylor, the plan had been simple. Athertone and Grady were to follow their man – it would not have been difficult because he had always been a cocky bastard who paid little heed to his safety. He had believed himself invincible – an IRA killer who had claimed the lives of at least six innocent Protestants – because he loved the 'kick' of the kill. Now the incompetent bastards who had allowed him to live had fuelled his own myth.

They had struck at the same time as Naylor and the other team had pounced on Kean and Gallagher. Early in the morning, as he made his way to the bookmaker's, they had grabbed him and taken him to the timber yard where he had once worked. There he should have died, four days after being released from the H blocks of the Maze – he had been near the top of the judge's list for retribution. They had pumped three 9mm bullets into the man's head. By any law of averages the man should have died, but miraculously he had lived – although he would be condemned to live his life as a mental cripple who would never be able to feed himself again, let alone commit murder.

Athertone and Grady had forged reputations for themselves as 'mad dog' assassins. Athertone, formerly one of the most active UVF killers in South Armagh, had earned his reputation in blood. He had been one of the men whom Naylor had been told to seek out. By contrast, Grady was a boy. But he had proved himself to be a killer with a baby face – a face that had once been engraved on every IRA gunman's memory. Ulster had been an impossible place for the teenage Grady to live any more after his single-handed attack on the social club in Turf Lodge that had rid the city of two of the Belfast Brigade's best bombers – and their sweethearts. A price had been put on his head and he had fled to the mainland. But with a little information from a friend within the RUC and Hursley he had become a valuable recruit.

Naylor listened as they pleaded that they had been disturbed by the yard's foreman opening up early. But they agreed that, even living, Gerry O'Connell would never again pose a threat to anyone.

'I suppose the message will still get through,' admitted Naylor. 'But when I say "Finish the bastard", I mean exactly that. I do not tolerate half fuckin' measures. It will not happen again!' he ordered as his eyes burned into the very souls of the two men. 'There is no room for failure in my outfit. I think you realize what happens to a man who cannot prove his worth to me?'

The two turned towards each other and each caught the other's look. They understood.

*   *   *

The war of words continued. The IRA immediately blamed the Loyalist paramilitary for the killings. They took it as a signal of intending war, despite the denials. Sinn Fein were busy blaming the British government or, more particularly, the British army for continuing a 'dirty tricks' campaign against their innocent men who had abided by the terms of the ceasefire. Whitehall squirmed and flatly countered the allegations. The delicate balance of the peace process was showing obvious signs of cracking, encouraged by certain sections of the press who were enjoying a field day, playing with the notions that the British army could be attempting to settle old scores – with or without the government's blessing. All sides held their breath for the expected maelstrom of revenge.

*   *   *

It had not been a good crossing. The seas had been whipped into anger by the force ten gales that had battered the ferry from the moment it left port at Liverpool. Only those with stomachs of iron had not been affected by the rolling of the decks as the sea tossed the vessel. The serving staff at the bars retained their usual cool, poker-faced exteriors, still managing to serve drinks to anyone who felt capable of retaining them.

The excitement of the day's preparation and the drive north from London for the night ferry were long since past. Scala had tried to comfort the queasy Noreen, but she could now feel resentment growing within her. For as others around him fell about in the corridors of the heaving vessel and the stench of vomit emanated from the crowded toilets below deck Scala had remained impassive, sipping the occasional bottled beer and even daring to tuck into an overcooked lasagne at the on-board restaurant. The sight had prompted an angry reaction from the pit of Noreen's erupting, empty stomach. She had cursed Scala; he had laughed.

As breakfast-time came and went, Noreen began to reflect on the daringness of her action. She was returning to Belfast almost as quickly as she had left it those seven years ago. She had left as nothing more than a girl. Now she was returning as a woman, with her lover at her side, to face the challenge of a new life. She was bringing her man to the land of her birth for all to see, and she felt good.

The two days since Scala had agreed to accompany her had flown by in an orgy of panic and packing. She had said goodbye to the few people whom she classed as friends. She had shocked the manager of the pub by announcing her decision to leave, and she had enjoyed telling the landlord of the grimy bedsit that she had laughingly called home what she really thought of his extortion racket, as she rebelliously flung the final rent payment at him. In that time she had hardly seen her man. He had told her that, if he was to come to Ireland with her, he would have things to do and people to see.

Matherson was relieved that the girl had taken the bait, but he had reminded Scala that there was no time to spare. He would be ready to send the merchandise to Scala just as soon as he demanded it, day or night.

Noreen had been ready with her pathetically few possessions. Scala had been punctual. And now the romantic adventure – which was how Noreen considered their decision – was under way.

But the sight of the quayside and the monstrous cranes of the Harland and Wolff shipyard which dominated the docks did little to enhance the notion of romance. It had been almost eight years since Scala had first seen the view when he had arrived with his soldier colleagues for their first tour. He still remembered the feelings of apprehension that he had felt at that time. This time his feelings were more than a little similar.

Noreen seemed at last to have recovered some traces of colour in the face that had been ashen throughout the trip, and gripped Scala's hand in excitement. She had known that she would feel excited at the prospect of setting foot on her native land once more, but now, as they prepared to disembark, she felt a strange sense of calmness and confidence in her new-found self that she would never have believed just a few weeks earlier.

The place seemed different now. Noreen insisted on taking the long route through the centre of the city. She remembered a time of soldiers on street corners; of vehicle checkpoints; of a feeling of fear and suspicion that hovered over the people as they attempted to go about their daily routines. But now the soldiers had gone. Occasional RUC Land Rovers, with Freephone numbers emblazoned on the sides for people wishing to pass on confidential information, still toured the streets; RUC officers still walked behind each other in two-man patrols, for fear of assassination; and retired men in security uniforms had replaced the troops at the numerous checkpoints and barriers that stretched across the streets.

All too soon the bustling city centre streets gave way to places more familiar to Noreen as they drove from the quayside along North Street and Peter's Hill towards the Shankill Road. The giant marble and stone buildings and the elegant green roofs of the public buildings were now replaced by red-brick terraces and grey pebble-dashed estates of boxlike buildings. The murals which depicted UVF power and history could still be seen at the end of terraced rows.

They drove past the community and health centres and then Noreen told Scala to take the next right turn, by the corner pub with the iron bars at the windows and metal cage at the door to protect it from bomb attack. The graffiti on the wall could have been the same as seven years previously, and no one had bothered to replace the missing letters on the pub sign that had been either knocked off during countless street scuffles or had simply lost the will to cling to the battered wood any longer. Scala noticed a narrow smile spring on to Noreen's face. Nothing had changed in the street, except the epidemic of TV satellite dishes that had spread along the walls of the terraces. She had often considered that, wherever in the world one went, no matter how poor the local community appeared to be, the spread of the satellite dish could not be halted. She had wondered if many people did not regard the erection of the ugly dish on the wall as a modern-day status symbol.

'Pull in just over here,' she told Scala.

The car came to a halt at the fifth house on the left in the never ending row of carbon copy homes. The red brick was identical to that of the house next door and the one next door to that. The flaking white paintwork of the windows was the same as on the rest of the eternal terrace. The light green of the paint on the door of her home was the same as she remembered: the door that she had watched her Da and her brother walk out of for the last time; the door that had been hammered by the men with the guns when they had come to ask for help on a dark winter's night, when she had refused and had been lucky to escape with her life.

Noreen had shuffled in her seat. She was wearing her best grey suit with the skirt that came down to the knees – the one she wore when she wanted to impress. She wore no shirt or blouse underneath; only the jacket fully fastened. Now she struggled to straighten out the skirt and jacket, and swept her wild hair behind her shoulders.

'Oh Jesus, Jim . . . I feel like a cat on a hot tin roof, I do. You'd never think that I was comin' home now, would ye? I feel more like I'm starting me first day at school,' she gabbled nervously. 'It's been so long, Jim – do you think she'll know me? Do you think she'll even remember what I look like? What do you think she's like now? Oh Jesus, Jim, I'm shakin' like a sack of bones!'

Scala placed his arm around her to calm her. 'It'll be fine – don't worry. You can't expect to simply pick up from where you left off – it's been seven years, for God's sake. It's bound to be strange at first. But it'll be okay, you'll see. You're home!' His voice sounded reassuring. 'But I think this next bit is something you have to do on your own. I'll wait in the car for a while – I don't think there's room for me there too. Now, go and get your life back . . .'

She turned, took a deep breath and walked the few short steps to the green door. Scala watched as it opened to reveal a small, fragile woman in mid-life with the face of someone made old before her time. It was the face of a woman who had known pain. Her man had gone, her son that she had borne was gone, both as a result of violence. All that she now held dear stood before her. The two women hugged and kissed on the step as if in a desperate attempt to make up for the last seven years. Scala thought of himself as an intruder in a personal scene of emotion as he watched the two women bonded by blood and their uncontrollable tears and laughter. Then, as if tearing herself away, Noreen turned towards the car and beckoned for Scala to come.

The older woman's face straightened to take stock of the man who walked towards her, mentally examining him. She wiped away the tears, determined to offer no sign of emotion to the stranger who had returned with her daughter. Scalà was aware of the slightest of movements from the curtains of the surrounding houses as a dozen pairs of eyes watched the scene. He switched on his warmest and most sincere smiling face. Still the woman's face gave nothing away.

'Jim, this is me Mam. Mam, meet Jim, he's the ... he's the ...' Noreen could not find the word to describe him. The word 'friend' was inadequate for what they had done together, yet she could not shock her mother by even hinting that they had been lovers. Mam did not believe in that. Only trollops did that kind of thing – the ones who were happy to be in the family way so that they could take the benefits that the state was prepared to give them.

'He's the man I told ye about,' was all she could offer.

'Pleased to meet you, Mrs Dillon.' Scala mustered his charm. She took his hand, nodded and bade them follow her inside.

*   *   *

The press had been forced to work overtime for the last ten days. The Sinn Fein party meeting with the US President had been worth thousands of desperately needed votes to the fragile administration. But there had been a price. Now, the so-called 'special relationship' that had existed between the United States and Britain was looking distinctly eaten away at the edges. The sight of the President socializing with the men whom America's oldest allies had deemed to be no more than terrorists had seen to that. They would have to work quickly.

So far, it was sufficient that the President's influence with the Irishmen had been strong enough for them to persuade the hot-blooded extreme elements of the IRA not to retaliate against the killings of the freed prisoners and the innocent Catholic girl. The Sinn Fein party, the British and the President knew that could not last. The President had begged for restraint; otherwise the work of the peace process would be dashed forever in a sea of blood – and the President needed the votes. He had at least appeared to try and persuade the Irishmen to give up their weapons.

Now he was upping the stakes. The telephone call that came from the Oval Office was short and clear. The Press Office would have the details on the wires within the hour, just enough time for White House spokesman, Bill Dane, to muster the familiar faces of the Press Corps together for the statement. Whether the Brits liked it or not, to paraphrase the old song, 'The Yanks were coming'.

*　　*　　*

Scala could face no more. Mrs Dillon must have spent two weeks' housekeeping money on the spread before him. The pies, whole ham, thickly buttered bread and a whole array of home-made cakes and pastries covered the lace-clothed table in the back room of the tiny house. The cups of tea had flowed like water pouring from a burst dam. It was Ma Dillon's way. There had been constant visits from neighbours who could not resist the opportunity to see what the girl looked like now, or eye up the man who had come with her. Now at last the three of them were alone.

'So what is it you do back in London, or wherever you work?' enquired Noreen's mother, still unable to use Scala's Christian name. It was almost an accusing tone, but she was trying her best to be sociable.

'I don't know if Noreen told you, but I specialize in leisure goods. I sell leisure items for youngsters. I suppose you could say I'm in the wholesale business,' he replied vaguely.

'And how long have you been doin' that kind of thing for?'

'It feels like a long time now,' Scala answered, then quickly changed the subject. 'It must be smashing for you to have your girl back. I hear you worked very hard for her – you know, trying to persuade people to let her come back. Noreen said – '

Mrs Dillon interrupted. 'There's little to be said about that now. That's all behind us – I only did what any mother would be doing for her own flesh and blood.'

Scala looked around at the sideboard that stretched the full length of the wall, and at the mass of photographs that adorned it. The pride of place went to the aged black and white wedding photograph of a younger Ma Dillon with a dark and handsome man beside her, whom Scala took to be Noreen's father. At either side were photographs of the children – a school picture of Noreen and one which featured a skinny, bright-eyed teenage boy, whom he assumed was her brother.

'That's a fine collection of photographs,' he remarked in another attempt to direct the questioning away from himself. 'Your late husband and son, I presume. A sad story indeed – it can't have been easy for you.'

'It wasn't, but I have had it no harder than many a woman in this place. We have learned to do without our men over here.'

'But at least there's the peace these days.' Scala sounded brighter. 'At least the killing seems to have stopped.'

'Does it?' she asked resignedly. 'I'm sure it does to you people across the water. But there are things that still happen . . .'

'What things?' Scala wondered if he had sounded too eager. 'I thought the killings were a thing of the past.'

'I shouldn't be saying that to anyone about the likes of that Kean man and Gallagher! I don't agree with what they were for – but I can tell ye, there are many that didn't shed any tears for what happened to them.'

It was Noreen's turn to change the subject.

'Mam, I thought Jim could use our Noel's room for the time being. He's going to stay for a while, and, well, it seems daft that the room stays empty. I told him that it would be fine with you.'

Ma Dillon stiffened. 'Well, ye had no right to be taking that for granted. It's grand to have you back, lass, but I'll not be rushed into having anyone else under my roof for a while. I'm sure that the man will understand – it's not right. The people round here would talk, and I'm not going to be giving them the chance. It's not right!'

Scala flushed. 'It's all right, Mrs Dillon, I hadn't really expected to stay here. I'll be happy enough in a hotel for a while. Don't you worry about me.'

Noreen looked embarrassed.

'In fact I was going to suggest that anyway,' he continued quickly, 'and maybe when I get myself fixed up you could come down and be my guests for a bite and a few drinks.' Before either woman had the chance to reply, Scala insisted. 'Look, I'll be off for a while and book in somewhere. You two have got a lot to talk about, a lot of time to catch up on. I'll be back later. Noreen, maybe you and I could have a drink later . . . that's settled, then. Say about a couple of hours. Good!'

*   *   *

Scala had been right. Connor had squealed. He had been questioned for hours on end, and the chief inspector in charge of the Drugs Squad had spelt out what he was facing. Connor had never believed until this moment that he could actually be sent to prison.

Then came the lifeline that the chief inspector was expert in throwing at the right time. Connor could be of use to them; he could be spared a prison sentence if he was prepared to make a deal. All Connor had to do was supply names – the names of the scum who peddled in the club.

Connor had no choice. He felt no remorse – he had barely known the man with the scar and slight limp who had appeared in the club. It didn't matter that Connor had made money from the man he was about to betray. Offering Scala's name was a small price to pay for his freedom. The deal was struck. Scala was a wanted man. There could be no turning back for him now.

*   *   *

He was glad to be in the fresh air again. He had never liked the atmosphere in hotels – too stuffy and too warm at any time of the year. But it was the best that Belfast had to offer, spacious and ritzy and with an image that defied the number of times that it had been the target for the bombers during the last twenty-five years. It was expensive, but money was no object. He had his earnings, plus the Gold Card. He could afford to live a little – possibly live while he could.

Scala decided to return to the Shankill on foot, to breathe in the atmosphere of the new Belfast. An occasional army Land Rover crept past, its rear doors open to reveal a squad of soldiers in full combat equipment who still registered the faces of everyone they passed, desperately trying to match them to photographs in the rogues' gallery in their barracks. Scala prayed that he had not been spotted by some eagle-eyed squaddie who might have recognized him from one far-flung place or another – a fluke accident that would wreck the whole plan.

As he slowly climbed the road that took him up the Shankill, the rows of terraced houses took him back to his childhood, to the rows of grimy red-brick houses that had been his world as a boy in Merthyr. God, he could be home again, to the world that he had once longed to leave behind to search for adventure.

It had been a long time ago, yet the memories and the pain were still fresh. He wished he could have held his father and apologised, then shared the time together that fathers and sons long for before they grow apart. It was all too late now. If only he could have been there to beg his father's forgiveness for turning his back on the family – the family whose only wish was that he would take over the greasy corner caff that had been their life. But it was all too late.

Momentarily closing his eyes, he found he could still recall the group of mischievous schoolboy faces that had been his cohorts. He wondered what had become of them all. He would never know, and he would never take the time to discover. He had left them behind for his new life, the life of the army, that had become his new family.

The Shankill Road is one of the best-known stretches of Belfast, running through the heart of one of its staunch Protestant areas. The very name has become a symbol of Protestant strength in the city, for less than a street away the Shankill gives way to the so-called Peace Wall which divides it from the Catholic stronghold of the Lower Falls. At this time of the early evening the Shankill was busy. As he walked, Scala passed the shops and supermarkets and the gaps where buildings had stood until the bombers had gone about their work. The signs of war were never far away.

Noreen was waiting. She did not ask him inside; they walked instead towards the main bars and pubs that lined the Shankill. Their names, deeply steeped in British tradition, were still familiar to her. They chose the one she had frequented most, the Regent.

They waited outside the locked thick wooden door for what seemed like minutes, as the lenses of the video cameras that kept permanent vigil monitored them and relayed their presence to the battery of TV screens behind the bar for approval. No one entered this bar who was not welcome. The damage to the brickwork of the side doorway paid testimony to the attempts of the bombers from the Falls to wage their war. Now the cage that shielded the door was the defence against their return, as were the standard iron bars at the windows.

Noreen had to press the bell again before being granted entrance. She had been in Belfast for barely five hours, but the news of her return had already been spread by the network of Loyalist agents and busybodies who thrived in the pub community.

The dense smoke stung Scala's eyes. He felt the atmosphere could have been cut with a knife. The deafening drink-fuelled chatter from the men that lined the horseshoe-shaped bar was silenced as if someone had pressed the 'off' button on a radio.

All heads turned to Scala and the girl. Noreen almost lost her footing through a combination of nerves and the slippery puddles of beer that oozed across the dirty tiled floor. Scala held out his arm to steady her. Then an elderly woman behind the bar, whose brightly coloured nose identified her as a person who was no stranger to matching her male regulars in drinking sessions, put down her glass and eyed Noreen.

'Welcome back, lass! It's good to see yer safe and well!' beamed the woman as she exposed the gap where her two bottom front teeth had once been. The greeting was treated as a signal for the chatter and shouting to erupt again. Noreen visibly gasped a sigh of relief and Scala gave one of the cheesiest smiles from his repertoire. She had been accepted.

The toothless barmaid would not take Scala's money and insisted that their first drinks were on the house. Six more rounds followed. The smoke grew denser, and – as if it had been needed – the crowd at the bar used Noreen's return as an excuse for an impromptu party.

'I tell yer, Jim, I've been dreading this. I was afraid I'd be made to feel like a leper. I can't tell you what a relief this is.' Noreen squeezed Scala's arm. 'You'll never know what I thought it would be like.'

But Scala knew exactly what a leper felt like. He would never forget his first moments hobbling into the mess at Hereford – the accusing looks that pierced his very soul from those who silently blamed him for Kearns' death. He too had known what it felt like to be an outsider . . .

It seemed like a challenge to the men at the bar to out-shout each other with incomprehensible, non-winnable arguments. To a man they were all speaking at each other, together. It seemed as if everyone was at loggerheads or involved in bitter dispute with the man next to him. In fact they were having a good time. Scala was unable to understand 75 per cent of what was being shouted, as the regulars became drunker and drunker.

'At least some thing's don't change,' laughed Noreen. Scala thought it was the first time that he had really seen her laugh all day.

'Is it always like this? How the hell can they hear what the other person's arguments are?' Scala grimaced.

'It takes years of practice and lots of drinking to attune yourself to it. Don't worry, you'll soon catch on to it,' she explained.

The doorbell rang continuously and more and more people crammed into the Formica-panelled bar. Scala and Noreen escaped to a tiny corner where they laughed and joked. At the same time Scala's eyes scoured the room for faces to store, or to check mentally against the countless photographs of 'players' that had been implanted in his brain. His instincts told him that they were being watched.

Few people took notice of the scrawny figure with the face of a cheeky schoolboy. To most people in the Regent, Georgie Armstrong was not worth the effort of consideration. He was one of the fixtures of the bar – always there, to be nodded to when seen, but worth little else. Georgie buried his pasty face in the glass of stout and reached for another tablet. It helped to reassure him. Despite what others might think, Georgie Armstrong considered himself as much a 'player' as anyone in the Shankill. He was committing to memory every detail of Scala's movements, features and mannerisms. He knew the people who would be interested.

Chapter Ten

Hursley was in no mood for pleasantries. 'So tell me, what the hell went wrong? It appears to have been a real balls up, don't you agree? You're not getting paid to balls up!'

Now it was Naylor's turn to be on the receiving end of a bollocking. He hadn't been in this position for years – not since the men with their heads up their own arses had booted him out. He didn't like it.

The two men strolled casually alongside the canal that cut through the centre of Birmingham. A brightly coloured barge occasionally ventured down the narrow stretch. Naylor went on the counter-attack: 'I've told you. Athertone and Grady felt they'd done enough – they put three bullets into the thick skull, after all. Most men with three soddin' great bullet holes in their skull would be six feet under by now. I suppose it's easy to miss the brain of a Paddy, though, even from point-blank range . . . Anyway, he'll be no use to anyone now,' he finished abruptly.

He was feeling defiant. It was fine for the likes of Hursley to criticize – too bloody easy! He was the kind of bastard who was good at giving orders, but he would not be so eager if he was called upon to put a gun to a man's head and send him to the next world.

'Let's just put it down to experience,' offered Hursley. 'The Boss is happy with the way things are going, and that's the main thing.'

The Boss was a man whom Naylor had only ever heard talked about. He had never met him and had not been made aware of his identity. It had been decided that things were better that way for the moment. Naylor had often attempted to imagine the man, what kind of world he lived in, what motivated him. Something must have hurt him a lot for him to fund this kind of operation. He wondered what it could have been.

'The Boss is certain that things will happen pretty soon. Our people have told us as much. No one will hold the IRA scum. I think we can safely say that the outcome is assured. So it's time to move on to the next phase. If we pull this off, I think it's safe to say that things will never be quite the same again. The Commander is waiting for you with the stuff. Are your people ready?'

Naylor's temper had settled. 'Yeah! I've got the right boyo for the job. He's a bit of a bloody idiot who no bugger will miss. But he'll do the job. Wants to be some kind of a hero or something. Can't imagine why!'

'Well, for Christ's sake make sure he doesn't just splash this around aimlessly. I can tell you, it's cost a small fortune – not that money really matters in this case. Just tell him to be careful,' added Hursley. 'The next point of business has also been confirmed. As we thought, the expected get-together should take place within the next month, so be ready. There's no time to be lost. The times, places and dates will be supplied nearer the time. That's all I can tell you for the moment, apart from the fact that it looks like everything we'd hoped for.'

As usual, in his position as paymaster Hursley now handed Naylor an envelope. Then he thrust a second envelope into the man's hand. 'The address and everything you require are in that one. You're expected. All being well, you should be back in Belfast by tomorrow night. Let's hope there are no more balls ups.'

*   *   *

The sun silhouetted the towers of the church against the pale clear sky, made hazy by the billows of smoke that came from the rows of chimney pots. Derek Macnamara prowled the path by the twelve-feet-high sheets of corrugated metal that made up the supposed Peace Wall of Belfast. The flimsy wall erected at the height of the Troubles separated the peoples of the Falls estate from those of the Shankhill. It acted now as a constant memorial to the hatred of people divided by a few yards.

Macnamara paced back and forth like a caged tiger as he waited by the clinic in Cupar Street. The corrugated wall towered above the short man in the long overcoat with his hands plunged deep into its pockets. He hated being kept waiting. It gave him time to consider, and considering his actions was not what was uppermost in his mind at the moment. He had always acted on impulse, and he had been right so far. He knew what the people wanted – and they would do what he told them anyway!

His instinct had been to fight, to seek revenge. He knew he was right. He believed in an eye for an eye – if they didn't strike now, the Prods and their Brit bastard backers would piss all over them. He had told Clancy and the other Sinn Fein bosses all that.

He had liked Clancy once, when he had been like Macnamara – a soldier, a killer who believed that the only way ahead was with the Armalite. The pair of them had inflicted so much pain on the bastards. But now he considered Clancy had gone soft and cared only for his own political ambition. Fuck Clancy, and fuck what Clancy tried to tell him to do! he thought.

He didn't care if Clancy and the others were being used as puppets by the Americans. Macnamara would never have wanted to share the same floor as the President of the United States in the first place. The prospect had never passed through his head. Macnamara had thought that the likes of Clancy would never bow to some Yank and not seek revenge. Macnamara himself would never do that. He was, after all, a soldier – he would leave the politicizing to the likes of Clancy.

All Macnamara knew was that he had heard of the possibility of a Brit from the mainland operating in Belfast, in his city, and that a girl might have died because of the Brit, and that he had two dead patriots on his hands and another of his soldiers who would never be able to utter his own name again. Derek Macnamara was not going to be told about restraint.

He cursed aloud as he waited. Then, from the corner of the nearby hostel building, he saw the two scruffy men in anoraks shuffling towards him. 'About fuckin' time too, you pair of bastards!' Macnamara gritted his teeth with cold and anger as he spoke.

The two offered their apologies. It would not happen again – they would see to that.

Macnamara examined the pair. They would do; they were new and eager, as yet unknown, not like the rest of his boys, who were all too familiar to every Brit, RUC man and Loyalist fucker in the city. The two newcomers had been accepted just days before Sinn

Fein had called the ceasefire, so they were untried. They were brothers just eighteen and nineteen who had carried messages and helped hide weapons when the men had wanted. Now they would have to do.

'Well, Billy boy, this is the moment when you'll get to be a man – when you can show us what you're able to do all right!' said Macnamara. 'I'm sure yourself and wee Kevin here'll not be up to letting us down. You've a chance to hurt the bastards, Billy.'

The brothers shook their heads. 'Don't worry, boss, we'll not let you down. We know where the bastard'll be and when. We know what to do, boss. You rely on us, boss – me an' Kevin are ready!'

The fire of youthful eagerness burned in their eyes, and Macnamara recognized the feeling. He had enjoyed that fire in his gut at the prospect of action the first time. He had not let his teacher down, either. He could still remember the sight of the twitching body of the policeman lying in the gutter as the man's life blood had spilled from him. He had enjoyed it. Now it was the turn of these two brothers.

'I'm sure you'll be fine, Billy. I'm sure you'll do me proud. Just don't miss, Billy. You'll only get the one chance – they'll not give ye a second go. You know the man, he deserves what's coming. Just remember that.'

The brothers went away with the words echoing in their ears.

*   *   *

She fought for breath. The climb had taken its toll, and now she was near to gasping. Scala, on the other hand, hardly appeared out of breath. She had tripped and groped and cursed her way to the top of the hill for the best part of an hour. Now it felt that every muscle in her body ached, and the pains from her chest worsened with each step. Yet her man looked as if he had simply strolled around the park on a Sunday morning. Noreen had appreciated Scala's lean, toned body. He had told her that he took pride in his fitness. Now she appreciated what he had meant.

She had dreamed of returning to this spot for seven years. To her, it was the best spot in the whole of Northern Ireland. It had been the place where as a small girl she had tugged at her elder brother's kite; where they had imagined themselves as angels looking down on the people below; where for a few hours at least, they could romp and forget the ugliness that was the city at war below. To Noreen, the Cave Hills to the north of Belfast held the most spectacular views of the city that she could remember. Now, as the puffs of cloud cast moving shadows over the moorland ridges of the Caves, she had returned with her man. The wind pressed her thick woollen jumper hard against her breasts, showing their perfect outline. She was unaware of the effect. Scala could only admire.

As they looked down at the red and white blocks of houses, the cranes that overshadowed the docks and the criss-cross of roads that made up the city spread beneath them, Noreen felt at peace. She placed her arms around Scala's waist and hugged him tight. She raised herself to her toes and sought his mouth for a long, lingering kiss. She wanted to tell him that she thought she was falling in love. Her heart wanted to say it, but her mind told her to remain silent . . . to wait like she had been used to.

He wanted her. He wanted her there and then, high on the hills above her home . Yet he wanted their lovemaking to be perfect. Neither he nor Noreen would be content with a quick screw on a damp hillside somewhere. As he fought to restrain his own desires, the thought crossed Scala's mind that he might be growing too old to play the kind of sexual stud that over the years he had always prided himself on being – a man who never considered the feelings of the woman. If he wanted her he would normally have her, no matter where or how. Yes, that must be it, he thought, age was taking its toll.

'Thank you, Jimmy, for being with me, for bringing me back . . . for trying to bring some meanin' to my life again. Thank you for being you,' whispered Noreen. 'I don't know of a reason in hell why you should have come with me. You could be with some other wee bird right now, back home – '

Scala placed his hand gently across her mouth to silence her. 'What if I told you that I chose to be with you? You've knocked me off my feet and at this moment in time I don't care about any other woman in the world. I chose to be with you . . .' The words came easily, he thought – possibly too easily. But he felt good about them. He saw tears welling in her eyes.

*   *   *

Colonel Aidan Massey came from a family that had all died well. They had given their lives in service for their country. His great-great-great-grandfather had been with the glorious Enniskillens who had fought and died so valiantly against the never-ending hordes of French cavalry and cannon at Waterloo. His great-grandfather had died under the blades of the Afghan rebels who had massacred the defenders of Kabul in the days of Queen Victoria's Empire. His grandfather had been awarded a posthumous Military Cross for single-handedly wiping out a Hun machine gun nest that had ravaged his company of Irish Rangers in the mud- and blood-soaked fields of Ypres.

To this day he could still remember his father telling him stories of how they had lost everything in the fire on the night the 'Patriots' of the Mid-Tyrone Brigade of the IRA had torched the family house. Everything had gone: the treasured gold dinner service that generations had eaten from, the paintings and the militaria of a family that had won its name in famous battles down the centuries. They had moved to England, but their tradition with some of the finest regiments that Ireland had ever produced lingered on.

Massey had been proud to serve. In true family tradition he had graduated at Sandhurst with flying colours and then volunteered to join the Rangers. His own men had died at the hands of the bombers and snipers of the Ballymurphy Estate and Turf Lodge. Massey and men from his regiment had often been attached to units serving in Northern Ireland. They had died to keep the Union. He had gritted his teeth and accepted the inevitable as one Irish regiment was eventually amalgamated with another. The regiments were being cut down like his own family who had fought with them on so many far-off battlefields. Now the people who had told him he was finished were talking to the men responsible for ending the lives of so many of his young soldiers on the cold, wet pavements of Belfast. Their memory too was being betrayed.

The Massey family had all fought and died well. Colonel Aidan Massey was the last in the line, and he was determined that his name would never be forgotten. He thanked God for the meeting with other like-minded men. They had planned and waited for this opportunity like so many of his previous military campaigns.

He watched the boys stable the horses that he thought of as his children – the children that his late wife had never been able to give him. They were the only things of beauty that touched his heart these days – the days that he spent as a virtual recluse on the stud farm near Cirencester since the army had told him that they had no further need of him, that the Massey family's link with them had been severed in yet another Whitehall cutback.

He saw the Range Rover drive along the track to the house, and watched the man he knew as Naylor step down. Naylor felt little pity for any man, but Massey had struck a chord with him. He too had known the pain and humiliation of being tossed on the scrap-heap after spending his life in the service that he loved and had bled for. He found it difficult not to salute Massey out of respect. Naylor thought that Massey had visibly aged since the last visit. The fifty-one-year-old man had let his normally immaculate white hair grow longer, which gave him an appearance of eccentricity.

The sight of the former soldier cheered Massey, in his turn. He too felt there was a bond, despite the differences in class and rank. They were stateless people in a world that had turned its back on them.

'Afternoon, sergeant!' grunted Massey, still using the old terms of rank. 'I'm hearing good things about your work. Old Niall was on to me the other day full of confidence. Keep it up, eh? That's all I can say.'

Naylor virtually stood to attention.

'The box is over there, all ready as promised. I received the gear the other day – bloody tricky getting your hands on the stuff now. Good job I still know a few people in low places. Privilege of rank, I suppose . . . Your Latin friend delivered ten pounds of the stuff . . . quite a bag, I understand – not that I know that much about that side of things. I prefer to leave that to you people. I suggest you go ahead and check the compartments.'

The giant horsebox looked more like a removal van than a livestock transporter. Massey and his troop of grooms and stable boys had become familiar sights at customs checkpoints between the mainland and both sides of the Irish border as he indulged his passion for horse breeding and trading. Naylor spread-eagled himself on the ground and dragged himself under the vehicle. There, unseen to the trained eye and sprayed by mud, was a metal hatch on which he pushed heavily until it gave way. Behind lay a specially made compartment, carefully welded inside the body of the horsebox. Naylor's eyes sparkled at the sight of the cargo. There, neatly racked against the side of the compartment, six 9mm Heckler and Koch MP5 sub-machine guns lay concealed, each with a dozen magazines of ammunition. They were the weapon of the world's elite forces, favoured by America's Delta Force and Britain's SAS as well as anti-terrorist groups in every corner of the globe. On the other side of the compartment he unlocked a smart black suitcase. He peered inside to view the weapon: a Parker-Hale M-85 sniper rifle, designed to give 100 per cent first-shot hit capability at ranges up to 900 metres.

Naylor smiled. He felt like a child opening toys at Christmas. In the far corner of the compartment he saw the thick, heavy box which carried his payload – the 30 lb of Semtex, the world's most powerful commercial explosive, so infamously used by the IRA. He replaced the hatch before sliding further underneath the vehicle to an identical compartment and feeling inside to check the package. The plastic container was strapped to the top of the compartment. Massey had been right: Naylor's Latin friend had not let him down. The 10 lb of heroin would be worth a million. It almost seemed a waste to him.

Naylor had seen everything. He was confident. These days, with the relaxed state of security across the border, he would have no trouble taking the concealed cargo in. Once in Ulster, it would all be put to good use.

*   *   *

There was no shortage of interest in Scala. As he waited for Noreen in the Regent there had been a steady stream of enquiries, ranging from 'How are you?' to 'What are you doing in Belfast?'

It seemed as though everyone wanted to know about him. Most had been passing, friendly enquiries, but others, he felt, had a more serious intent. He had known they would come to him: Matherson had briefed him.

At one point he felt he had been outed. The friendly faced guy from the bar with the mop of greased-back black hair had been too pushy. Scala had coped with 'How are you?' and 'How long are you staying ?', but when the apparently friendly questioning about his work back in London grew too intense he decided his interrogator was a security man, probably one of the cloak and dagger merchants working with Fourteen Int, the British army's specialist intelligence unit which had always remained a closed shop even to those within the army world. They were the eyes and ears of the security forces. Scala felt compromised and backed away, changing the subject.

Then he saw the pasty, nervous face of the man at the end of the bar. He had seen him the night before. He had been alone then too, as if everyone had bypassed him. There was something odd about this figure with its piercing stare. Scala stored his memory away. Georgie Armstrong too had seen Scala again.

As Scala sipped his stout he failed, however, to spot the thick-set man move from the shadows to sit alongside him. The unshaven face with a nose that had been squashed beyond recognition in too many street fights or boxing matches turned to him.

'So the name's Scala, is it?' said the hulk.

He did not respond, unsure if the words were meant as a direct question or a statement.

'And what kind of line would you be in then, Jim Scala?'

Scala turned slowly and grinned. 'Well, I think that's for me to know, isn't it, Mr whatever-your-name-is! Wouldn't you agree with that?'

The inquisitor was not to be put off. 'I hear tell that you're here with the Dillon lass, the one who was allowed to come back. Sad thing that was – sending her away like that. Still, it could have been worse. Should've known better than to ignore the Lads . . . I hear you're a bit of a big man back across the water – a bit of a flash guy with the money.'

Scala dropped the grin. 'Am I now? Well, you seem to know a

lot about me – or think you do. And here I am not even knowing your name.'

'The name's Healy, and I hear that you've been a bad boy back home. That's the real reason that you wanted to get away from the place – not simply because you went chasing the skirt. We know a bit about you, Jim Scala!'

Scala fixed on the word 'we'. 'And who the bloody hell might "we" be then, Mr Healy, my long-lost friend?' he challenged.

'Oh, I doubt if we'll ever be friends, Mr Scala. But I do have some friends who might be interested in what you can offer. I'm assuming that you're still in the same line of business? We think that there might be possibilities for a man like you . . .'

There he went with the 'we' bit again, thought Scala. 'Let's just say that I'm into supply and demand,' he bluffed.

'We hear that you might be able to supply what we demand, if you get my drift,' Healy said. 'Course, we could have entirely the wrong man – in which case no harm done.'

Scala's mind was racing. He had told himself to tread gently, but his instinct told him not to hesitate too long for fear of losing this bite. 'Let's just say I'm willing to listen to any business proposition. I do like to know exactly who I'm dealing with – so get it out of your fuckin' head that I'm about to go around dealing with a monkey like yourself. If I'm going to go into any business then I want to deal with the "wes" of this world, whoever the fucking hell they might be. So I suggest you carry that message off to your we pals.' Scala felt bold. His adrenaline was rising and, to his surprise, he found himself enjoying it.

Healy seemed confounded. He had not expected this counter-attack. Gingerly, he took a swig from his own pint glass.

'Be here tomorrow dinner-time now!' he half ordered. 'I'll tell yer more then . . .'

Scala noticed that the pale-faced youth in the corner still had his dead eyes fixed on himself and Healy. As Healy made to get up, Scala thought it was his turn to become inquisitor.

'Who's the creeping Jesus in the corner with the eyes?'

Healy looked up. 'It's only wee Georgie Armstrong – he's nobody. Sure enough he would like to be someone, but he hasn't got the bollocks. No use to anyone, man! Had a stint in the British army, but didn't have the bottle – they got rid of him. Done a bit of petty thieving . . . gone down the line a couple of times . . . still lives with his Ma. Best ignored.'

Scala liked the instant appraisal, and wondered how they had appraised him.

The doorbell rang again and Scala could see Noreen's face being screened on the television behind the bar. Perfect timing.

'Till tomorrow then,' Healy reminded him.

* * *

It was Wednesday night. Kevin O'Grady was a creature of habit. If it was Wednesday night, then it was country and western night at the Alma bar. Kevin O'Grady never missed it.

The brothers had waited in the darkness behind the drab, dimly lit building which proudly boasted the title of Shankill Leisure Centre. Billy delved into the pocket of his thin windcheater and pulled out the half-bottle of Irish whiskey. The pair each took a sip, feeling the liquid slowly burn downwards into the pits of their frantic bellies, in a desperate bid to ease their nerves. It was the first time they had been called on, and they could not let Macnamara down. The face of Kevin O'Grady was etched on their minds; Macnamara had told them how the plumber lived a double life and was also one of the most notorious hit-men for the Ulster Freedom Fighters. He had to die.

They each slipped a tablet to give them the courage: the 'buzz' would soon be on them.

The band was still busy tuning their instruments, the girl singer hoisting her buckskin skirt that would give the aging customers a tantalizing glimpse of thigh. The crowd was noisy, shouting at the bar staff to order their beer, stout and lager before the girl started singing.

The 'buzz' was on the brothers. They felt good. They were right. At last they would be men! The two burst through the double doors at the front of the pub. Each brandished a Webley revolver held high in his right hand. There was a moment's stunned silence in the room as the pair scoured the bar for their man. Shit, fuck, he was not to be seen!

Wild eyed with Speed, Billy shouted his challenge. 'Kevin O'Grady! Where is the murdering bastard known as Kevin

O'Grady? Come out, you cock-suckin' bastard, show yourself!'
His voice had risen to a screech as the two waved their guns
aimlessly around the room, seeking their man. 'We're here for
you, Kevin O'Grady! Murderin' time is here for you!'

He sat there powerless to move, as two madmen whom he
had never seen before waved their guns towards him shouting
the name of a man he had never known. It was not his name –
everyone in the pub knew he was Jimmy Daly. There was relief.
He had come to listen to the music. He had never heard of a man
called Kevin O'Grady.

Suddenly Bill lined his gun on the frozen man and fired. If
O'Grady was not here, then some other Prod bastard would
take his punishment. The bullet passed through Jimmy Daly's
left side, spinning him round. There were screams and people
dived to the floor. Billy kept firing as the man lunged towards
the doors, frantic to escape and clutching his side which was
pumping blood through his thick woollen jumper.

The brothers ran after him into the street. They could hear his
footsteps running down the alley that ran along the side of the pub
to the open play area behind. Like mad dogs chasing their quarry
they ran screaming after the staggering man. In the middle of the
play area Jimmy Daly stumbled and fell to the ground. Baying for
blood, the brothers were on him. Kevin thudded a kick into the
screaming man's wounded side. The blood squirted on to Kevin's
jeans. They stood over him, half laughing, half screaming. They
aimed their revolvers and pulled the triggers. They continued
pumping bullets into the riddled body at their feet until they were
brought to their senses by the clicks of the empty chambers. There
was no life left for Jimmy Daly: the execution of the man who had
taken the punishment intended for another was complete.

The brothers ran. They disappeared into the night, to be
swallowed into the back streets of the Lower Falls.

Three streets away, in the back bedroom of one of the grey
pebble-dashed terraced flats that had sprung up around the
Shankill, Kevin O'Grady sat up in bed. The bout of flu that
had kept him indoors for the last two days still gripped him.
Unknown to him, it had saved his life.

* * *

Across the road, further up the hill, the sound of the shots even pierced the mayhem of the Regent bar. It was a familiar sound. The drinkers spilled out on to the pavement to see for themselves the expected horrors. Scala was with them; in vain Noreen attempted to hold him back. She was screaming, for she felt in her heart that nothing had changed in the city to which she had returned since the days when she had been sent into exile. The thing that she could see lying like butchered meat in the playground opposite might have been her brother or her father.

Scala stood at the back of the circle of inquisitive bystanders who came to look at Jimmy Daly as the boy's blood spread along the ground and streamed down the hill along the gutter. Revenge had come to the Shankill Road.

Chapter Eleven

Jimmy Daly was rapidly becoming a national figure. Much as the assassination of the Archduke Franz Ferdinand was held to be the spark that started World War I, so Jimmy Daly was taking his place in history as the man whose death brought open Warfare to Ulster.

Declan Holmes was quick to point this out. Prepared for the eventuality which he knew must come, he had moved fast to seize the opportunity. The lobby correspondents of every national newspaper received an invitation to meet him within minutes of their arriving at the House of Commons. Holmes, the mad extremist regarded as a virtual outcast by his own party as well as by most normal-thinking MPs within the House, was now basking in his role as prophet. With a practised air of solemnity and foreboding he appeared before the television news cameras to decry the cowardly and senseless murder of an innocent man by the people to whom the British government were insisting on talking round the peace table. He was well versed in the phrases – he had had twenty-five years of blood-letting in which to practise them.

The press crowded into one of the Commons committee rooms to hear the hastily prepared briefing. Holmes wore a black suit as a mark of respect to the dead man. He had decided to speak without the aid of a prepared statement. His words would seem more impassioned that way, he thought.

'Ladies and gentlemen, I thank you for attending this conference at such short notice. Needless to say, the cold-blooded slaying of this young man in Belfast has stunned me, as it has every decent-minded individual in this country and indeed around the world. Within the last hour, we have received confirmation from the police in Belfast that a unit of the Provisional Wing of the IRA have admitted responsibility for the killing. They have further compounded the savagery by claiming that the murder was in fact an error, and that the man who was killed was mistakenly identified.'

He studied the expressions of the journalists before him. The IRA's admission of an 'error' in these cases always prompted cynical comments from the Press Corps, who felt contempt for the words of apology that generally followed. An apology would always help the wife and children of Jimmy Daly.

'The Provisional Wing of the IRA have apologised for the error.' Holmes emphasized his words carefully. 'The murder of this innocent young man, who had no connection with any paramilitary organization whatsoever, is said to be a retaliation for the deaths of at least two known IRA terrorists.

'Ladies and gentlemen, I'm here today to publicly denounce this so-called tit-for-tat and cowardly action by the people who, as we speak, are claiming their willingness to sit at the peace table and hold talks with British ministers and all parties concerned with the future of Northern Ireland. They are the people who have openly claimed to have declared a ceasefire in the name of peace . . .' Holmes' voice rose. 'I am here today to repeat my message that so many of you reported recently . . . the views which led to my expulsion from the floor of the Commons, that these people have not, and have never had, any intention of renouncing violence.

'I repeat, we would be blinkered by these bloodthirsty murderers into thinking that their aim is ever to talk of peace. They have refused to give up their guns, and now we see that they intend to use them to slaughter more innocent men, women and children. I have already received calls of support from members of my own party who had shown a willingness to negotiate with these people. I am here to tell you that forthwith we have already prepared a statement calling on the Prime Minister to break off forthwish any form of negotiation with the men behind the killing . . .'

He knew that the demands would be rejected. But he also knew that the headlines would do more to fan the flames of hatred than a dozen keynote speeches that any minister could offer to calm the terrified communities on either side of the Peace Wall. He would win the sympathy, for he had been proven right.

He felt good. Today was the first day of the rebirth of the political career of Declan Holmes.

*   *   *

The stench of stale whiskey and smoke clung to the air and filled the nostrils. It was still mid-morning and the club had not yet opened. In the main lounge the steward tried hard not to listen to the shouting that bellowed from the back room.

Eamon Clancy smashed his fist on to the table, sending papers flying and spilling the whiskey in his glass. Few people in the room had ever witnessed him in a rage like this, and they felt genuine fear rising within them. He paced back and forth and used his hands to toss back the hair that sagged into his face with each violent action. Macnamara sat at the table, impassively refusing to display any sign of nervousness. He knew only too well of Clancy's reputation.

'Jesus fuckin' Christ, man – by what right did you sanction it? What fuckin' right do you think that you, Derek Macnamara, have to go it alone and order some fucker to be blown away?' spat Clancy. 'All the work and all the planning that have gone into this, and you have to come along and stick your fuckin' dick into things that are bigger than Derek Macnamara! Jesus, I know how you feel – but this is a big game now! There are some big bloody players involved. It's not just up to one fuckin' bitter little bastard to give the nod and somebody dies!'

Macnamara could restrain himself no longer. 'That's *exactly* how it always has been. If I say somebody dies, then somebody fuckin' well dies – that's the way of things, that's the way we've ruled. That's why people have respected us. I'll not be told to give that up because some ambitious arse-holes have forgotten their roots and are more interested in having their strings pulled by some fuckin' Yank who tells us how to run things. For God's sake, man, think of all the coffins we've walked behind, the coffins of men *you* once fought alongside. I'll not betray that memory – even if you find it easy to do so.'

Clancy spun on Macnamara, his eyes wide with rage. 'Well, you won't have to think about fuckin' well betraying them any more. You're out, Derek, you've blown the shit out of it all. There's been talks – it's been decided, and they want you out. You're a fuckin' mad dog that we can't afford. Just pray to Jesus that we can salvage this situation. We're in no position to be seen beating the bastard war drums. The people are sick and tired of it. It's getting harder to get their money – and from the States too. For Christ's sake, man, can't you see we're in stalemate? There's more than your bloody ego at stake ... You'll cease to command from immediate effect. The men will be told to take no further instructions from you – is that clear?'

The words were like a knife to the heart. Macnamara had expected to be disciplined, but never this. He could find no words in defence. Argument was in any case futile. He reckoned that he could count on a small faithful following, but the rank and file would feel duty-bound to obey their masters. Jesus, even the Army Council had given Clancy their backing. Macnamara, the man who had lived for the fight and had been good at it, was now unemployed. But they would hear from him again.

* * *

Healy arrived early, but Scala was already waiting. Healy still did not trust the man from the mainland. Scala felt the same about the man with the crushed nose. The events of the night before were still on everybody's lips, yet Healy refused to mention anything about the killing. Instead, he beckoned Scala to follow. The Welshman carried a small leather shoulder bag which he gripped tightly.

'Where are we going?' Scala asked.

'Wait and bloody see!' came the monosyllabic reply. 'Not far.'

The two men stepped out into the busy Shankill Road, where the women shopped and talked about the death of the boy Jimmy Daly. His mother was taking it bad, they assured each other. An only child as well.

After barely fifty yards Healy stopped and signalled Scala to cross the road. They halted outside what Scala took to be a closed shop. The sign above the darkened window declared the building to be the premises of the Shankill Road Society of Friends. Two men in anoraks stood outside the closed door and nodded their acknowledgement of Healy, but reached to examine the stranger's shoulder bag before allowing them to enter. Scala held tight. Healy and the two men glared, but Scala stood firm. 'Fuck it! Let him go!' snarled Healy finally.

The passage leading to the back of the building was cluttered with ancient photographs and newspaper cuttings that told of how it used to be in the days before the present Troubles.

Scala would like to have studied them, but found himself being ushered into a dank, empty office.

Healy and one of the doormen stood in opposite corners. No one spoke. The sounds of the waiting were deafening. The doorman struck a match to light a cigarette; Healy's stomach groaned from the beer he had taken the night before. Behind him Scala heard the door open slowly, then felt the light touch of a hand on his shoulder.

'Ah, Mr Scala – so I understand you wanted to speak!' came the quick-fire greeting. 'Let me see here, you're here with the Dillon gal. Caused us a lot of trouble, that wee gal. Still, that's all in the past now, eh?'

As Scala turned to look at the man his mind galloped through the record files that Matherson had set before him. He fought to recall the face. Shit – he remembered!

'Well, who would I have the pleasure of speaking to?' enquired Scala in a calm voice.

'That's a fair question, so it is, especially if we're to do business. The name's McConachie. I suppose you might be right in thinking that I run things around here.'

Scala's mind recalled the pages of the file. 'Kenneth McConachie, commander of the Ulster Volunteer Force of Belfast ... suspected of a string of sectarian murders all of which were unprovable. As fanatical as any terrorist of either side in Ulster,' the report had said, adding that he was 'thought to be the brains behind the racketeering and fund-raising for the UVF.'

The chair moaned under McConachie's giant frame and he stroked his neatly trimmed ginger beard. 'We've done our home-work, Mr Scala. We like to keep a check on the new faces on our patch – and, let's face it, you did have something of a high-profile entry. I wonder if that was on purpose now? Still, it's a good-looking lass that you've come back with, I'll grant yer that. Our friends in London have told us that the police might be interested in knowing your whereabouts. It seems they want to talk to you about some involvement in the peddling of drugs – seems someone fingered you for it. We know all about touts over here, too!'

Scala grinned inwardly. Good old Connor – the little bastard had come up trumps!

'Now we know that selling stuff like Ecstasy over there is small fry, Mr Scala. Child's play, so to speak. But allow me to assure you . . . that things are different over here. There's a lot of money to be made – although I feel pretty sure you already know that.'

Scala interrupted. 'But I thought the Church and others made it a virtual cardinal sin to deal – '

'True! But even organizations like ourselves and the Provos have to move with the times, as I'm sure you agree. The thing is, Scala, the demand is sky-high, and I believe in giving people what they want. The young 'uns want their stuff – can't get enough of it. There's not a bloody club in the city that isn't a marketplace. They've got a craving for the shit. They seem to like the crack it gives them – they seem to want to forget their worries. Well, I for one think we should give them as much as they want. They deserve it.'

'And you rake in the profits – the more the merrier!' agreed Scala. 'Let me guess now . . . so that you can stock up your bloody arsenals and go off shooting again.'

'Fuckin' right we can, Scala, and we will. There's enough friggin' weaponry on the market from Eastern Europe and South Africa to start World War III, and we need it. You saw for yourself what happens when we drop our guard, as the wee Daly boy found out.'

'Yes, but you're not doing too bad as it is now, are you? What about the Provos that got it after coming out of the Kesh?'

'Those fuckers were nothin' to do with us, I tell you. But I'll weep no tears for the Provo scum. No, someone else took them out – someone else who wanted justice . . . The thing is, Scala, are you willing to help?'

The room went silent. Scala looked as though he was considering.

'Best prices?'

'Best prices okay. Say £25 to £30 a tab,' agreed McConachie.

Scala reached into his shoulder bag, pulled out a manilla envelope and threw it down in front of the UVF man. McConachie opened up the ten plastic sheets and smiled at the thousand tablets.

'Take them,' insisted Scala. 'Let's say it's a sign of good faith. You'll have more later, but I'll expect cash on delivery every time. Let's hope we both get what we want!'

* * *

'Yes, sir! He took the bait ... and I'll need the rest of the stuff sent to me immediately,' Scala told Matherson. 'Things are hotting up here. Sure enough the Provos took out Daly, but McConachie says that no Loyalists were behind the other killings. It looks like you might have been right.'

Unseen to Scala, Matherson smirked down the telephone. 'Does anyone suspect you?' he quizzed.

'Probably only half of the Shankill Road and three-quarters of the Falls, but apart from that they haven't got an inkling,' Scala replied, before considering that he might not be joking any longer.

* * *

The President had moved quickly, much to the annoyance of the British who felt they had been backed into a corner. He had told them that it was the only way ahead, to avoid the stalemate and the danger of the whole process collapsing. He had told them that they and the others involved could not afford to ignore the invitation. They would have nothing to lose and everything to gain. He had told the Prime Minister that the world would be grateful to them both – and, of course, the President would have the votes.

The Republic had agreed, and Sinn Fein had not placed any obstacles in the way. It was down to the British and the Unionists to accept. History would judge them as the men who squandered the chance of peace if they didn't accept, he told them. The publicity machine had already begun to gather momentum. Once started, it was as difficult to stop as a runaway train. Bill Dane had done his work well. The move had been unexpected, but there had been no way the Limeys or the so-called Loyalists could reject it. The date was fixed. History was in the making, and the President was the man who was leading the way. It was guaranteed to boost his ratings.

* * *

The man with the bulging gut felt like puking. He took another giant mouthful of the gassy beer and once more fixed his icy stare on the group at the far side of the room. She was a whore: it was as simple as that, he thought. She was a goddam whore. Wiping the dribbles from his unshaven chin, he ordered another beer.

The music started up again. The tall man with the scar rose to take the girl to the dance floor. They slipped into an easy body movement together, knowing that the eyes of the entire lounge were on them. Noreen felt the urge to show off, to show her man off, but a look across to her Mam persuaded her against it.

Scala had played the gentleman, a role which hardly came naturally; just ask the people in Merthyr or Hereford. He had joked and charmed, paid false compliments and shown patience. He felt it had paid off. Mrs Dillon was warming to him – or was it just that she was not as hostile as she had been? At one stage in the evening he actually imagined he had seen her smile.

It was Ma Dillon's night. She rarely made an appearance at the club these days. Tonight she was back with her daughter, and she didn't mind who saw it. She was not averse to a little showing off herself. The strains of familiar country hits and ballads filled the room, prompting many of the younger girls in the lounge to form themselves into dance groups. The men preferred to drink and argue.

Noreen knew that the eyes of the neighbours who regularly used the club would be on her. She wanted to make the effort to dress up, for both her Mam and her man. She had chosen a simple, plain, close-fitting dress, which plunged at the back to reveal her unblemished, milky skin. It was a cheap dress, one she had treated herself to on one of those wild days in exile, yet it proved effective. With her mass of black curls she would have seemed at home on a dance floor in some southern Italian town. The dark-haired, dark-skinned man dancing so closely with her completed the picture. Ma Dillon felt the warmth of pride swelling within her as she watched.

The man at the bar watched too. His festering mood was now reaching boiling point, aided by vast quantities of beer. She had walked straight past him as they walked in. She had forgotten the boy who had confessed his schoolboy love for her as they had walked home; ignored the pimply-faced teenager who had given her that first real kiss as an adolescent; walked past the young man who had cried when she had been sent into exile. No one paid any attention to the unshaven, overweight man at the bar. Few people could have imagined the humiliation mounting within him as he stared at the dancing girl and her man.

But one man saw. Georgie Armstrong, the eyes and ears of the Shankill whom people treated as a joke, saw and understood. He could see the volcano that was about to erupt. He said nothing, but merely continued to watch as he did every night.

The song came to an end and the groups of girls and couples returned to their seats. The man with the belly slipped on to his feet from the high bar stool, hoisted his sagging jeans and pushed his way through the corridor of tables and people across the lounge to where Noreen sat. His frame cast a shadow over the table as his eyes blazed towards her.

'I heard you were back,' he spat. 'So you'll not be remembering me now, I suppose? I suppose the years over there wiped us all clean away – ye'll not be wanting to have anything to do with the likes of meself now!'

A nervous smile stretched Noreen's mouth as she searched her mind for recognition. Thoughts flashed across her brain. It couldn't be . . . he had been a slight youth . . . not this!

'Aye, it's me, Michael – Michael Fitzgerald. Can't even speak to me now, eh?'

There was silence in the room. Michael took it as a signal to speak even louder. Ma Dillon was ashen. Scala attempted to calm the scene.

'Listen, friend, why don't you sit – '

'Piss off, you ponce – coming over here throwing your money round. Why don't you piss off back to where you belong? We don't need the likes of you flash bastards here, coming over here with our . . . with our . . .' He desperately searched for the word. 'With our whores – that's right, the whores who can't be bothered to take up with the likes of their own . . . the ones who can't even remember their names!' He slammed his fist on the table, spilling drink over the black dress.

The blood surged in Scala's veins and the blindness came over him. It was too late to control himself. Michael didn't see any hint of the head butt that struck him on the bridge of the nose, sending him reeling, arms flailing, into the tables behind. Blood spurted from his face on to the dresses of the two girls sitting there. Still the madness remained. As Michael attempted to rise, Scala's knee caught him under the chin and sent him sprawling again. Instinct led Scala now, and the fingers of his hand closed around the man's windpipe. In seconds he would be dead – the end of another piece of shit. The rage was still on him, but then Scala heard the echo of his name repeating itself within the depths of the turmoil that was his mind.

Noreen was tearing at his arm in a desperate attempt to make him release his grip. 'Jim, Jim . . . for the love of God, Jim . . . let him be . . . Jim, you're killing him . . .!'

The rage lifted, like curtains being drawn back to reveal the light. Scala was suddenly aware of the face in front of him, now bright blue and in the last stages of life. He released his grip. Michael still lay there frozen, gulping in air, but rapidly his terror forced him to stagger to his feet and lurch coughing from the lounge.

Noreen stood before Scala speechless. She had never dreamed that this man had an ounce of violence in his body. How could she have been so wrong? Her man had acted like a killer! Silence still echoed around the lounge. Ma Dillon was the first to regain her composure. Gathering up her bag and coat, she took hold of Noreen and led the sobbing girl out of the room. Scala now held centre stage. He breathed deeply, openly apologised to the people around him, and left.

The walk back to his hotel was an eternity. There was no sign of Noreen. He could picture her sobbing uncontrollably in her mother's arms. His brain bubbled with remorse. Shit, he had blown it, he had lost control – against everything the manual said, against everything he had been taught. A split second later and the guy would have been dead – and all because he had sworn at a woman. Scala had never acted that way before because a woman was being called names. But the names had hurt – they had hurt Noreen and they had hurt him. Christ, what was happening to him? All for a woman – this woman. Why this woman? Did she mean anything to him?

Then he thought rationally. So much for not sticking out too much – half the bloody Shankill had just seen him nearly crush a man's windpipe. He would be the talk of the area. How bloody stupid he had been! He had lost it all for the sake of a girl! Yes, they would be talking about him now okay.

140

Chapter Twelve

'I tell ye, the man nearly throttled Fitzgerald with one hand. It was all so quick it was like he was some kind of expert,' Georgie Armstrong gushed. He was excited. In his fantasy world, it was the kind of thing that he would be capable of. 'I thought Fitzgerald was a goner for sure – the fat fucker went bright blue. I tell you the man was like a bloody tiger!'

Naylor was only half listening. 'What bloody man?'

'You know – the fella from England that I told yer about. The one that's with the Dillon woman.'

Naylor vaguely remembered. He paid little attention to the rantings of Georgie when he was like this: the boy got too carried away with himself. Naylor reckoned that the so-called 'scrap' he had talked about was probably nothing more than two snotty-nosed kids slapping each other around. Georgie Armstrong wouldn't have an idea what a real 'scrap' was all about. And anyone worth worrying about wouldn't be coming to make trouble under the cover of a woman's skirt, would they? Naylor was too preoccupied sorting out the stuff to bother further with Georgie's ramblings.

The others were not at the boat yard today. Naylor wanted Georgie never to see them. It was better that way. The less he saw of them and the less he knew, the happier Naylor was.

The boy had his uses, though. He was a good spy; nothing much happened in the area without him knowing about it. He was always hanging around, so no one paid him much heed. He had also proved the perfect errand boy who asked no questions but lived in his dream world where he longed one day to have power. Naylor fuelled those dreams. Georgie had been easy to recruit. Naylor had seen his type before in so many shit-holes around the world where their services had been needed. He knew where to find them and how to run them. Naylor had convinced the boy that, with the growth of crime in the country, he would become a big man in the organization. That was what Naylor and his cohorts were there to promote, he said – a few drugs here and a little fraud there. There was big money in it for someone who could keep his mouth shut.

Georgie had agreed, partly because he wanted to believe in his dreams, and partly because he was afraid to say no to the hard man Naylor, whom, even in his fantasy world, he recognized as deadly. To Naylor, Georgie was a slavish puppy dog that rolled over on its back when told and did whatever was asked without question. That was the kind of loyalty that could be of use to him.

The boat yard was organized like a miniature military barracks. Everything was stored in its rightful place: weapons were hidden away, the cot beds of the men who lived there were always made tidy, and there was even a rota stating who would act as dishwasher for the day. It was the only way Naylor knew how to operate. It was the way of the army. And worked.

Now Georgie was about to face the biggest and most important test that Naylor had set him. So much would depend on him. Naylor would give him only a portion of the stuff now, as bait.

'Okay, now look!' Naylor commanded Georgie's attention. 'There's the money – say around £100 to begin with. There'll be more just as soon as you need it. I think you know where to start.'

Naylor set out a large metal container on the table. Inside, it was divided into sections crammed with dozens of tiny paper sachets. Each contained a tiny amount of powder – the white powder that was now the scourge of the Western world, that had ruined millions of lives; that people had died from and died for. Now Naylor had a use for it too.

Georgie gazed into the container. This was the stuff that dreams were made of. It was the stuff that brought nightmares too.

'Start tonight after school . . . Spread yourself around – keep on the move, there's less risk that way,' explained Naylor slowly as if talking to an uncomprehending child.

The stuff was good – his 'Latin friend' had seen to that. He praised himself for his good sense in maintaining relations with the people in South America. It amused him to think that once he would have been against these people.

Georgie looked apprehensive. Naylor saw the tension rising.

'Do this right, Georgie boy ... do this right and the world will be at your feet. All those people who laughed at you, Georgie – just think about them. You'll be laughing at them by the time you've finished. They'll all be wanting to know Georgie Armstrong then.'

Georgie felt bolder. If Naylor thought he could do it, then, Jesus Christ, he could bloody well do it!

'But remember, Georgie,' Naylor's tone became more sinister, 'not a word! If I hear anything that might have come from your mouth, Georgie, then I'll come for you. Day or night, I'll come for you. There's no crossing in this job, Georgie.'

* * *

The knock at the door stirred Scala. No one came to see him at the hotel, and he was not expecting visitors. He quickly gathered up the parcel that had arrived from London that morning and stashed it away in the bottom of the wardrobe before answering the door.

She was the last person he had expected. Noreen stood in the corridor giving the appearance of a lost child in a crowded store. Her eyes were red as if she had been crying all night, and her face was pale. She looked a pathetic figure, and Scala could barely resist the temptation to take hold of her, hug her and tell her that everything was going to be good.

'Come in,' was, in the event, all he could muster. 'I'd planned to come and see you later this morning. I wanted to say sorry to you and your mother.'

'I don't think Ma wants you around the house at present,' replied Noreen. 'I think she was a bit shaken by what happened. She reckons she's seen enough of trouble to last her a lifetime, and she doesn't fancy the risk of any more.'

Scala shrugged. 'I understand. But I think I should have at least been heard. I couldn't just sit there and let some fat bugger like that start calling you names – not those names. Something inside me gave way and I had to stop him.'

'But you nearly killed him – you would have killed someone you'd never set eyes on before just because of a few names,' spluttered Noreen as she sat on the edge of Scala's bed. 'If you'd lived my life, Jim, then names like that wouldn't mean much to you. When the people you've grown up with turn their backs on you because you stand up for what you think is right and refuse to help men who claim they're killing for the likes of me, then that is the really hurtful thing. Names don't matter much after that.'

He thought he was beginning to understand what she must have gone through.

'But you, Jim . . . I thought you were different . . . a gentle person . . . the tenderness that you've always shown me . . . the lovemaking. . . And then last night you show me a side of you that I never dreamed existed. It scares me, Jim. I tell yer, I'm frightened of it . . . and I don't want to be frightened of you. I thought I loved you – but now I wonder if I even know you.'

Scala was taken aback by her confession of love. He had never thought, never planned anything like this. She was a job – that was all. But he could not shrug off his uncertainty over why he had reacted so violently against the fat man who had called the woman he was with a 'whore'. Deep inside the worrying suspicion grew that he might actually care for a woman whom he had set out to trap and use. Yes, that was it. Damn it all – he cared for her. He hadn't simply gone through the motions of screwing her – he delighted in her vulnerability and her readiness to take on the world no matter what hand life dealt. He was in trouble.

'I can't explain, Noreen. I wish I could . . .' The words sounded pathetic as he heard them flow from his mouth.

'Oh, Christ, Jim, I want to believe in you, truly I do. I hoped we had something. But I want to know you, Jim. I'm not even sure what kind of work you do, Jim.'

'You will in time – all it takes is time. You'll know everything about me that there is to know. Trust me! I'm one of the good guys . . .' He was bursting to let her know more.

Don't be a twat, Scala, he thought. Cough now and you're dead! Get a bloody grip of yourself, man. She's only a bit of skirt. But the thoughts that ravaged his head failed to convince him.

He took her in his arms as a protective father takes hold of a crying child and hugged her. He gently kissed her forehead, then her nose, working his way to her mouth. She did not fight. She needed to believe in this man. They collapsed on to the bed urgently tearing each other's clothes off as if there was no more time left in the world for lovers like themselves. Their lovemaking was violent and passionate. She had never known it like this – she had never known herself like this. She needed her man.

* * *

The plan had worked before. There was no reason that it should not have the same results now. Naylor had drilled Georgie in the way it used to work so effectively, so cruelly. He had told him how the nightmares that had been started those years before had led to the horrors that still existed today.

Even in the late 1970s the scheme had seemed outrageous. Dublin had been free of drugs then. The elders of the Church and even the IRA had seen to that. Then the Iranians had come, escaping vengeance in the wake of the revolution that had ousted the Shah. Seeking to create a new empire, they had brought with them drugs. There had been those in Dublin willing to help . . . at a price.

It had been easy. They had paid children as young as nine years old a fiver a time to come and try the stuff, to inject themselves with heroin, to see what all the fuss was about, to get the 'buzz'. There had been no shortage of takers, eager for the fiver. They had come again and again, and brought their friends, and they had still had to come when there were no more fivers for them – because they needed to. The whole epidemic had taken just weeks to sweep the community.

The Church had been helpless, as had the hard men of the IRA. Many of those who had dared to take the initial fiver were still victims. Heroin was in Dublin to stay. Now, if Georgie did his work correctly, the youngsters of the Lower Falls and Turf Lodge and Andersonstown and Ballymurphy and a host of other Catholic enclaves would know the same pain that those of Dublin had known in the seventies, and who still lived the drugs nightmare. That nightmare would live with the Catholic community for generations to come.

Georgie saw himself in a position of power. He knew that many of the children on the impoverished estates and tower blocks thrown up by ill-thinking officials in the fifties and sixties could never resist the temptation of 'easy money'. A fiver and a needle would seem a perfect combination, and Georgie had a ready supply of both. It would be like giving them sweets. Naylor had told Georgie of the money that it would bring and of the empire to be created. He would be a big man.

The Boss and Hursley, Holmes and Hennessey and the others were intent on bringing down a plague on future generations of Catholics: one which the cardinals, the self-made politicians of Sinn Fein and the killers of the IRA would be powerless to prevent. Justice would finally be theirs.

*　　*　　*

'It's only rumours, of course. None of us know for sure – none of us really wants to.' McConachie was feeling more relaxed now, more talkative.

'Yes, but if it was true there'd be shit to pay, wouldn't there?' asked Scala. 'I tell you, I wouldn't like to be the bugger once the British got their hands on him – or, come to think of it, if the Provos got to grips with him. That's about as close to treason as it comes – you might as well go and shoot the Queen.'

'Well now, if he did that then we would be bothered, wouldn't we?' laughed McConachie, dipping his head into his glass of stout which left a rim of white foam on his beard. He liked this place. It was not only a place of business, but one of the few spots where he felt at ease.

Until now Scala had only heard of such places: the shebeens were drinking dens that existed throughout Belfast and operated on the pretence of being clubs – any kind of club, from pigeon fanciers' to bricklayers' apprentices'. The message at the hotel had instructed him to take himself to an almost derelict hall behind an almost derelict former government office which rejoiced in the name of the Belfast Greyhound Breeders' Association, situated off the Donegal Pass in the midst of the

Protestant stronghold of Sandy Row in the centre of Belfast. Scala discovered it to be little more than an excuse for a drinking club that would remain open for its loyal regulars at any hour of the day. The steward who ran it openly admitted that the nearest he had ever been to an actual greyhound was the aging photograph of a distinctly decrepit-looking beast that hung defiantly on the wall behind the bar.

The ramshackle place was full, even in mid-afternoon. It was here that McConachie held court. Scala had handed over a packet containing enough tabs for almost £15,000 worth of business. By the time he had drunk his first pint the Ecstasy tablets had been distributed to an army of anonymous couriers around the room, who in turn would use their network to get them to the rave bars and clubs within a few hours.

McConachie had a hidden admiration for Scala. He had been a man of his word. McConachie liked that. No copper would ever part with drugs, and his credentials had been checked out in London. He could use this man. Scala, for his part, needed some leads, and McConachie seemed a perfect starting-place for information. 'What I don't understand is,' he began, 'if it wasn't you who knocked off the pair of Provo jailbirds and the girl, then who the hell would have the balls to do it? I'd love to meet the man.'

'As I said,' came the careful reply, 'it's only a rumour. Whether or not he's here to even old scores official-like – if you get my drift – or whether he's totally independent I can't tell you. What I do know is that the main word is that there's a Brit over here who's willing to make the bastards pay, whether the bloody government like it or not.' McConachie felt as though he had made a speech. 'Whoever he is, I'll know eventually.'

Scala wasn't satisfied. 'But why the hell would they knock down a chopper and take out the security men? It doesn't make sense.'

McConachie rose to the bait. 'Course it fuckin' does, man! Knock off the bleedin' security men and a Brit chopper and who will automatically get the blame? The Provos – some die-hard Provos, that's who. Doesn't look good, does it? Certainly wouldn't look good in America or at the bloody peace table. Course, we can't complain. We look like the saints that we know we are – until the Provos come to knock the shit out of us again. Then we'll have to have a go back. Then, we're all back to square one, only next time it'll be worse – a lot, lot worse. We've had time to restock and plan . . . but so have they. I tell yer, the blood'll flood the drains.'

Scala thought of the consequences. 'Surely no bugger in their right minds wants that? With every passing day of peace, things will get harder to start up again!'

McConachie was losing patience and wanted to end the conversation. 'You sound like a fuckin' priest, man. There's plenty out there who'll not lose a night's sleep if it starts again. Bollocks to what you see on the TV, man – feel the hate. It's there, man. You can almost reach out and touch it. You'll never know what it's like until you've had your kin or a mate blown away by them bastards. You'll never understand.

'To be honest, there's no way that we can control all of our people. Some of them didn't like the idea of the ceasefire and just want to fight on – they won't wait. I've heard that some of the boys have gone independent – it has been known, you know! They'll not rest until every bastard Provo is face-down in the gutter. That's the only kind of reason they know. For example now, there's stories goin' round about one such fella by the name of O'Grady – a bad man, a real loner. He was one of us for a bit, but he was real hard to handle. Took out a Provo social club single-handed he did. He hates the bastards, you see – just hates them. The city got too hot for him. Every Provo was gunning for wee Kevin O'Grady. I heard tell he had to go to England. But I've also heard he's back. People like him just don't change because some fuckin' politician says, "Let there be peace", I tell ye.'

Scala stored the name away. 'So you think he might have come back to carry on the good work?'

The drink was starting to tell on McConachie. He liked a man he could trust, but he was getting tired of the questions. 'Oh, shut the fuck up and drink. Let's drink to a healthy business – or more to the point, an unhealthy business – and stop all these shit questions or I might think yer a friggin' spy or somethin'.'

Scala laughed. He knew when not to press his luck further. Just smile and drink to business: the business of peddling misery for the sake of being able to buy a few more guns. Life, it seemed to Scala, was as simple as that in this new city of peace.

* * *

It would be a day that would live in history. The President would see to it. The British had effectively been told to tow the line. There had been the usual talks about diplomatic niceties. But the President could ride that. He did.

Phrased in the way that Bill Dane explained it to the press as they gathered in the White House in the afternoon, there was no way that the British government, the Ulster Unionists or the Ulster Defence Association could convincingly argue. It was agreed that the first all-party face-to-face meetings in the history of the Troubles of Northern Ireland were set.

The British delegation would be headed by the necessary junior minister, while Eamon Clancy would head the Sinn Fein delegation, with the support of the Irish Republic. Few but the United States of America had the influence to be able to broker such a meeting, insisted Dane. To that end, the historic talks would take place on neutral ground – the United States Embassy in Belfast – where no one party could claim impartiality. It was a historic breakthrough. The talks would be held within the month.

The news was flashed around the world even before Downing Street had had time to mould its own statement of events, even before the Unionists had been able to voice their reservations. Peace was on the move.

* * *

Matherson had a name. It was a clue that might, God willing, lead them in the direction of the renegades who appeared hell-bent on setting Ulster on the road to a bloodbath. His team checked and rechecked for any trace of the man Kevin O'Grady. He was known to Special Branch and he was known to the Met. There had been possible sightings of him in Manchester, Bristol and even Glasgow. Now he had disappeared, and immigration were unable to assist.

Matherson ordered his team to work around the clock to find

any trace of O'Grady. At least he could tell Jacobson they had a name – whether it was the right one was immaterial at this point. If only Matherson could be certain of his other information he could tell Scala, but it was impossible. It might even save Scala's life. But at present, it was only guesswork and poor intelligence-gathering. It was better that Scala learned what he was up against for himself. Until then he would have to blunder on in blissful ignorance.

*   *   *

He was The Pied Piper. He had spent days befriending these youngsters. They trusted him. They were too young to worry about whether Georgie Armstrong was a Catholic or a Protestant. He had kicked a football with them on the playing fields of the Falls Park, he had waited for them as they left the primary schools of Ballydownfine and New Barnsley in West Belfast. And now they had followed him to derelict factories and secret hideaways amid the peeling tower blocks.

Few had been able to resist. The older ones of eight and nine had more appreciation of the fiver, but just as much ignorance of the needle that accompanied it. The small sachets of powder were diluted with water. Georgie told them it would make them feel good, make them feel funny and happy – they would be in a dream. Over fifty had been willing to believe in the dream within the first two days, and there would be many more.

Now Georgie sat alone in a bar, sipping beer. He felt good. Naylor would look after him. He had promised.

Chapter Thirteen

It had started as a game. The other kids had dared each other. The man had said it would be fun, and there was money to be had too. There was nothing to it. Everyone else had done it – just a small prick and it was done. There had been a world of colours and of floating, looking down on the others from high above. The man was right, it was fun. It was better than being chased away from the shitty, broken-down flats by the miserable grown-ups. It was better than the drudgery of listening to the boring teachers at the St Teresa's Primary School. This was a world away from the grey misery of the estate, and there was money to be had too. The man had said there would be more money if you brought a friend to share the fun with you.

How long ago had it been since the man first came? It seemed like an age, even though it had been no more than ten days. To Danny MacMichael it seemed like a year – although time, as his teachers and his Ma and his Da had explained it to him, meant little now. To Danny, and his two friends who had also followed the man, time didn't exist any longer. At nine years old, the hugs of his Ma meant little, the warmth and security of his home on the estate in Whiterock meant nothing. What mattered now was seeing the man who made dreams come true.

It didn't matter that the fivers were gone. It didn't matter that Danny MacMichael had now become a thief, stealing the money from his mother's purse to give to the man who met you at the back of the flats after school had finished and took you inside the houses that had been empty since the people went away. His friends had done the same. It didn't matter because the white stuff he gave you took you away to a funfair far away in your mind. It didn't matter that each time the white stuff was a little stronger than the time before.

No one had noticed the unthinkable. Nobody saw the start of the plague.

It had been like every other day. Danny had waved goodbye to his mother, like he had every other day. He waited for his friends at the end of the road, like every other day. Together they had gone to the same classes given by the same teachers that they did every day. He sat at the same desk in the crowded school, and listened to the pretty red-haired teacher who was kind to them. But today was different. It was hot in the classroom but Danny felt cold, yet he was also sweating and shaking uncontrollably, almost violently; his eyes blazed uncomprehendingly.

His friends smiled at first, then realized it was no game. They stared and screamed. The caring teacher turned and watched; fear and panic struck her. She shouted to the other children to bring help; she tried to hold the shaking boy in her arms. She noticed the tiny bruises on his arm, yet still did not comprehend. It would have been unthinkable.

The ambulance was there within minutes. The Royal Victoria Hospital, which had witnessed so much horror over the last twenty-five years, was about to receive the latest victim of the struggle for Ulster.

* * *

Scala thought they must be like ghosts – phantoms who appeared in order to take life and then disappeared again. He had sent the name to Matherson in the hope of getting a result. But there had been none. There was still only talk of the lone Brit. Everyone whom Scala attempted to quiz believed that the man must be working for the British army. If not, they would have known him.

McConachie was getting suspicious of Scala's questioning. Healy had never liked Scala and was only too eager to fan the flames of suspicion. But Scala had delivered the goods – the tablets that would raise thousands more for the UVF coffers. The peace talks might have been scheduled, but if permanent peace was around the corner then it seemed to Scala that no one had told the Loyalist quartermasters. It had been over three weeks since his arrival, yet apart from suspicions he had nothing. His reputation as a dealer was also starting to spread. He was no longer anonymous, and it could not be long before he was compromised. Noreen was still suspicious, but he comforted himself in the belief that love was blind. Business was good. If Scala had been a bona fide dealer, he could have been set up for life. The prospect did not make him feel any better. He sat alone in a corner of the Regent, unaware of the world around him and not caring for it.

'I saw yer scrap the other day with the Big Man. Pretty bloody impressive – taught the fat bastard a lesson or two, eh?'

The words jerked Scala back to reality. He recognized the gaunt, pale-faced figure that always sat alone at the end of the bar – the one who never spoke, just stared.

'Like to shake yer by the hand, mister. I like to see a good scrap and meet a man who can take care of himself.'

Scala stretched out his hand.

'The name's Georgie. I've seen yer in here a lot, haven't I? Yer with the wee Noreen girl, are you not? Aye, a fine-lookin' woman.' Georgie had started drinking early that day. His new-found role as ace drugs peddler had emboldened him. He had been given the first instalment for the job and now he felt the need to talk to someone – someone who was his peer, someone who was a big man like himself.

'I've noticed you before, Georgie. You're in here a lot, aren't you.' It was a statement, not a question. 'My name's Jim.'

'I know,' responded Georgie sharply. 'I know everyone around here. It's like my job, you see. I like to know who everyone is. It started as a kind of hobby, but now I make it me business.'

Scala studied the shabby figure. He knew why few people had time for the man.

'And who do you do your business with? Anyone in particular?'

'I suppose you could say that I'm a freelance, but I'm on a retainer at present.'

'Sounds interesting.' Scala could smell the drink on Georgie's breath.

'Where did yer learn to fight like that then, Jimmy? Yer wouldn't be an army man, would yer? I was an army man meself, yer know. I got pissed off with it, though. Too many people telling yer what to do with yer life. That's not for me, Jimmy, I tell yer . . .'

'I couldn't agree more, Georgie my friend. You'd never catch me in the army for the same reasons. I picked up a bit of fighting knowledge along the way. I'm no great expert, but I can hold my own. Anyway, the fat man was hardly any challenge.'

Georgie felt the budding of a comradeship between the two men. 'I suppose in your line of work a bit of fisticuffs is inevitable really, if you get my meaning.'

'And what line of work would I be in, then, Georgie?' enquired Sçala.

'Well, from what I hear we're very much in the same line of business. Shall we say supply and demand? I happen to know that yer a dab hand at supplying the tabs . . . there's not much of a secret about that kind of thing and the people who are offering them about. If you live in the bars, then you get to know!'

'If you say so, Georgie.'

Georgie wanted to talk. He now considered that Scala and himself were from the same world. 'Well, let me tell you, Jimmy, the kind of stuff that you're into is fuck-all compared to what I'm about. I know the people, you see. I have the right contacts. I know your type, Jimmy. Come over here from the mainland, a bit flash, likes to get yer leg over wherever ye can and fancy yerself as a bit of a hard man, sure enough. And good luck to yer, Jimmy.'

Scala was resisting the temptation to smash the man's nose. Instead he made himself listen.

'Yes, Jimmy, I think we're very much alike, you and me.' Georgie leaned forward to whisper. 'Yer see, Jimmy, I know a lot about the drug shit meself – that's why I say we're very much alike. I tell yer, Jimmy, it's the future of this place! Well, I can tell ye that people will be talking about my shit for a long time to come – especially them Catholic bastards over there!' He motioned beyond the Shankill to the far side of the peace divide. 'Aye, Jimmy, what we're doing will teach them to mind their shit for a long time.'

Scala became more attentive. 'You said "we", Georgie. You said, "What *we're* doing." Have you got a partner or something?'

Georgie considered. 'Clever bastard, aren't ye, Jimmy? A hard man and a clever bastard sure enough! What if I do have a partner? He's a hard man too! Very fuckin' hard, I'll tell yer. You'd never cross him, Jimmy – and live! He's got plans, Jimmy. He came from the mainland like you. He's got plans and he wants me to help him, Jimmy! He's going to make me a big man around here, Jimmy . . . He's a clever man as well, sure he is. He reckons that just six good men could change the whole fuckin' future of this country . . . that's very profound, that is!'

Scala was intrigued. 'So does this hard man come in here? Tell me how you met him. Would I know him, Georgie?'

Georgie blinked studiously. 'What the fuckin' hell is all this about? You a cop or sometin'? All these fuckin' questions. He's my man . . . ye'll get no bloody name from me, Jimmy boy.'

'Sorry, Georgie. Course I'm no bleedin' cop . . . you brought the matter up. Let's just forget about it, shall we?'

All of Scala's senses were now on the alert. A sixth sense told him that the young drunken fool who nobody talked to, the man who had proved a failure all his life, might well at this moment be the most important man in Belfast.

*　　*　　*

It was the only news of the day. The headlines screamed a shocking new story from Ulster. There was no room for mention of the peace talks or distant wars, or of the latest revelations of adultery amongst MPs in Westminster. The news was of the five cases of heroin addiction amongst primary school children in Belfast. But no one knew the full extent of the addiction. These were not isolated cases, and there could be countless more. All had been aged between eight and ten. All had been Catholics from the estates ruled by the IRA. The talk was of an epidemic that was sweeping the city.

Churchmen, politicians, social workers and leading community figures queued to say their few minutes' worth to camera, while the children who had shown adverse reactions to heroin lay fighting for life in the Royal Victoria Hospital. The communities on both sides of the sectarian divide felt the same revulsion. For years the churchmen and even the gunmen had been united in the belief that drugs should be outlawed. Ecstasy had arrived: there had been a demand. But heroin had never found a place or a demand in Ulster. Now the nightmares that accompanied it all over the world had arrived in the Falls, Ballymurphy and the other Republican strongholds where the patriots of the IRA had boasted to keep the streets clean of such evils.

The Deputy Chief Constable of the Royal Ulster Constabulary, Philip McGann, interviewed on television, was first to point the finger of guilt. In his prepared statement McGann insisted that 'we must look very carefully at the growth of organized crime in Ulster, and in particular the growth in drug-trafficking. For some years the growth has shown a steady increase. We expect the problem to double within the next two years. We already know, of course, that elements within the IRA are already much practised in the dealing of drugs to fund their terrorist operations. It is they who have already soiled their hands with the use of heroin in numerous deals. It is true that, until this moment, such deals have been restricted to foreign soils. Now, as funds for their efforts are somewhat restricted, it may be fair to assume that they have turned their attentions to similar dealings on their home territory. We must all be vigilant for the sake of our children . . .'

Until now the IRA had been thought of as the safeguard against the spread of heroin. Now it seemed that the men who had fought in the name of nationalism against the British were more interested in making the fortunes that came with organized drug-dealing on a huge scale.

But even before the IRA mouthpieces of Sinn Fein had had time to counter McGann's accusations Declan Holmes had joined his voice to those who blamed the Republican sections of Belfast life. In a number of public statements Holmes declared himself unwilling to sit at a table with anyone who might be responsible for poisoning the children of their own kind for profit to buy more weapons of war. This time the man who had been expelled from Parliament for voicing his extremist notions found a growing audience.

* * *

There had been dreams for Danny MacMichael. He had been born into a place of war, a place where one child was taught to hate another without asking the reason. However, many of his generation could now at last look forward to a time when there might be no war; when Catholics and Protestants could share in a new prosperity and hope for the country that would come with the peace.

But because of the man who had come with the fiver and the needle, and who had enticed the children to follow and sample new dreams, Danny MacMichael would not be allowed to share in that peace. He had never regained consciousness. Danny MacMichael became another statistic on the list of death in the land that had seen so much.

Chapter Fourteen

The Range Rover snaked along the coast road and came to a halt by the ten-feet-tall electrically operated gates. The weekend always brought a steady stream of traffic escaping from Belfast towards the resort of Bangor or the picturesque coastal town of Donaghadee a half-hour's drive from the city. It had taken Naylor just ten minutes to reach the house from where he and the others were billeted at the boat yard. The instruction for the meeting had come from Hursley. It had to be important. Naylor had thought the job almost completed. He had thought he would never get to meet the Boss.

The gates opened to reveal a long driveway which cut through a carefully manicured lawn. At the end of the driveway stood what Naylor considered to be one of the most magnificent houses he had ever seen – a stone-built mansion in traditional style with a pillared porch and what he estimated to be at least six bedrooms upstairs. Behind it the Irish Sea acted as a shimmering backdrop. The land at the rear of the house sloped down to the water's edge, from where a small private jetty jutted out into the clear blue sea. At the end of the jetty, Naylor spotted an elegant all-white cruiser which bobbed in the water and shone against the brightness of the sunlight.

'Sweet Jesus – some bastards know how to live!' he muttered under his breath.

As he pulled up in front of the porch he took in the matching metallic blue Jaguar XJSs, one soft-topped, which he assumed belonged to the Boss, and a further array of sleek cars, presumably owned by the other 'guests' who he had been told would be here. A plump, elderly woman opened the door and beckoned him to follow her. Naylor gawked at the trappings of luxury within. A wide red-carpeted staircase festooned with old family portraits wound its way from the first-floor gallery to the open hallway below. The hall opened into a sumptuous room furnished with shining leather chairs, well-stocked bookshelves and in a far corner the biggest piano that he had ever set eyes upon. But even Naylor felt the tingle of unease in this house.

As he moved he felt he was being scrutinized from the scores of photographs which were displayed in every possible crevice and shelf in the room. Each contained the laughing, handsome face of the same young man in one pose or another – a young man with dark good looks, neat white teeth and clear blue eyes. Above the open fireplace, where a massive log burned, hung a huge oil painting of the same young man in academic robes. The eyes from the photographs and the portrait seemed to focus on Naylor wherever he moved. It occurred to him that the room, or perhaps the entire house, had been turned into a gigantic shrine.

'Mr Naylor, I presume? Sorry to have kept you waiting.'

Naylor spun round at the sudden interruption, to be confronted by an elegantly clad woman whom he guessed to be in her early fifties, but who, with the aid of wealth, had been able to stem the march of time. The woman of the house, he presumed.

'My husband and the others are waiting for you. If you would like to go out through those French windows and along the jetty, they're all gathered on the boat.'

Without speaking, he made his way along the jetty to the bobbing cruiser which appeared to grow in size with every step. He was welcomed aboard by a man who directed him below to a wardroom before returning to the bridge and starting the engines. Naylor opened the double doors and viewed the men before him. He knew the familiar faces of Hursley and Massey. 'Christ!' he thought, 'a real boys' outing.' He nodded politely in greeting. The figure in the corner he recognized from the newspapers and television as Declan Holmes, a man whom he classed as a total extremist as crazed as any Provo he could come across. The remaining man had his red face dipped into a glass of whiskey. He was introduced by Hursley as His Honour Niall Hennessey, one of Ulster's foremost judges.

Now he understood. Everyone had played their part. Of course, Hennessey must have fingered the men whom Naylor and the others had taken out. It was as if he had drawn up a death list and meted out his own kind of justice.

'I have to say, Mr Naylor – or shall I call you Mick – your

efforts in this latest phase seem to have paid off in spades,' beamed Hursley. 'You're to be congratulated on the idea. I doubt if there's one sane person of any creed who doesn't doubt that the IRA have taken to poisoning their own children at this moment in time. The seeds of doubt are growing every day – even across the water, from what I understand. As if pushing them into action again hadn't been enough – no one could possibly trust them now for years.'

The others muttered their agreement. Naylor felt the boat move and begin heading out into the bay. Suddenly the doors behind him opened and a man with a stooped frame and shock of white hair entered the room. From the silence that followed Naylor assumed that at last he had come face to face with the Boss. The deeply lined face and heavily lidded eyes were familiar even to Naylor, who had never been one to indulge in the gossip pages of the tabloids; but he knew the man, by reputation at least.

He finished the details from memory. Noel Caffrey was probably the richest man in Northern Ireland. It was not an inherited wealth: the newspapers had always been quick to point out that Caffrey was a self-made man. His empire, which stretched from the construction industry via export to even a national chain of bookmakers' shops, had all been the result of his own labour. He was a multi-millionaire of his own making, the kind of man whom Naylor respected.

A flash of inspiration passed through Naylor's mind. He remembered now: Caffrey had had a son who had died – killed in an explosion at a factory owned by his father at Newry in Armagh, in the heart of Republican land. The IRA had claimed responsibility . . . it flooded back to Naylor now . . . they had apologised because they had believed the factory to be empty at the time. But Noel Caffrey had stood firm. He had refused to pay the 'protection' that the IRA had demanded. He had bragged that he would always stand up to extortion.

That had been six years ago. The IRA team had honestly believed that the factory would be empty. They had recruited a girl, who had unwittingly driven the car with the bomb from Belfast; a girl who had dated one of the team of bombers on a few occasions. He had told her that he would pick the car up later.

Martin Caffrey had been a bright boy, his parent's only son. He had done well at university and was a fitting heir to the empire built by his father. He had insisted on being at the factory that day: there was work to be done. The car bomb had taken out half the street as well as the entire floor where Martin had been working. Noel Caffrey, the man with everything, had never recovered. He was now considered a near recluse: a man with millions and no future.

'Well, Mr Naylor, I see you recognize me!' said Caffrey. 'Are you surprised?'

'Not really, Mr Caffrey. Everything fits into place now. If you'll pardon my bluntness, it would seem that you don't really care too much about disrupting the peace process – it might appear that you're more interested in revenge.'

'Perhaps, Mr Naylor, there is a way of doing both. We all have to live with our various reasons,' said Caffrey. 'I think in this particular instance all of us here – with the possible exception of yourself – are of a like mind. You see, in one form or another we have all been betrayed. We are being asked to stand idly by while those who have brought us so much pain and have deprived us of so much bask in glory. Well, thanks to you, Mr Naylor, it is going to be difficult for them. They can hardly bask in the glory of killing their own children, can they? It will be years before the stigma detaches itself. But some of us can have the pleasure – one of the few pleasures left to us these days – of watching their generations of loved ones being tortured and taken from them, like ours have been. For that, Mr Naylor, we thank the endeavours of you and your colleagues.'

The general chatter resumed. Naylor sat back and observed. The gathering gave the appearance of a party, as if celebrating death itself, for they had each played their own role in the deaths of so many – and possibly many more to follow. He wondered if any supposed cause could justify those deaths.

Caffrey, seeing Naylor lost in his own thoughts, went over to join him. 'Mr Naylor, you were blunt enough with me – now allow me my turn,' he began. 'I have often wondered what drives men like yourself to do this kind of work. If it is painful, please don't answer, but I am curious to know what makes a man become involved and risk dying for somebody else's struggle.'

Naylor had grown used to such questions by now, and gave his practised response. 'I think, Mr Caffrey, we have all been betrayed in some form or another – you in yours and me in mine. What does a man like me do after a lifetime of being told how to take a man's life in so many different ways – but doing it for Queen and Country? I believed sure enough in what I was doing. I was wearing the uniform of my country and proud of it – I was ready to die for that uniform, you see! But what do you do when somebody from high above, somebody in Whitehall who has never met Michael Naylor, decides that you're no longer right to wear the uniform? When they decide that after twenty-two years of serving your Queen and Country then you're not required any longer? Because, on one occasion, I did my job too well, they decided I wasn't wanted any longer.'

He appeared to lose himself in thought for a second as he recalled his past. Then he continued: 'After that you can't exactly go down to the Jobcentre and ask for a job for a man whose only experience is spending twenty-two years killing people. I was good at my job – very good indeed. The army was my life: the boys I worked with meant more to me than the woman I was married to for fifteen years. So the most natural thing left was to make myself into what the government would like to think of as one of Britain's "small businesses". I decided that if I was going to kill, then the only person I would have to justify it to was myself – and take the profit from it.'

Caffrey had expected such an answer. 'Do you find it easy to justify what you do for your pay cheque? Do you have a price list for different men's lives?'

Naylor fought to control his anger. 'Listen, Mr Caffrey, I'm not one for following causes. Don't tell me that you're backing this little lot for a cause. You are a man simply taking revenge for someone whom he lost. Now I can understand that a damn sight more than I can asking someone to die for any bloody cause.'

Caffrey forced a smile. 'You're right, Mr Naylor. These people robbed me of my only reason to live when they took my son, and I think every man needs at least one reason to live.'

Naylor considered carefully. 'Or more to the point, Mr Caffrey, maybe everyone should have a reason to die for. I know what mine is now – it's not for some bloody flag any more or some country that turns its back on you because you do a dirty job too well. I know my reason for dying, and it comes in any currency you would care to name. I believe in myself and money, Mr Caffrey. So far they are the only things that haven't let me down in life.'

Champagne was opened. Naylor preferred beer. They toasted the success of the campaign thus far. The former soldier had the feeling that more was to come, something he might not like.

He knew Hursley's and Massey's backgrounds and understood their various reasons for throwing in their lot with Caffrey. It had not been difficult for Caffrey to find 'like- minded men'. They had all wanted to hit back. Listening to Hennessey, Naylor gathered that the man's sole reasons for entering the little consortium were greed and power. He guessed right. A little blackmail about an illicit affair, and Caffrey had had little problem persuading Hennessey of his use in providing details of the jailed IRA men. After all, Hennessey shared the anger; he had presided over each of their trials and delivered his justice, but the politicians had seen fit to over-ride his power. Caffrey had known Holmes for years and shared his beliefs to a great extent. In turn Hursley had made no secret of his feelings to Holmes during many evenings in the lobby bars within Westminster. Hursley had met Massey at one of the demonstrations of British army technology at Aldershot, when Hursley had sat in a junior role on the defence committee. That had been in the days before the cutbacks. Massey had been an easy recruit. This would be his last war.

Caffrey interrupted the gabble. 'I am afraid, gentlemen, that our gathering is one member short. Our colleague from within the ranks of the constabulary has come down with a sudden attack of cold feet. Therefore I thought it better that we carried out the meeting without the pleasure of our Mr McGann. I have arranged to see him later.'

So, thought Naylor, it had been McGann, the man who by an apparent fluke had escaped death on the helicopter – the helicopter that he, Naylor, had brought down – who had provided the information about flight times and schedules. Christ! How many more surprises would lie in store during the afternoon?

*   *   *

The brothers had expected to revel in glory. Instead they had been forced to hide and were shunned. They had waited for years to prove themselves, and thought that the killing of the Prod in the bar would be easy. They had expected to feel like the great freedom fighters they had heard of in the stories of old. But it had all turned out different. Their baptism in death had been a messy affair: the man's blood had splashed over their clothes, and when the buzz of the Speed had left their bodies they had puked and suffered and had nightmares of the man's pleading eyes staring at them as they had pumped their bullets into him. There would be no celebration for the killing of Jimmy Daly.

They had hidden in the safe house that Macnamara had told them of. But they had not felt like the heroes they expected to be. Instead they felt fear – not of capture from the green-uniformed men of the RUC, but that their fate would be sealed by a man with a gun who would step from the shadows one dark night to claim revenge. They took courage, however, from Macnamara. He had fed them stories about the fight against the Brits and the Prods, and about the dream of one Ireland. He would look after them.

But now, as Kevin and Billy ventured into the back room of the club and sat waiting for more words of encouragement from their champion, Macnamara appeared a different man. The fire in his eyes had been dampened; even his ruddy skin held a grim pallor. He was a man who had been gutted; a man who still had the fight, but did not know where to unleash that fight.

'It's true, I tell you, sir,' insisted Billy. 'I'd not come to you with a pile of bullshit. There's this man, a Brit sure enough, a shitehawk called Scala who is making a fortune from the drugs. He's proud of it. He's come back with a Prod bitch they allowed to come back to the city. We know some fellas who've told us that he's made no secret about his dealing, I can tell yer – and we did not have any of this shit with our kids till he turned up here. Our fellas in the clubs reckon that the cause of all this is a fella from away. They'd said all along that there was a Brit behind all these things. There's no other bastard who would have the guts to try it here. The Prods would know we'd knock the shit out of them. They'd never risk it . . .'

Kevin felt the need to add his evidence. 'It seems that this fella Scala has also been seen with a fella called Armstrong – Georgie Armstrong, thinks he's a big player sure enough. Some of the kids have talked about mixing with a wee shite that fits Georgie Armstrong's description. It could be that he's the runner for the man Scala. They're probably working it as a team, two shite-peddling bastards together. I bet yer, if we got wee Georgie aside for a bit he'd spill his guts to cover his arse quicker than a ferret down a rabbit hole.'

Macnamara was a general with no troops to command. The brothers at least still regarded him as their officer. The least he could do was listen, and listen he did intently. What they had said made sense. There could be no other explanation. Nothing would be lost if they were to pull Georgie Armstrong, he agreed. Macnamara felt the darkness that had shrouded his heart and soul lift. He had always been a hero of the cause. Now there was a chance to return in glory.

* * *

'She had to go – she was the bitch that drove the car. Nothing else matters,' insisted Hennessey. 'McGann gave us the name. To put it in military jargon, we felt her a legitimate target, you see!'

Hennessey was feeling comfortable. The champagne was taking its effect and he wanted to talk. Now, as the boat returned to the jetty, Naylor felt he was feeling the need to justify their decision to target Sheena Maguire.

'The police found out that she'd driven the car that took the bomb. She'd been persuaded by that bastard Kean, sure enough. Course, when I jailed him they couldn't pin the factory bombing on him for lack of evidence, but I knew he'd done it and so too did McGann. Noel was so badly cut up about it – that they couldn't pin Martin's death on the little bastard and his whore. And how do you think he felt when they decided to let him go free?'

Naylor listened in silence. He was a soldier. He followed orders. He did not allow himself the luxury of thinking about why he was doing these things, why he had killed the people he had been told to. He didn't want to know. He was being paid a cool £500,000 that would see him okay for years, set him up in South America. That was all Mick Naylor wanted to think about.

'From the pictures, though, I guess you could have had a nice time with that little tart!' Hennessey went on. 'She looked like she could have done a turn or two!'

Naylor could stomach no more. He had heard enough of the man's alcohol-fuelled rantings. Naylor felt pity for Hennessey's wife. He wondered what kind of woman would tie herself to such a sick-minded little bigot. In disgust, he moved to the other side of the wardroom. As he sat alone there, waiting for the cruiser to moor once more at the jetty, Hursley took a seat next to him.

'I gather you've been getting a little background information on our proceedings,' he said, smiling. While the others were beginning to show the effects of the afternoon's drinking, Hursley appeared completely in control of his faculties. 'Yes. Kean was the man who made the bomb okay, and the silly bitch delivered it for them just because he'd screwed her a couple of times.'

'What about the others, then?' enquired Naylor.

'Part of the same team, Mick. They were part of the team that came with the IRA's head man at the time to deliver the ultimatum to Mr Caffrey. Sure enough Noel gave their descriptions to the RUC, but they had watertight alibis, and even our Mr McGann had to agree that there was bugger-all they could do.'

'And Caffrey's been turning his guts over with anger ever since – until you got me to play the avenging angel bit, eh?'

'Something like that, Mick. But you won't forget you've been well paid in exchange for your expertise, will you?' insisted Hursley. 'And I'm afraid there's one more task for you before you're finished with us here – one which Mr Caffrey is very happy to pay for, and pay for very well indeed!'

Naylor looked up with interest.

* * *

The door of the Shankill Road Society of Friends slammed shut behind Scala. McConachie walked with him, carefully surveying the street. Healy and one of the other guards walked behind.

The two men were locked in conversation, and Scala did not see Noreen watching from across the street.

She had been touring the local shops and chatting to long-lost friends when she saw the two men step into the street. She had wanted to shout to Scala, but then she had noticed the bearded man by his side. Noreen recalled that night seven years earlier when the same man had knocked on the door and told her and her Mam that their Noel would not be coming home. He had also been the man who had banished her for her 'disloyalty'. She remembered him.

She watched McConachie laugh and share a joke with Scala, her man, and her heart plummeted to the bottom of her stomach.

* * *

Caffrey put down the folder in front of Naylor, who opened it carefully. 'You will be paid a further £500,000 for your trouble, Mr Naylor, you and your men. From then on, there will be no more contact,' said the Boss.

Naylor's eyes skipped through the contents. 'I can understand why, Mr Caffrey. There's a very good chance that we'll all be dead anyway!'

Caffrey pointed to a photograph in the folder. 'I suppose you could call this a double-header, Mr Naylor,' he continued. 'The meeting has been scheduled for 23 April. It's a blow that neither side will recover from – there'll be no peace, there'll be no surrender to these scum. This will do the job for good. The consulate – a soft target these days, but one that will have impact. I suppose it means you're going out with a bang, anyway! But make sure of the man, Mr Naylor. Make sure!'

Caffrey knew from his reputation that Naylor would not be able to resist. He stabbed at the photograph of Eamon Clancy as his mind returned to that grey afternoon six years before when he had arrived with his henchmen to speak to Caffrey – to deliver the ultimatum that Caffrey had refused and that had resulted in the death of his son. The pain was still etched on Caffrey's face.

'And let justice be mine!' muttered Naylor.

Chapter Fifteen

The narrow lanes of County Down sped by. It felt good to be out of the city and in the open countryside: Scala felt imprisoned if he spent too long in the restrictive streets of any urban jungle. This had been his idea – an opportunity for them to be alone, without a dozen pairs of eyes focused on them at any given time. Scala had wanted to tell her he had realized just how much she meant to him. He had tried to shrug away his emotions, but without success; today was the day he had chosen to tell her.

But Noreen today was a different person from the one he knew. Barely a word had passed her lips since they had left the city behind. She had chewed her nails and shuffled in her seat uneasily. Scala's jokes had met with stony silence.

'So what is it then? What's going through your head today? Come on, tell me – there's something bugging you,' begged Scala as he pulled the car to a halt at a remote spot where a bridge crossed a near-flooded stream. 'If it's something I've done, then tell me and we'll sort it out. But don't give me the silent routine!'

Noreen got out of the car and stood on the bridge. Scala followed. She looked nervous.

'I saw you the other day . . . with that man,' Noreen spluttered as she stared into the flowing water below.

'What man?'

'The man McConachie. I know him, you see. He was the man who came and ordered me to leave Belfast. He was the man who told our Noel how great it was to shoot Provos. He's a man who deals in death . . . and I saw you with him the other day. I saw the man I'm supposed to love walking with him and joking with him . . . and I don't know what I'm supposed to think, Jim Scala.'

Scala fought for an explanation. What had she seen? Where had she seen them? There was nothing to be gained in lying to the girl – that would merely fuel her curiosity.

'Oh, I see.' It sounded pathetic, and Scala was furious with himself at his inability to explain. 'It's business, Noreen. That's all I can tell you at the moment – simply business.'

Noreen turned sharply. 'Just who the bloody hell are you, Jim Scala? Just who the hell is the man I brought back and who within days is talking to the man who runs the Ulster Volunteer Force? Who are you that you'd be mixing with a killer like him? And don't give me that crap about dealing in so-called leisure – the only piece of leisure that McConachie knows about is the body bag! Why do I get the feeling that the man I brought back is using me? that he doesn't care a shit about me? that he screws me and uses me. Are you a Brit spy or something? Are you a cop? just what in the name of sweet Jesus are you, Jim Scala? I told you I can't be hurt any more . . . I can't take the pain. I thought you knew that.'

'I know it's hard Noreen,' he replied gently, 'but please trust me. I'm not here to hurt you or anyone else. Far from it – I want to stop people being hurt. But you can't know. All that you need to know is that I care for you, Noreen Dillon. Truly and deeply, I care for you . . . and that's a confession that I thought I'd never make.'

The tears came. Noreen could hold them back no more.

'I just ask you to trust me for a little while longer. Trust in me because I'm one of the good guys . . . and trust me when I say I care. God help me, I never thought I would care for anyone.'

She turned to him and threw her arms around him as her tears flowed uncontrollably.

His words were inadequate. But they had to do for the moment.

*　　*　　*

Ambassador Mitchell Cain was making the final preparations for the meeting. It would be the high point of his career. It would be enough to take him out of this god-forsaken hole and off to another posting, either Stateside or possibly to one of the major capitals of Europe. He had voiced his support of the President. It had been right to welcome the men from Sinn Fein. That's what he had said, even though in his heart he had doubts. He had lived amongst the bombs and bullets and murders for too long. It was fine for the President who sat up there on Capitol Hill; it was the likes of Cain who had witnessed the blood-letting at close quarters in his five years of running the consulate in Belfast. But if he played his hand correctly now, he could wave goodbye to all that.

He would do his best to preside over the meeting. He had dealt with the stiff upper-lipped British before. They simply wanted to preserve their image: he could play them. The Loyalists, however, would be different. They had good cause for scepticism, especially after the recent wave of violence. But Cain knew that the people in the street would not allow them to throw away this opportunity for permanent peace. Finally, Cain knew Clancy. He knew him to be a hard-nosed sonofabitch. But this latest thing with the drugs and the kids had blemished the Republicans' image. According to the latest opinion polls, their own people were withdrawing their support: the people didn't like the idea of their kids being killed by drugs peddled by the IRA in order to raise money for guns. Cain knew the IRA would be difficult to handle. They were rapidly getting to the point where they would openly revert to the Armalite. If that happened, Mitchell Cain could kiss goodbye to his political future.

He would have to be careful how he dealt the hands when they met. In just two days' time he would know if he had dealt them correctly.

* * *

Scala had left Noreen with her mother. Their day out had been abandoned, and he knew that he was losing her to doubts. He needed a drink now more than he had for many weeks.

He sat alone at the end of the bar in the Regent, nursing his whiskey. He was in a shit country doing a shit job that no one really cared about, and for the first time in his life he had serious doubts about his own capability. He wanted to tell Noreen everything and beg her forgiveness for using her as cover because, against all odds, he had fallen in love with the girl.

As usual, few people took any notice of Georgie Armstrong

entering the Regent. No one acknowledged him as he sidled over to sit by Scala's side. He was sure they were kindred spirits. The death of the boy had frightened some of 'his' children. But he was confident they would return; all he had to do was wait.

To his surprise, Scala found himself pleased at the interruption. It would take his mind off Noreen and, he hoped, focus him on the job. The two men talked as if they were lifelong friends, unaware that outside eyes were monitoring them.

* * *

Noel Caffrey prided himself on his expertise on the golf course. It had been the one challenge that had given him solace since his son's death. Philip McGann was no match for him but Caffrey tolerated the man's ham-fisted attempts to play a serious game. Today, as usual, McGann had tried his best and Caffrey had restrained himself from making the man look a complete fool. Now the two men put on an air of cordiality as they walked towards the clubhouse.

Throughout the game McGann had waited for Caffrey to open the sniping. But the Boss had waited his moment.

'I was sorry you missed our little gathering the other day, Philip,' he said at last with an air of sincerity. 'But, considering the circumstances, I'm sure you realized that it would not have been proper.'

McGann nodded his understanding.

'Your decision has been a cause of great personal regret to me after all these years of friendship, although I do understand your reasons. I thought we were like-minded people until this moment.'

'That we are, Noel,' responded the policeman, 'but this latest episode with the kid dying has got to me, I'm afraid. I told you as much. I could justify the other stuff without too many problems, but since the boy died I haven't been able to look at myself in the mirror. It was as if I'd given the little sod the needle myself.'

McGann was now being tipped as successor to the chief constable who had met his fate along with senior other figures in the police helicopter crash. It was an appointment that he had thought he might never achieve. He had felt cheated. In the violent days of the seventies when the Provo power was at its height, Philip McGann had been one of the most powerful and successful men in the Royal Ulster Constabulary. One of the most feared opponents of the IRA, he had been a man with power who was destined for the top. The various ministers and heads of government had told him that there should be more like him. He had believed them – but their praises had never materialized into office. And now the man of power had been sidetracked into a position as consultant. The peace had reduced the need for a man like Philip McGann. He had been cheated and betrayed by the people to whom he had given his life.

McGann had always been a sceptic about the intentions of the IRA and Sinn Fein. But no one had listened to his reservations. He considered the men who ran Ulster these days to be charging headlong into a valley of disaster.

Caffrey and the others had given McGann his chance to change all that: to feed his own power and needs and to influence the course of history in Northern Ireland. He had believed he was right when he had supplied snippets of information on known terrorists or had run checks on suspects. And he had shown little remorse about providing the details of the helicopter flight from Aldergrove that would rid Northern Ireland of its senior security staff who might meddle in the plans of Caffrey and his fellow conspirators. Their deaths would, of course, leave the door open for McGann finally to obtain power.

'I respect your opinions Philip. Believe me, I do understand. It's simply that it's come at a slightly awkward time,' insisted Caffrey.

'For that I apologise, but it would appear that you have achieved the kind of mistrust and created the background where an open renewal of violence is assured. The other day my men discovered a massive cache of weapons from a Loyalist hideaway which was surely destined for a new offensive – and the mad dogs of the Army Council are so thoroughly pissed off with their Sinn Fein buddies that they're going it alone. It's going to be back to good old bad old days, just you wait and see – just as soon as this charade of an all-party meeting is over. So I think the time is right for me to head off into the sunset.'

Caffrey dropped the air of civility. 'Your decision would have nothing to do with the fact that you look certain to be made the next chief constable, would it, Philip? or is that simply a coincidence? I would hate to think that you merely used us to achieve your own personal gains!'

McGann's face reddened. 'Frankly, I don't really give a damn about coincidences. I think I've gone as far down the road as I'm prepared for. I'll honour my commitment to you as far as maintaining my silence – but I can't get involved any more.'

The smile returned to Caffrey's face as the two men stopped short of the clubhouse. 'No hard feelings . . .!' he said. The hand of friendship was seized once more. McGann had made his decision. So too had Caffrey.

*   *   *

The world spun as Georgie Armstrong lay on his bed and stared at the ceiling. The night's drinking had taken its toll and, as he lay in the tiny room that had been his since childhood, he was unable to separate reality from the fantasies that visited each night. His mother, a widow for the last fifteen years, occupied the main bedroom at the back of the tiny house in the cul-de-sac that bordered the Westlink trunk road which cut through the centre of the city. There had been no response from her as Georgie tumbled into the house. She had grown used to his drunken stumbling each night, and chose to ignore it. The sound of the traffic from the nearby road interfered with Georgie's fantasy, in which he saw himself in a tuxedo and a fast car with a pouting, painted woman on his arm. The clock downstairs chimed midnight. Georgie was unsure of the reality of the sound.

Once more the shrill sound of the bell cut through the night. He heard his mother cursing and descending the stairs, then fumbling with the door chain. There was a pounding at the door, followed by the shouting of men's voices and the panic-stricken cries of his mother.

Georgie shot bolt upright, his mind still swirling, and staggered to the window. The sound of his own heart thudding in his ears added to his panic. Gingerly he summoned up enough courage to peer down at the commotion below. Barely showing his face, he saw two young men, their faces covered by black balaclava

174

helmets, hammering against the door. With each blow his mother screamed more.

One of the men glanced upwards and caught sight of him. He raised the Webley revolver. As if by instinct the other hooded man looked too and aimed his own pistol. They opened fire at the petrified figure simultaneously. One wild bullet smashed through the window while Georgie felt the wind of another skim by his face and thud into the woodwork.

Panic gripped every muscle in Georgie's body. They had come for him, but in his blurred mind he could not fathom out who or why. He darted back from the window and bolted from the room, down the stairs past his screaming mother as she lay crumpled behind the door, desperately attempting to keep it shut. She cried to Georgie to run – run for his life!

The beating at the door continued, followed by the sound of splintering as the door was knocked from its hinges. Georgie flung himself through the darkness of the kitchen at the rear and frantically tried to find the lock. A crack and a flash, and another bullet smacked into the wood of the door. He shot a glance over his shoulder as he screamed in terror, and saw the shapes of the two hooded men push aside his yelling mother and charge along the short passage towards the kitchen.

At last he found the lock and the bolt, jerked them back and catapulted himself into the tiny back yard of the terraced house. In a few steps he was at the wall and opted to hoist himself over it into the narrow alley rather than risk fumbling with the lock on the gate. The footsteps were gaining on him. He dropped into the alley. Fear and exertion had given him a crippling pain in his chest, but he still launched himself forward.

Billy reached the wall before Kevin and vaulted to the top. He snatched the balaclava from his head to give himself better vision and took a steadier aim. But the glare of the street lights reflected off the wet pavements temporarily dazzled him and he fired wide. The bullet crashed off the wall as Georgie ran towards the open street, dodging the shadows in the alley. His hard breathing was broken by the sound of his sobbing.

'Oh, dear Christ . . . Christ help me . . . save me . . . for fuck sake save me!' he cried out loud in panic and in the vain hope that someone might offer him salvation. The lights came on in the houses as he crashed past, but the doors remained closed. They had heard the sound of shots at night before, and had known they meant death to anyone who meddled. To them it was the turn of some other poor bastard to take his chances tonight – best not get involved.

Georgie could see the steam of his own breath billowing out in the cold air. He panted, and prayed for his legs not to give out. Cramp was already on him. He could not stop. He hid in the shadows of the alleys and saw the two men, still clutching their guns, follow into the open street.

The brothers stood for a moment in the middle of the road, regaining their breath and composure. The street was awake now. It would only be a matter of minutes before the cops and the soldiers arrived. They turned and ran, disappearing into the night. Georgie Armstrong would have to wait for another time. But he was a dead man living on borrowed hours.

Georgie cried. The fantasy had turned into a nightmare.

Chapter Sixteen

The dawn brought an eerie light from the water of the River Lagan that snaked its way through the centre of the city. At this time of the day, even the docks had not burst into life. Georgie sat huddled between the rows of containers stacked up along the harbour front ready for loading. The steam that rose from the cold water created a haze that wafted over the docks like an icy sheet.

Georgie shuddered with cold and fear and exhaustion. He had run for hours, often aimlessly, finding himself at the docks by mistake rather than intention. He felt alone and haunted like an animal. In his dreams it was not meant to be like this.

Each time he had tried to recall the events of the night he had sobbed like a child, just like he had for those months when he had been alone and picked on by the other young soldiers when he had joined the army. They had been some of the worst moments of his life. His head ached and he wondered how his Ma was, and if the men in the hoods had hurt her. He told himself he could not think of that now; he could only allow himself to think about how Georgie Armstrong was going to survive. His mixed-up mind could not even work out for him who the two men in the hoods worked for; but he told himself that they must surely have been IRA. They had come for him because the little bastard kids had touted on him. The men with guns and hoods had come for revenge.

Daring to peep from the makeshift security of his hideaway he could see some of the earlier traffic beginning to flow over the Queen's Bridge. Somewhere, he thought, people were going about their ordinary lives as if the world was a normal place. They were not being hunted like an animal. He had pissed his trousers and his mouth felt caked with dryness – the dryness that came with fear. He wondered how low he could sink, how long could he hide from the men with guns. If only he could think.

There was someone who could help – someone who had to help. He would not turn his back on him. After all, he was a hard man!

*   *   *

The sound of the mobile telephone echoed off the bare walls of the boat yard building. The men had already stirred from their cots and were busy brewing tea. Moore was frying bacon. Naylor had risen earlier and was now shaving. He had always insisted on being clean-shaven: it had made him feel cleansed and fresh. He grabbed the telephone and punched the receive button.

Georgie was gabbing incoherently, but Naylor managed to pick up something about men with guns who had come to his home and had shot at him.

'Okay. Take it easy, for Christ's sake! Where are you now? . . . Good! How many were there? . . . Did you know who they were? . . . Did they say anything?' Naylor fired the questions, but Georgie had no answers. 'No, not here – definitely not here!' snapped Naylor. 'Keep calm, man. For God's sake keep calm! Of course I'll come for you. Leave it to me, trust me. Meet me tonight, by the warehouse at the docks. Now stay out of sight!' Naylor switched off the telephone.

The others looked at him enquiringly, at the same time smirking because they already knew the answer.

'The little shit has gone and got himself compromised!' snarled Naylor. 'Seems that our Al Capone got himself shot at his house and he's shitting himself. He's on the run out there now. I'm afraid there's only one thing for it – we'll have to pick him up ourselves. Still, the little arse-hole has fulfilled his usefulness, I think. We can't take the risk anyway. I want no loose ends left behind after this little caper.'

He turned to the two men nearest to him, Brent and Morrisey, and told them to join him that night. Ray Brent had been a proud member of the Royal Ulster Constabulary until the day that a gunman found him and his partner as they walked behind each other through a crowded high street. The gunman had rushed up behind Bren's partner, placed his pistol at the back of his head, pulled the trigger and then disappeared into the crowd as the man lay dying on the street. They had pulled in the suspect, but no one would give evidence and the gunman has walked free. Brent had decided otherwise. He had beaten up the suspect and fractured his cheekbone so badly that the man's mouth had to be wired. They had kicked Brent out of the force for that. Since that day, two summers ago, he had nursed his anger and his vengeance. Naylor had given him the opportunity to unleash that anger.

Carl Morrisey was different: he had followed no one. He had graduated from petty thieving as a child to develop a taste for violence, and had earned his reputation with a gun of any description. He simply enjoyed the kill. Naylor had been the only man ever to tap that passion for killing.

These two would do what he had in mind.

* * *

Georgie could stay hidden no longer. As the dockers and workers turned up for the early shift he had decided to break cover. He walked towards the city centre, seeking protection and anonymity amongst the crowds on the streets.

Fatigue and fear had fuddled his brain. He could smell the terror and dry sweat on his own body as he wandered through the shopping malls and narrow streets of central Belfast. His greasy hair clung tight to his head and the stubble on his face itched. As he walked he stared into the faces of passers by, suspecting each one and preparing himself for the moment when one of them would draw a gun and fire the bullet that would end his life. It crossed his mind that in some ways the latter might be a blessed release from the terrors of living a life of fear as he was now, but he shook the idea from his head. It would be hours before he could meet Naylor and he was desperate for a drink; anything that would calm his fears. Instinctively he found himself heading from the busy streets along St Peter's Hill towards the Shankill Road.

The bar was familiar. It had a reputation as a meeting-place for many of the UVF commanders and their foot soldiers. A huge Union flag hung from the pole over the door. Surely no Provo would dare to venture into such a stronghold? For the first time that day, Georgie considered he was thinking rationally.

The door was open and the sounds of an ancient juke-box greeted him as he weaved his way towards the bar. It was only mid-afternoon but the place was crowded with jabbering, laughing and shouting men, all trying to talk as one. Georgie felt the warmth of the whiskey burn down into his stomach, soothing him. He was not normally a whiskey drinker, but today was different. His hands were still shaking and his belly ached from hunger. But he wanted more drink, not food.

Suddenly he felt the hairs on the back of his neck rise. An uneasy feeling gripped his body. As he looked at himself in the mirror behind the bar his instinct told him he was being stared at. The group of men at the end of the bar were speaking in muffled tones and looking at him. He smiled a nervous smile in their direction and nodded. There was no response. A small weasel of a man with a chiselled face was engrossed in conversation with a giant next to him. Both men's heads turned towards Georgie as they inspected him, then continued their conversation. The topic of conversation was Georgie Armstrong. Other pairs of eyes were on him, too.

Georgie's head pounded; the drink was not helping. Sweat was trickling down his face even though it was cold in the bar. Everyone knew about the shooting in the street the night before. They had also known that Georgie Armstrong was the target. Yet there had been no support, no sympathy, no outstretched helping hand. They despised him and he knew it. They would sooner the Provos had put a bullet in the back of his head.

Suddenly the noise around him seemed deafening. His head was spinning. He felt that if he stayed in that place he would die, probably at the hands of one of the men at the end of the bar – he would escort him through the back, and Georgie Armstrong would never be seen again. He wanted to be sick. The vomit was rising in his throat and he bolted for the door just in time.

*　　*　　*

Everything was in place. Nothing had been left to chance, and Moore had shown why he was regarded as one of the best in his field. The first of two Toyota vans had been resprayed and carefully loaded. It was ready to move. Moore would drive it to

Belfast that night, park overnight and await Naylor. The other men would bring the second Toyota tomorrow and give support if needed. All hell was sure to break loose afterwards, and Naylor wanted to make sure that his escape route was covered. Weapons had been checked and cleaned. It had been planned like a military operation, and Naylor was confident. Now, all that required attention was to tie up the 'loose end'. Naylor and his chosen men took the Peugot and headed to the docks for their planned rendezvous.

* * *

The policeman outside the house had gone. The broken door had been temporarily repaired and a board replaced the broken glass in the upstairs window. The place seemed to have returned to normality. May Armstrong had taken herself away to her sister's across the river for the sake of her nerves. The house stood dark and empty.

Georgie crept along the alleyway behind his house, hiding in the shadows of the doorways. Cautiously he opened the door to his own yard and entered the house. Without turning on the lights, he felt his way to his bedside cabinet and grabbed his passport before making his way to the bathroom and opening up the toilet cistern. The plastic container he had hidden away was still there: the cops had been too busy with the bullet holes to worry themselves about what Georgie Armstrong might have stashed.

He untaped the container, took out the sachets of white powder that it contained and crammed them into the top pocket of his leather jacket. Then once again Georgie Armstrong faded into the night.

* * *

Brent and Morrissey were in position between the containers. Naylor preferred to wait in the shadows by the warehouse. He had chosen the spot well because of the lack of light which favoured the stalker and not the prey. The stretch of quayside was deserted and the slightest sound echoed amongst the empty containers piled there.

In the distance, the silence of the night was broken by the sound of footsteps approaching the quay. The three men waited. In the dim light of the lamps that lined the water's edge they could see the shuffling figure coming towards them, hands deep inside his jacket pockets. He was no more than a hundred yards from them, his steps growing quicker. Naylor took the Beretta from his belt and cocked it. The others too had their weapons ready.

Naylor had agreed to meet Georgie alone. The frightened man was looking for any sign of his saviour, the hard man who would save him from the hands of the Provos. But just as Naylor was about to step from the shadows his attention was grabbed by a commotion from the side of the warehouse building to his right. The teenage boy gruffly pulled at the struggling girl and dragged her towards the containers. She shrieked with laughter, then he ran his hand over her backside and pulled her even harder as the two headed for the comparative privacy of the containers where he would have her.

Their shouting startled Georgie, who squinted with tired red eyes to make sense of the noise amid the containers. As he narrowed his eyes he heard the complaint from another male voice as the hidden figure was disturbed by the teenage lovers. The man stepped from the darkness to ward off the young intruders, and even in his exhaustion Georgie could see the gun. The teenagers ran in fear as Morrisey broke cover.

Fearing the Provos, Georgie turned on his heels. As he did so, Naylor ran from the shadows into the light and shouted after him. Georgie recognized the voice and glanced over his shoulder to see the man who had come to protect him. Then he saw the gun in Naylor's hand. It was as if a bolt of comprehension struck Georgie at that moment. He saw the gun and the other man, and as he did so the third man rose from behind more empty containers. It was clear – they had come for him. The man who he thought would protect him had now come to kill him. He ran.

'Georgie, me boy. Come back! It's okay – we're here for you. We're here to help. Come back!' shouted Naylor in vain.

But Georgie's adrenaline was flowing and he was thinking clearly for a few precious moments. His life depended on thinking clearly, on making the right choice. Refusing to heed the voice behind him, he continued to run.

Naylor raised the Beretta and, taking a two-handed position, fired, cursing as he shot. The bullet missed Georgie by no more than an inch and ricocheted off the quayside in front of him.

'Stop, you little bastard!' he spat. 'Goddamn you, I'll make you pay – you'll not get away from me.'

Morrissey raised his gun to shoot, but Naylor could see that the desperate figure was now out of effective range. He cursed the man's seemingly charmed life and pledged revenge. It was late now. Morrissey and Brent must return to the boat yard to join the others. But he would stay in Belfast.

*   *   *

The news was of the conference and of the hope that went with it. It was being hailed as the most historically significant meeting of the century. According to the reports, it was already being seen as a last-ditch attempt. Feelings were running high. No one could afford for the meeting to break down. The result would be open civil war that not even the power of the Americans could prevent. Tomorrow was going to be one of the most crucial days in the history of Ireland.

Scala sat alone in the darkness of his hotel room, wearing a glazed expression and watching the news bulletin preview the meeting. The light from the screen bounced shadows around the wallpaper. He took little notice of the debate, lost as he was in a world of self-doubt and misery. He had been sent to find a man who was a ghost, whom no one was even certain existed; he had dealt in a trade that he despised and he was on the way to ruining the life of a girl who, against all odds, he had grown to care for. That was the only thing he knew for certain. Why in God's name had Matherson singled out him, Jim Scala, the boy from the valleys, for a no-hope job like this? Give him an enemy soldier to kill and he'd do it time after time. But this was something else.

Scala sipped at his bottled beer and sighed. His attention was taken by the report of the funeral of the boy Danny MacMichael which appeared on the screen. It appeared that half of Belfast had turned out for the occasion. The boy's mother had walked behind the coffin unable to hold back the tide of tears and comforted by the sobbing man who held her arm. To Jim Scala, it seemed certain that nothing would end the killing in this city.

The hammering startled him. It was no gentle tap but a sound of urgency. He leaped to his feet and stiffened his body for action before warily opening the door.

Georgie Armstrong was nervously skipping from one foot to the other. 'For God's sake, Scala, let me in! Please, for pity's sake let me come in. I need your help. For Christ's sake help me. You're the only person I can turn to,' he sobbed.

Wide-eyed with shock, Scala pulled him into the room.

Georgie shivered as he sat head in hands on the end of the bed and snivelled. 'Scala, they're trying to kill me – I'm a dead man. Oh, Jesus, I'm a dead fuckin' man . . . I don't know what to do . . . They're going to shoot me. They've tried – both of them have. Everyone wants me dead. But it wasn't my fault, you see, Scala. It really wasn't my fault. He told me to do it!'

Scala took hold of Georgie and shook him. 'What in Christ's name are you talking about, you stupid little shit? Make sense, man. How the hell can I help if I haven't got a bloody clue what you're talking about?'

Georgie sipped at a miniature bottle of whiskey that Scala handed him and slowly began blurting out the events of the previous day. He told him about the men he assumed to be an IRA team who had come for him because he had followed instructions and begun dealing the heroin, and about the man whom he had trusted turning on him and trying to kill him.

'So who is he, this man who took you on board in the first place?'

Georgie gulped. 'He's a Brit sure enough – a mean bastard, I can tell you. He scares the shit out of me. That's why I did what he told me. He found me and asked me if I wanted to work for him and his team. I thought they were drugs men over here like you, out to make a fortune. But I tell you, this man is more – he just looks straight through you and twiddles that bloody ring!'

Scala's interest was aroused. 'What ring? come on, you've got to tell me everything if you want my help.'

'It's a special ring. It's like a gold nail with a death's head kind of thing on it. He just keeps playing with it . . . and he looks straight at you with those deep eyes . . . it's as if he's looking through you! He shot at me, Scala. I went to him for help and he fuckin' well shot at me . . . Oh, Jesus, I'm a dead man – if one lot doesn't get me the other – '

'Shut up for a bloody minute, will you!' interrupted Scala. 'Tell me about the man – his hand. Tell me, has he got a finger missing? What's the man's name, dammit? You must know!'

'Yeah! He has half a finger missing, the one that he wears his ring on. How did you know? I know the fella as Naylor – I don't know if it's his real name. I've only seen him a few times. He came to me, you see . . . He said I'd be a big man in town one day. Oh, Christ! A big man – yeah, a big man in a fuckin' box!'

Scala snapped: 'Christ Almighty, man, shut your snivelling. After what you've done you're lucky I don't kill you myself.'

'But why, Scala, why you too? We're alike, aren't we? We both want to make money – that's why I've come here. I've brought you some stuff . . . I need the money . . . I have to get away. For God's sake take the stuff and give me some money so I can just piss off out of here.' He held out some of the sachets from his pocket, but Scala pushed them aside.

'Put them away, you stupid sod, and talk to me. Then I might help you. The man Naylor – where did you meet him? Do you know where he hangs out?'

Georgie told how Naylor had found him sitting alone in a bar one night, had made friends and begun talking of the 'big time', and how Georgie could share in it too if he wanted. He told Scala of his only trip to the boat yard where he had met Naylor. From the outside the place had looked almost deserted, but inside it had looked different, lived in yet orderly – like a military barracks. 'He said he'd kill me if I ever talked to anyone about it,' squealed Georgie. 'I guess it doesn't matter much any more, does it?'

Scala sat back, letting the thoughts fight in his mind. It had to be him, he concluded. This had to be the man he wanted.

'Bastards!' he hissed. Matherson, Carter and the others must have known all along. That's why they had sent him. They were using him too. 'Bastards!' he repeated.

Then Scala ordered Georgie to wait in the room. He would be safe there, but Scala had to plan, to think and to make some telephone calls.

*   *   *

It was the call that Matherson had been waiting for. He had expected it each day for over three weeks. But he could cope with Scala's rage. He would explain fully when he saw him.

'I need to know now, you bastard. Don't fob me off with any of your shit stories now!' Scala bellowed down the phone. 'Why the hell had it got to be me, after all these years. Why me? Why couldn't you tell me?'

Matherson felt he might attempt an explanation. 'Firstly, dear boy, we were not 100 per cent certain that it was our boy. As you can imagine, there haven't been too many details to go on. There was this anonymous tip – that was all. I needed somebody who knew him, and I needed someone who hated the man so much that he would have no qualms about putting a bloody end to him. It had to be you. Let's face it, there aren't exactly queues of ex-soldiers willing to execute the man who taught them all they knew – someone who had been their friend! That's why we chose you . . . Now work quickly. Put the boy Armstrong on the next plane to here. We'll take him from there. I'll also arrange some assistance.'

Chapter Seventeen

Georgie had gone. By now he would probably have been picked up at Heathrow by the men he was told would be friends. He would be behind bars now, Scala hoped. It would be one peddler in death off the street.

He sat back in his room and sipped the strong black coffee that he hoped would clear his mind. The images of the man he had known in the years when he was a basic trooper with the SAS were haunting him. It had been so different in those days, so clear-cut. As he looked down from his window to the early morning traffic in the street below, Scala's mind drifted back to a faraway world in 1989 when he had embarked on his own personal crusade. He had volunteered for the special training that he would require to join the SAS's anti-drugs teams. Subsequently he had been instrumental in numerous busts on the British mainland and had assisted in raiding a sea-going tug in the docklands where a massive haul of narcotics had been made.

The Americans of the Drug Enforcement Agency had been impressed when they had visited the Hereford camp, and it had been Scala among others who had assisted the DEA teams in several drug swoops as part of an exchange deal with the States. When, in the eighties, President George Bush and Prime Minister Margaret Thatcher had agreed to provide help to fight the all-powerful Medellin cartel in Colombia, who had helped turn the narcotics trade from a small cottage industry to a multi-billion-dollar racket, it was Scala and other members of the SAS's anti-narcotics team who were sent into the steamy jungles to train the local anti-narcotics police.

Scala had never lived by morals, but he had believed in this job. He also had faith in the man who commanded him, his veteran sergeant Michael Naylor. They had made a good team. The two of them had trained the men hard and given them valuable tips in technique such as how to carry rifles crooked in the forearm

– a position known as the 'Belfast cradle' that allowed quicker use. Naylor and his trooper had joined the anti-narcotics teams, fought alongside them and won. Naylor, the veteran of the Falklands, had boasted that that campaign was the last real war that he had fought in and loved every moment of, and he was eager to pass on his experience to the likes of Scala. He had taught his eager pupil to leave nothing to chance, and would always insist on a back-up plan as a safeguard.

Away from the jungles, they had lived life in Colombia to the full. The women had been plentiful and magnificent. They had shared them and wallowed in the drink and fast living that Naylor told Scala went with the job. Had it not been Naylor who had paid for the birthday surprise that Scala would never forget, when six nubile local beauties had turned up at the Welshman's door? For a year, in their own way, Naylor and Scala had been the toast of Bogota. They were super-heroes fighting a blacker-than-black foe.

They had been good days, true enough. Scala looked down into his coffee cup. There was more. There had been the girl Lena, the girl whom Naylor had taken from the bar as his woman and looked after as his own property. She had been long-legged, with hair the colour of night and eyes to match. To Naylor she had been the most beautiful woman in the world. Lena had taken him to the jeweller's in Bogota where they had designed his ring. She had insisted he had it blessed at the church – it would keep him safe always. To Naylor, it was *her* ring.

'Call me the luckiest man in the world, Jimbo!' Naylor had boasted. 'Here's a job worth doing, with a bird that's walked straight out of a James Bond movie and a mate who's as straight a guy as you could ever ask for. What more could a man ask for, Jimbo? I've died and gone to heaven, I tell you. And when Queen and Country have finished with me, then maybe I'll come back here to see out my days, Jimbo – you just watch me.'

Then the girl had died. They had come for her that night in revenge for the lost millions of dollars' worth of cocaine. Raul Escobar – the man hailed as one of the country's most infamous cocaine barons – had ordered her to be taken because Naylor and Scala had been good at their job. They had found Lena two days later with her throat slit. Escobar's men had enjoyed Lena before killing her and discarding her body by the dusty road that led into Bogota. Scala had seen Naylor cry for the first and last time in his life as he looked at her body, at how this creature of beauty had ended her life.

From that day Naylor had changed. Scala watched the hatred grow within him as some thing that a man could almost touch. The jokes had stopped and his moods grew blacker. Any compassion that he might have felt for the world had been buried with the girl. Naylor had become a man who lived solely for retribution.

Scala remembered how he had almost beaten one of his own rookies to death after the terrified young lad had accidentally dropped an ammunition box on Naylor's hand as they prepared for a jungle exercise. Naylor had punched and kicked the man senseless in front of the horrified Colombian anti-narcotics team before Scala had been able to intervene to save the boy's life. The doctors had been unable to save Naylor's finger and had insisted on amputation, yet the man had recovered like a lion and insisted on staying with the campaign.

Scala considered how many times he had wished that he had followed his instincts and reported Naylor to his superiors as being 'unstable' and a risk to others. Instead he had chosen to turn a blind eye to the worsening situation because of his friend's fine record and dreadful personal loss. Then had come the mission that Naylor had insisted on leading – the mission to trap Raul Escobar.

The twenty-man team, led by Naylor and Scala, were to act on the word of a police informant that Escobar would personally be supervising the movement of a consignment of cocaine worth millions of dollars from his ranch near the Nechi River to the north of Medellin province. The force had landed by helicopter and waited in the designated area by the well-worn path traditionally used by Escobar's men. Naylor had been like a rabid dog as they waited, yet, as predicted by the informant, the convoy had made its way through the jungle area and straight into the trap.

The firefight was short lived but effective. At the end of the ten-minute shoot-out Escobar, his teenage son and ten of his faithful followers lay dead. The police team had been jubilant; for them it had been an important victory. But Naylor had demanded more.

They had gone on to Escobar's ranch in the hills, with its gleaming white walls which resembled a fairy-tale castle against the thick green carpet of the surrounding jungle. Naylor ordered the place torched; Scala had half-heartedly protested. There was little opposition: what few guards remained died in a hail of bullets. The storage buildings that housed millions of dollars' worth of cocaine sent plumes of smoke billowing skywards through the dense foliage. But Naylor was nowhere to be seen.

Scala had yelled for him and searched the rooms of the palatial residence. As he climbed the enormous staircase that wound to the first floor Scala had seen the first of the sights that had come back to him on dark nights ever since. For there, at the top of the stairs, stood Naylor clutching his razor-edged machete. The man's fatigues were drenched in blood, his eyes glazed, as if looking at a distant place that could not be seen by any other man.

It had taken Scala just minutes to find the room of horror. Escobar's wife and two teenage daughters, half Lena's age, had hidden there from the narcotics police led by the two Europeans. It had been from them that Naylor had exacted his retribution. The butchery was such that Scala could not contain his stomach. He had lunged at Naylor in anger, but the man did not hear him. The shocked men of the narcotics team had restrained Scala and led Naylor away.

Ever since that day Scala had lived with his failure to report Naylor before the raid. His indecision had led to the murder of a family by the man he had called his friend. Instead he had done the next best thing, and reported the slaughter to the commander on their return. Naylor had been returned to Hereford pending the inquiry, with Scala as chief witness against the man whose balance of mind had been tipped in the jungles of South America. It had been Scala's evidence that had made certain that Michael Naylor was banished from the British army all those years ago.

Certainly Naylor had sworn vengeance on Scala too. As far as Scala was aware, Naylor had returned to South America some years earlier and had not been heard of since. Now it looked as though the 'mad dog' who had once been his friend had returned. But the reason for his return remained a mystery. But

Scala was quite certain that, wherever Michael Naylor emerged, death would follow.

*   *   *

The duty officer took the call and relayed it immediately to the room further along the corridor. Captain Terry Kirby had been told to have his men ready to move as soon as the call came. There were to be no uniforms. This was to be a 'civvy' operation. The man on the telephone identified himself as James Scala, gave Kirby the location and agreed a rendezvous point.

Within five minutes the sixteen men of the SAS's Ulster troop found themselves crammed into the two Wessex helicopters and lifting off from the heavily fortified former mill that was now their headquarters in Bessbrook, South Armagh. To them, the peace process appeared a very farway option.

Chapter Eighteen

An early morning sea mist shrouded the area around the boat yard like a thick cloak. The four men inside had risen early, unable to sleep as their stomachs tightened with anxiety and their minds turned over the uncertainties of the following day.

Naylor had left his orders, and each man went about his allotted task with precision. The M-85 sniper rifle was stashed under the rear seat of the van, wrapped in sacking, while each man took personal charge of his MP-5 sub-machine gun. As instructed, each of them wore blue overalls so that they would pass as workmen going about their jobs. Each knew his role. The four would split into pairs: Brent and Grady would form one partnership while Athertone and Morrissey made up the other – a mixture of youth and experience in each team. At the exact time they would park the van at the end of the street, and the pairs would then position themselves at either end to give cover should the need arise. As the best marksman, Athertone was designated to use the M-85 from the protection of the van.

Despite their anxieties, the four felt buoyant. They joked as they went about their preparations: they would cause a bang today that would be heard around the world.

The gentle, wooded hill to the front of the boat yard shielded them from noise and their view of the track that led from the building was interrupted by a stone wall. The four men therefore were unaware of the choppers that came to rest on the golf course two miles up the coast road. The sight of the two machines landing on the seventeenth green startled the two early golfers, who watched open-mouthed as the sixteen men dressed in varying civilian outfits and equipped with an arsenal of weapons scrambled out.

The men ran to the agreed rendezvous point on the road where Scala was waiting. He had driven like a madman along the A2 from Belfast to get there on time. Now, clad in jeans and roll-neck sweater, she greeted the group and began the kind of briefing that he had given so many times to men like these. Georgie had told him of the boat yard and had attempted a description. Scala and his men would have that information as well as detailed maps of the area to help them formulate their plan. The troopers of the SAS squadron were heavily armed, some with Heckler & Koch G-3 assault rifles, others with M-16 rifles and with at least two general-purpose machine guns. Scala himself took a Browning high-powered hand gun. The party split into three groups. Two sections under the command of Kirby headed across-country towards the boat yard, where one group would take up position with one of the general-purpose machine guns in the copse overlooking the track and the boatyard, while the other took position along the wall. Once there, they would wait. Scala and two other men would take the direct route, driving along the track towards the boat yard, and use their vehicle as a roadblock to prevent anyone escaping.

The trap was about to be sprung. Scala now prepared himself to come face to face with the man who had tormented the back corridors of his mind for over five years; the man whom he had once deemed a friend, but was now the man he would have to kill – or be killed by.

*   *   *

No one had paid any attention to the brightly painted blue Toyota van that had been parked overnight by the Queen Quay station on the east bank of the river. There had been too many other trucks and vans parked alongside to make this one stand out.

Moore had spent an uncomfortable night in the vehicle, but had managed an hour's deep sleep. On schedule, Naylor arrived at the station to make his rendezvous. Together, the two men made a last-minute inspection of the boxes in the back of the van. They paid special note to one of the boxes.

Then it was time to move. The two men changed into their designated outfits; Naylor into his light-coloured overalls while Moore made the necessary final adjustments to his, which should, on a day like today, allow him to blend into the background.

It seemed a solemn occasion. The two shook hands and separated. Now Naylor took the van and headed towards the city.

*   *   *

Eamon Clancy readied himself. He felt good. No matter what happened, today would be a day of history-making and he would be part of it. The Sinn Fein headquarters in the Andersonstown Road was a hive of activity that morning. It seemed as though everyone was preparing to make history . . .

Across the city, Mitchell Cain's wife gave a last-minute check to her husband's tie. The image of her man would be screened all over the world today and would be in all the newspapers tomorrow; for that, he had to look right. The telephone call from the President the night before had boosted Cain's morale. Before, he had been apprehensive. Today, he too prepared to play his part in history . . .

Athertone made one final check before taking his position in the front passenger seat. Grady was already at the wheel and the others had been complaining about being uncomfortable in the back for the last five minutes. It was time to move. The mist had started to clear and the visibility was good.

The van set off down the curved track that led from the sea. From the copse, eight pairs of anxious eyes watched the vehicles progress. Kirby watched nervously; he eased the safety catch off his G-3 and slowly moved the weapon into a comfortable firing position. He could feel his heart pounding and the adrenaline flowing through his veins. He knew the other group were in position behind the wall. Shit! Where the hell was the man Scala? It could all get bucked up any second now! As if in answer to a prayer Kirkby saw Scala's car bumping its way down the track – on collision course with the van.

Athertone and Grady saw the car at the same time and cursed. Intuition told them that it spelled trouble. The two men in the rear reached for their weapons and began scouring the surrounding area.

'Jesus Christ! Bang on the bloody nose!' yelled Scala as he pulled the car to a screeching halt and turned it sideways across the track. The two men with him crawled out of the rear passenger door, took position behind the vehicle and aimed their M-16s.

It was like old times for Scala and he found himself enjoying it. To him, this was what soldiering was about – good guys versus bad guys. At least now he knew who the good guys were for the time being.

As he raised his own weapon he yelled a warning to the van to stop in accordance with the rules of engagement of the security forces in Northern Ireland, which dictated that no one could open fire unless he felt that his life or those of other colleagues were at risk. The van ground to a shuddering halt. There was a moment of silence as Scala drew breath. Then the passenger door of the van sprung open and Athertone leaped from the vehicle, firing wildly towards the car.

It was the signal for all hell to let loose. Gunfire erupted from the copse and from the waiting troopers behind the wall. The rear doors of the van were half opened, but the barrage of firing from the copse made it impossible for the men to get out.

Kirby emptied a magazine from his G-3 and clipped a fresh one in the weapons receiver. Grady attempted to dash from the van towards the comparative safety of the boat yard, but was cut down before he could run ten yards. Bullets continued to hit his lifeless body as he lay on the track.

Athertone took shelter in a nearby ditch and fired short bursts towards the copse, before a heavy bullet from an M-16 smashed into his shoulder, almost severing his arm. Blood pumped from the wound, but his cries were lost in the sound of the firefight.

It seemed as if every trooper was directing his fire at the van; they were reacting instinctively: squeeze the trigger, reload. Empty cartridge cases flew everywhere, while in the background the rippling fire of the two machine guns beat out their message of death. Everyone inside the van would be dead.

Athertone crawled along the ditch towards the boat yard, still clutching his weapon. Scala ran forward, breaking from the cover of the car, and headed toward him. The rest of the troopers ceased firing, and the sudden silence was deafening. Still Athertone crawled along the ditch, every movement agony. He saw the man running towards him and, with his last ounce of determination, chose to stand to meet him. He screamed with pain and defiance as he raised himself to his feet and shakingly took aim.

Scala saw it in slow motion. 'Drop it, you bastard! I said drop it – it's over!' he screamed. The gun in Scala's hand rose almost without his knowledge. His subconscious heard the three shots that followed and saw them tear into the man's chest, flinging him into the ditch. The sounds echoed against the distant hills around the bay.

Cautiously the troopers emerged from their positions, weapons still trained on the bodies. Kirby carefully opened the rear doors of the van to peer inside; the floor was like a butcher's table, smeared with blood and shreds of human tissue. Brent and Morrissey lay riddled with bullets: the expression of surprise on Brent's face would stay with Kirby for a long time. He signalled and, in one swift movement, the troopers took up position around the yard, covered by the men on the machine guns who prepared to rake the building with fire.

Scala stood alongside Athertone, whose body lay partly propped against the stone wall. The man was spitting the black blood of a lung wound and was fading quickly. Athertone turned his near-colourless eyes towards Scala and smirked as blood bubbled from his mouth. In his thick Ulster accent he hissed, 'Child's play, you bastard . . . fuckin' child's play . . . you'll see!' He laughed, coughed and Scala could hear the wheeze as the final air left his body.

Scala strained to hear the man's words. They had meant nothing – perhaps they had been a sick private joke. He had almost forgotten what it was like to kill a man, yet he had just shot someone whom he had never seen before in his life. It had come naturally. He knew then that the 'skill' would never leave him.

The troopers had entered the yard and declared it empty. Scala scoured the scene of carnage, searching for the face of the man who had visited him in dreams for years. He scrutinized each body, hoping to see that familiar face. But Naylor's image was nowhere to be found. Yet Georgie had said that he would be here!

It was 10 a.m. The ambush and firefight had been over in less than ten minutes. Kirby contacted base. A convoy of soldiers and armed RUC officers were en route to replace the SAS team. The Wessex choppers were on their way to carry out evacuation.

Scala frowned as he toured the inside of the boat yard. As Georgie had explained, there was an air of military exactness about the place. Scala could almost smell Naylor's presence. He stepped into the back room that had once been used as an office. By the side of the table he caught sight of a waste bin overflowing with paper, and tipped the contents on to the table. Desperately he searched through the scraps and pulled out an enlarged segment of a street map of Belfast: the Castle Street and Queen Street area of the city. It meant nothing to him. His foot skidded on the floor as he slipped on a thin broken stencil which outlined the letters 'OYS'. Again, it meant nothing.

A beam of sunlight suddenly burst through the window that overlooked the bay. The rays spotlit a line of photographs on the wall that began with one of a blonde girl alongside the faces of men whom Scala found familiar. All had a red cross marked on them. Scala froze as he focused on the last photograph. He had seen the man recently, but he could not recall where. He was balding, with a thin face and a dark, Mexican-style moustache. Scala cursed himself, desperately attempting to recall the face from his memory. Where had he been? Who had he spoken to? He mentally recounted his steps.

He had it! Moments before Georgie had thudded at his hotel door he had seen the man. He had been on television and he had worn a uniform – a green uniform, the dark green uniform of the RUC.

'You dosey bastard, Scala, it's McGann,' he cursed himself. 'They're going to hit McGann . . .' Then he attempted to recall why the man had featured on the news. 'Holy mother of Christ! That's it!' McGann had been talking about the bloody meeting – the one being held today.

Scala was like a man possessed as he fought to recall details. Where was it being held? What time? He stared at the table – the map! An idea darted into his mind. The consulate – that was it!

Kirby entered the room. 'Don't know if this is any use to you, old boy. One of my lads found it stashed in one of the bins outside, along with a bit of old wire and stuff,' he said. 'Seems like our boys got a bit careless in their haste

– not that they'll be running anywhere else now.' He felt smug.

Scala glared. All bloody officers were the same, he considered. He looked at the tattered briefcase in Kirby's hand. It bore a crown seal and the initials 'P.A.M.' The side of the case had been ripped open and discarded as worthless.

It had to be McGann.

*   *   *

The consulate of the United States of America in Belfast is an anonymous building. On any other day a person could be forgiven for walking by without realizing its existence. Only the sight of the American flag dangling limply from the flagpole over the glass door, sandwiched between restaurants and shops, indicates its presence.

Normally, shoppers would file past the building in the centre of Queen Street in the heart of the city, oblivious of the upper four storeys that housed the consulate. But today was an exception. The reporters and television news cameras had been camped outside since early morning, waiting for their first glimpse of the history that was about to be mad. No one could miss the consulate today.

A busy stream of officers from the RUC station opposite shuffled in and out of the building. These days, even the civilian security staff that had manned the entrance to the consulate had been disbanded: in these days of peace the American staff felt no necessity for their presence. For this occasion, two burly United States marines stood smartly at ease in the entrance, more as a display of pomp than as a counter to any threat.

The cars that were normally allowed to park directly outside had been banned for the day. But those parked on the side of the street by the RUC station would be permitted to stay. History was about to be made, but the RUC had decided that everything should seem as normal as possible.

Mitchell Cain looked down on the newsmen from his third-storey office. Today would be his day, he decided. In thirty minutes' time, the gathering of the people who would shape the most important day in three hundred years of Irish history would begin. He sucked nervously on a cigarette as his aides waded through the pages of paper to ensure that the correct levels of protocol would be observed. Cain gave them no heed. He was dreaming of what lay ahead for him. The President had assured him.

* * *

It was almost 10.40 a.m. Scala looked at his watch for the hundredth time as his BMW dodged slower-moving cars ahead and hurtled along the A2 towards the city centre. He was riddled with doubt. What if he were wrong? Maybe they had simply been unlucky to miss Naylor at the boat yard – after all, luck was crucial in warfare. But McGann's photograph was on the wall alongside the others – the others that were dead. Then again, was he certain that McGann was to attend the conference? Was that what the television news had reported?

He considered calling RUC headquarters – but what would he tell them? That a group of terrorists who were not IRA or Loyalists but led by a psychotic Englishman were planning to wipe out the IRA and Loyalist representatives at the conference, and that they were going to use the acting head man of the RUC to do it? They would think he was a madman himself – and maybe they would be right! The questions hurled themselves around his mind as he headed for the Queen's Bridge that would take him across the river and into the centre.

Christ! They'd crucify him if he turned out to be wrong!

* * *

The black cab that was the official staff car of the Sinn Fein party left the headquarters, and headed in a stately fashion along the Andersonstown Road towards the city centre. Eamon Clancy felt good as he surveyed the drab streets en route. He had done well for himself since his days as a bricklayer's labourer, in those days before the present Troubles. The Troubles had been good for him. They had given him a platform to display his skills, whether it be on the streets with a gun in his hand or now, as a skilled negotiator.

The car turned right into the Falls Road, the heartland of the Republican cause in Belfast, and took Clancy directly past the street of his birth. 'From humble beginnings . . .' he muttered. Clancy glanced at his watch. It was 10.50 a.m. Ten more minutes, and the one-time bricklayer's labourer would begin to prove himself the saviour of a united Ireland.

* * *

The traffic lights remained on red for an eternity. His head was pounding – he needed sleep, but his body was being fuelled by adrenaline. It was sales time. The shoppers were scurrying about their business looking for late bargains.

Scala could wait no longer. He pressed the accelerator and surged down the high street before the lights had time to change.

'Tough shit!' he snarled. Every second might count now, if he was correct.

* * *

The ambassador was already giving his opening statement to the reporters waiting on the wide pavement in front of the consulate when the deputy chief constable began to make the short walk across the road to take his position. He carried the same briefcase that he had carried for the last two years, the one embossed with his initials which stood for his full name: Philip Arthur McGann.

'Ladies and gentlemen, I am hopeful that the events of today's meeting will prove a positive step along the footpath of permanent peace in this troubled land,' declaimed a beaming Mitchell Cain. He was at his most pompous, and he knew it. 'If there is any part that I or the United States can play that will further that cause, then we stand here ready to fulfil that role. We see it as a hope that must be grabbed. The President is being kept closely informed of everything that takes place here today . . .' The reporters were busy scribbling shorthand notes and the television crews jostled for position.

McGann stood within the glass doorway, directly in front

of the portrait of the President which hung between the two marines. He placed his briefcase with the uniformed officer who stood by the table. Suddenly all attention was shifted on the first black limousine to arrive outside the consulate.

The British Home Secretary, Douglas Hamilton, arrived with the Secretary of State for Northern Ireland, Sir William Harmer, to be greeted by Cain. McGann saluted as they passed him and entered the building. Minutes behind, the leader of the Ulster Unionists arrived with the representative from the Ulster Defence Association. The cameras clicked. Ireland's Foreign Minister was next to arrive, with a close friend and colleague from the moderate Nationalist party. All were ushered inside.

Scala was listening to the events being relayed on the car radio. A street away, the traffic had ground to a standstill to allow the official vehicles access to Queen Street. He decided to abandon the car and run.

As Belfast's clocks prepared to sound the hour of eleven the black cab that carried Eamon Clancy turned from Castle Street into adjoining Queen Street and pulled to a halt in front of the growing crowd. Clancy nodded his greetings to the cameras and was met by Cain. The two strolled directly into the doorway, passing the two marines and the grim-faced McGann. He would follow the procession to the second-floor conference room where the talks would be held. McGann reached for his briefcase and was handed it by the tall uniformed officer.

The procession of representatives had already started to fill the two huge elevators that would take the party to the conference hall as Scala burst through the gaggle of journalists outside. He caught sight of McGann, clutching the briefcase, and leaped towards the doorway. He had no identification and little authority. There was no time to convince anyone of his credentials.

The doors of the elevators slid shut. McGann waited along the corridor, flanked by two other senior RUC officers who would make the next trip. The sound of the commotion in the hallway startled McGann as Scala stormed past the two RUC constables who took position by the door.

'Sir, Mr McGann sir . . . British intelligence, sir . . . please sir, listen!' shouted Scala as he charged towards the group of stunned men. 'For God's sake, sir . . . no time to explain. Please throw down the briefcase – get rid of it, sir!' Then in desperation Scala yelled: 'For Christ's sake . . . I'm telling you to put the fucking briefcase down, you thick Paddy bastard!'

The two marines were after him, but their burly size hampered them. Scala was nimbler and more agile. Still they chased him. A searing pain shot through Scala's injured leg and he stumbled. A split second later one of the marines was on him and they grappled on the floor of the corridor.

'Sorry, mate!' snapped Scala, as he lashed out with a full-bodied chop of the hand into the man's windpipe, which sent him sprawling in agony.

Lorcan Moore stepped from behind the table in the doorway. His huge frame filled the green RUC uniform perfectly. He had no clue who the man was. Everything was going well. It had been easy to walk into the consulate; no one had questioned him as he stood there. He had taken McGann's briefcase – it had been easy to switch it with the identical case to which Moore had applied his special talents. Everything was going well – just a few more minutes and they would have all been gathered. Then this bastard had charged in, shouting like a madman!

Moore pulled his pistol. He could still silence this idiot before he completely ruined everything. The bullet smacked into the second marine as he was about to lunge at Scala, catching him between the shoulders. There was silence as everyone turned to stare at the man who had fired the shot. The former UDR man took stock and bolted for the doorway.

Scala saw Moore with the identical briefcase, and the pieces of the deadly jigsaw slotted together. He fired his Browning twice. The second bullet took Moore just above the left temple and he crumpled like a rag doll. The two officers with McGann pounced on Scala, and took him by the arms.

'Please, Mr McGann' he screamed at the top of his voice as he fought against the two men, 'check the bloody bag before you do anything else . . . it's a trap . . . it's a bloody bomb, I tell you! That man's no policeman – he was a bloody bomber out to get you. He's got your real bag . . . for God's sake, man . . . just look . . .'

McGann froze to the spot as the words of warning began to pierce him. 'Wait!' he shouted to the other officers as more green uniforms flooded into the corridor. 'Check the other bag quickly – see if it's mine. Quickly, damn you!' he shouted, as beads of sweat began to form on his brow.

An RUC man by the glass doors stepped over Moore's body and cautiously took the briefcase, then opened it. The papers inside were all either signed by McGann or addressed to him. His face turned ashen and he fixed his eyes on the case in his hand. Any second now he would lose control of himself.

'Get the bomb squad here, *now*!' he shouted as the men in the corridor backtracked. The officers released their grip on Scala.

Within minutes the RUC specialists from the nearby station had arrived and taken hold of the case. McGann's legs finally gave way and he sank to the floor, sweat flooding over his body. The events of the recent weeks flashed through his head; he saw the faces of Caffrey, Hursley and the rest. The men nearby tried to hear his murmurs as he repeated: 'Bastards! Oh, the bastards – after everything I've done . . .' He appeared to be jabbering names and curses. 'They wanted me dead . . . they were going to use me!' The shock of realization gripped him now.

The people in the second-floor conference room were told of a commotion below. There had been shots, and an investigation was taking place. Everyone should stay where they were, everything was under control.

The RUC men formed a cordon outside the doorway as the journalists pressed forward. This was better than anything they could have hoped for. There were questions, lots of questions, but no answers.

McGann's composure was further shattered when the chief of the bomb disposal team reported to him. As the deputy chief constable fought to quell his shaking limbs, he was told that the case had been booby-trapped to explode on opening. The five pounds of Semtex inside would have taken out most of the second floor. McGann imagined the scene, and saw his body being blown into a hundred pieces.

'We've no clue who the dead 'un is, sir.' He's no police officer, that's for sure.

He could not control himself any more. He had been betrayed, almost murdered – it was worse than fighting the IRA. 'I know who's behind it!' McGann muttered as he interrupted the officer.

* * *

He had just wanted it to end. Scala had been prepared for all eventualities except these persistent questions. They had dragged him to the first floor and fired question after question. He could tell them nothing – Christ, they had nearly shot him until he had agreed to hand over his own pistol.

He was worried that he would now have to run the gauntlet of the bloody press outside. He was angry with himself . . . he must have been wrong. The self-doubt was creeping back into him now that the rush that came with action had subsided. Maybe he had been wrong about Naylor . . . but his senses told him there was more. His gut was a tight knot. Scala's mind overflowed with possibilities and theories, none of which fitted the scenario. Naylor was nowhere to be seen. It was just a short walk across the road to the police station, but Scala refused to leave by the front door – no member of the SAS, past or present, would ever do that.

As he prepared to leave by the rear exit of the consulate, Scala saw that the RUC were attempting to close the street.

* * *

Away from the furore directly outside the consulate, people were trying to continue as normal further along Queen Street. The shops had remained open, feeling that they might benefit from the extra custom that the excitement of the peace talks had brought. Life went on as normal for these people who had been used to turmoil for so long. It was hardly a surprise that no one took particular notice of the brightly coloured Toyota van that had pulled into the street as the official cars drove away.

The man in the bright overalls agreed that it was an unscheduled delivery, but the paperwork must have been fouled up. The assistant in the toy store could only agree: she was more interested in the events that were unfolding just two doors away. The man with the close-cropped hair had brought in some boxes and taken them, as directed, to the warehouse at the rear of the store. The paperwork could be sorted later.

Naylor worked quickly. He had heard of the shooting at the

consulate; soon the ambulance would arrive and the street would be closed. He would just have time.

* * *

Scala fixed his eyes on the carpet as he walked the corridor which led towards the stairs, down to the rear exit. The two RUC men followed him. He was still troubled. He had known Naylor for a long time, and knew he was a man who left nothing to chance. He had always drilled the need for a back-up plan into Scala, in the days when he had been Naylor's protégé.

Scala was lost in thought: the excitement of the last half-hour had taken its toll. Upstairs, the members of the conference were still settling down to negotiate. Casually Scala glanced from the window to the street below. Everything appeared as normal as possible under the circumstances. He had just killed a man, and yet moments later life was going on as normal. He shook his head. Everything was normal, a man lay with a bullet in his skull, upstairs men talked of peace and outside a bloody van delivered toys.

Scala stopped in his tracks as he saw the name on the delivery van. In bright yellow letters the name 'CHILD'S PLAY' was emblazoned on the side of the vehicle – a Toyota van like the one the others had used at the boat yard. Underneath the name the words 'Specialists in Toys' formed a strap line ... Scala recalled the broken stencil on the floor of the yard with the letters 'OYS'.

He turned and shouted for the two RUC men behind to follow as he sprinted for the doorway. 'Give me your bloody gun, man! Quick ... for Christ's sake ... no time to argue! And follow me!' he barked. His tone of command struck a chord with the policemen and they followed. One handed Scala his pistol.

The rear exit led to a narrow road which came up beside the toy store. Scala could hear himself gasping, but still he ran.

* * *

Naylor stacked the boxes high. Only one remained. The assistant saw him struggle with the weight.

'Do you want some help?' she asked genuinely.

Naylor snapped back, 'No, I'm fine. Just let me get on with it – this is the last one. Mind your own business now, that's a good girl!' as he disappeared into the store room. The box was heavy, true enough – but then over forty pounds of Semtex *was* heavy. After he had connected the wires to the timer, it would be ready. It had been Moore's idea to fashion the bomb in such a way, to ensure that the blast travelled upwards. It would work as long as the box was placed high. All Naylor had to do was position it high enough to stop the blast being absorbed by the ground. The result would be similar to a mini-atomic bomb going off in the centre of Belfast, he had boasted. The consulate would be ripped apart, and anyone above the bomb with it.

Just a few seconds more, and the scene would be set for Armageddon. The timer would give Naylor fifteen minutes for a getaway. It was ample.

He afforded himself a brief moment of congratulation. The team had been right. From the moment they had chosen the name of the store and the name was stencilled on the van, it had become a running joke. It would be child's play to wipe away the months of careful negotiations and to bury the hope of millions to live in peace. Naylor could almost smell the far-off shores of Rio.

The sound of footsteps racing through the store behind him and the shouts of the customers and staff shook him from his momentary dream. He was furious with himself for his lapse. He spun and crouched to meet whatever lay behind him. He saw the uniforms of the two officers, but failed to see the third man dart into the store room. The policemen, unable to see their prey, shouted a challenge for the man to surrender. Scala knew it was futile.

As if straight from the training manual, Naylor reared up, clutching his 9mm pistol with both hands and with legs astride. He took deliberate aim at the uniformed men.

'Oh, sweet Jesus! Have pity,' muttered the first as he caught sight of Naylor taking careful aim at the man's head. His partner turned to face the challenge. Naylor fired twice, and the men died.

There were screams from inside the toy store as shoppers and staff ran in terror. Naylor made for the box.

'Don't, you bastard!' Naylor's head turned in recognition of a voice from the past; a voice that he had heard condemn him; a voice of an old friend who had betrayed him, and on whom he had sworn vengeance.

Scala stepped from the shadows, his pistol already cocked and aimed at the centre of Naylor's forehead. Naylor straightened as if to defy the challenge. Scala looked different now.

'Long time no see, Mick!' whispered Scala in a voice filled with menace. 'I thought you were dead. Correction, I *hoped* you were dead. Now, put down your cannon . . . *do it now*!' he shouted.

At last Scala was confronting his own personal nightmare. He felt good, with nothing to fear. He had faced his mistakes of the past that had cost the lives of innocent people, and could make amends.

Naylor placed the gun on a packing case and began to finger his ring and his mutilated finger.

'Dead give-away that, Mick. You should learn not to be so sentimental about jewellery. Georgie couldn't wait to tell me about it. Very helpful, that Georgie. You should learn to look after your employees a little more carefully,' Scala smirked. 'Oh, I forgot . . . you always *do* look after your employees!'

'Of all the people they might have sent it had to be you, didn't it?' grinned Naylor. 'I suppose they thought they'd send one treacherous bastard to catch another. They send the man who stitched me up and got me thrown out of the only life I'd known, because he didn't have the bottle for a bit of getting even. You know what they did to my girl – and still you sided against me, you bastard!' Naylor edged forward.

'Whose side are you on now, Mick? How many more people have got to die to satisfy your cravings? Georgie told me about the kids, that it was your idea. And now this! For Christ's sake, Naylor, when does it stop with you?' shouted Scala.

'Smart bastard, aren't you?' growled Naylor. 'Always one of the good guys. I thought by now you'd have learned that there are no good guys any more, Jim. I don't know who the good guys are – and if you're honest, neither do you.'

'At least I don't murder people for the sake of it, Mick.'

Naylor laughed. 'Of course you do, you stupid bastard, but you call it duty and hide behind your shit morals. You know you've murdered people, like I have. There's no difference between us, Jimbo!'

Naylor's use of his name momentarily took Scala back to Colombia, to another time and another place, when they had been united.

Now Naylor showed his teeth. 'The only difference between us is that you haven't got the balls to pull that trigger – and I have.'

'Try me, you bastard!' Images of the mother and children butchered by Naylor's machete and the memory of the coffin of the boy killed by drugs flashed into Scala's mind. His finger squeezed the trigger.

Suddenly a voice behind him, the voice of an officer in dark green calling for his colleagues, distracted him. Naylor leaped and brought his knee into Scala's groin. The pain shot through Scala's body and he sank to his knees. Naylor grabbed the gun and put it to Scala's head. The RUC officer stepped into the warehouse from the shop and saw the scene. It was his last vision. Naylor lifted the gun from Scala's head and fired.

Scala seized the moment and jumped to his feet to smash a punch into Naylor's windpipe. The blow sent the man reeling in pain. Scala followed it with a head butt which caught Naylor a glancing blow to the nose. Still fighting for breath, Naylor saw Scala lunge towards him and drove an upper cut which caught him squarely on the chin. Then, slipping on the blood of the dead men, he broke through the shop and on to the street. Scala recovered his senses, grabbed the pistol that Naylor had dropped in his haste and charged through the store, sending displays of toys crashing to the floor.

He followed his quarry on to the street. Screams from passers-by alerted the troop of journalists and TV cameramen who still gathered outside the consulate to his left. He guessed that Naylor must have gone right.

Ten paces to the right lay a narrow alley. It led to a rear car park for the row of shops and restaurants, bordered by a high brick wall. The sound of running footsteps came from the end of the alley. Scala followed recklessly – too recklessly, he knew, but it was as if he did not care any longer. All that mattered was facing the man from the past.

The wall was too high to vault, and Naylor had failed on two attempts. Blood oozed from his scraped fingers. Scala stood at the entrance to the car park. Wild-eyed, Naylor turned. The two men raised their guns together, arms straight and deliberate. It was as if Scala had never been able to see more clearly in his life. His senses had never seemed better. He was alert to everything alive. The two men fired simultaneously, and Naylor crashed against the wall as the bullet caught him below the ribcage. He lay paralysed on the ground in a pool of his own blood.

Scala could hear the sound of running footsteps behind him. The curious press pack that had waited outside the consulate had sensed the possibilities of a bigger story. A crowd was gathering. Slowly, deliberately, Scala moved towards the man sprawled on the concrete and stood over him.

Naylor mocked, 'Bastard! Think you can take me? You had your chance a long time ago and fucked it, Scala . . . I told you, you haven't got the bottle. . . . I defy you to pull that trigger . . .' he snarled.

The images and memories returned – of Lena, the friendship, the man who had taught him so much. Then they were replaced by those of Danny MacMichael and Sheena Maguire. There would be more if the man lived . . . there would always be more. Scala's head throbbed. Was Naylor right? Did he have the nerve? Was he any better than Naylor?

It was a mechanical movement. He knew it had to be done. Scala placed his feet on either side of Naylor's head and lowered the gun to aim directly at the middle of the man's forehead. Naylor's eyes stared at the end of the barrel. There was no fear, only anger. Scala fired the two shots in the traditional manner of the SAS. A woman screamed from behind him. He heard the click of cameras. He could not move. It was as if he were glued to the spot.

'Get your bleedin' head down, you stupid young bugger!' came the thick Ulster accent. 'Can't have yer puttin' on a show for them bloody hounds . . .'

The policeman threw the coat over Scala's head and led him away, past the shouting journalists and screaming women. He did not struggle – he had no fight left in him. He just wanted to be left alone with his demons.

Chapter Nineteen

The newspaper headlines said it all. In huge black type, in newspapers on both sides of the Atlantic, they spelled out: 'EXECUTION'. Most used an out-of-focus photograph taken by a panic-stricken snapper at the moment of Naylor's death, which revealed a shadowy figure leaning over a man and pointing a pistol to his head. The shock waves of revulsion were instant. Even the President was outraged. The telephone between the White House and Downing Street had sizzled throughout the night. The President demanded answers. The man from British intelligence – or 'sub-intelligence', as he nicknamed it – had made his consulate seem like the OK Corral. This incident could cost him votes.

Eamon Clancy had never been one to miss an opportunity to seize the initiative. His statement had made it clear that he believed the entire affair was a continuation of the British 'dirty tricks' campaign against the people who demanded a united Ireland. There had been no way that he could sit at the same table and talk of peace when the 'out-of-control' gunmen of the British army were involved in what he dubbed 'a return to a shoot-to-kill policy'. The scandal of the possibility that the IRA had begun selling heroin to children as part of the expansion of its criminal fund-raising activities was conveniently dismissed.

And it mattered not that a plot by militant extremists to destroy the continuation of the peace process had been averted – and in so doing had saved Clancy's own life. The entire affair was valuable ammunition in the war of public relations. It was, according to Clancy, clear that Loyalist factions would stop at nothing to avoid talking peace.

For his part, Mitchell Cain had the worst day of his political career. His consulate was being used as a gun range. Someone – no one knew who for sure – had tried to blow him up, and he fancied that his political future and the chance to be the historic

211

peacemaker had walked out the door along with Eamon Clancy. It had been a day to remember, sure enough, but not for the reasons that Cain had envisaged.

It would be a long time before the negotiators of all parties would sit around the same table again.

*　　*　　*

Scala felt empty. He had faced one of the demons from his past and won, but felt no relief. Perhaps it would always be like that. He sat alone in the room at the rear of the RUC station, feeling dirty in both body and soul. He wondered if the SAS team that had carried out the killings of the three IRA suspects on Gibraltar had felt the same back in the eighties.

The newspapers had quizzed police sources for his identity. They had not seen his face – the quick-thinking RUC man had seen to that. The usual whos, whys and what ifs of the press had been dealt with appropriately by men in pin-striped suits. The press still had no clue to his identity or who he worked for. But they had called him an 'executioner' – perhaps that's all he ever was, mused Scala as he sat alone.

The door opened, and Scala's reddened eyes opened wide with anger. 'You! What the bloody hell are you doing here? You must have some balls to show your face in front of me!'

There in the doorway stood the immaculately dressed figure of Matherson. Behind him stood another 'ghost' from Scala's past – the tall, grey-haired Alex Carter whom Scala had met briefly in Hereford, and who had recommended him for the job.

'I don't know which one of you bastards to kill first!' snarled Scala, lurching towards Matherson to stand virtually nose to nose in front of him, spitting anger. He wanted to place his hands around the man's throat and squeeze. 'You used me like a child uses a bloody toy, you bastard! You knew about Naylor all along – you knew how we felt about each other!'

Matherson stepped away from Scala. 'There's an old saying that it takes a thief to catch a thief. I simply altered the nouns a little. I wasn't certain if you had the bottle for the job, so I had to keep you in the dark.'

A smile came to Scala's face. 'The last person who didn't

think I had the bottle now has some extra ventilation in his head!'

Matherson ignored the comment. 'The thing is, Scala my man, you've caused me a lot of bloody problems. I send you in to catch a weasel – a weasel who, it transpires, is hell-bent on buggering up the peace effort – and you end up doing the job for him! Admittedly you kept your end of the bargain – but at what a cost! What am I going to do with you, Jim Scala?'

Scala dropped his voice. 'You can leave me alone and let me go home, that's what!'

'Can't do that, old boy. Things are not quite as simple as that in my little outfit. I'm afraid, once you're in, it's a lifetime commitment – none of that gold watch and handshake when you're sixty-five crap. I'm afraid the only real way out is dead. The truth is, I wasn't really sure you'd make it through this far. I had visions of yet another lonely unmarked grave in some far-flung vestige of our shrinking Empire being occupied by your good self. But it would seem that the novice has beaten the odds.'

The words cut into the Welshman like a knife. They had expected him to die – that was the reality of it. Even he had not prepared himself for the truth. He felt caged, and fell silent. Then he remembered that there were still some loose ends to tie up.

*   *   *

Philip McGann talked. He had not stopped talking since the Special Branch officers had brought him in, still shaking at the realization of his betrayal and near death. He had not known Naylor or the other man in the RUC uniform who had switched the briefcases. But he knew the men who employed them. McGann was finished – but he would ensure that his fellow conspirators would fall with him.

*   *   *

The envelope smacked on to the table in the darkened back room. Scala reached forward to inspect it.

'Don't worry, it's all there!' said McConachie. 'I think we

agreed on ten grand, didn't we? Now where's your bit of stuff?'

Scala reached into the leather shoulder bag that he invariably carried when he came to the Society of Friends premises and placed the plastic sheets of Ecstasy tablets in front of him. 'As promised, five thousand tabs!' he said drily. 'There's a few AK-47s for you. Soon be able to start your war, won't you?'

McConachie ignored the cynical remark. 'Fancy a wee drink now?'

'Not for me – got some unfinished work to get on with,' he explained as he took the money and passed the usual two doormen as he brushed by into the street.

Scala had walked less than a hundred yards before he was aware of the scuffle behind him. The first officers from the RUC'S Anti-Racketeering Squad pounced on the doormen as soon as Scala had walked away. Others stormed into the building.

From the barred window of the Regent Scala watched as, moments later, McConachie emerged held by two green-uniformed policemen. Healy was being dragged behind.

For the first time in weeks Scala felt really good. He would not be responsible for destroying someone else's mind tonight, at least. But elsewhere the door had been opened, a need had been found, and he wondered how long it would be before the men with sachets of white powder began infesting the estates and alleys of Belfast to prey on those with a hunger for the self-destruction of heroin. There would always be another 'Pied Piper'; of that he was certain.

* * *

Margot Hennessey sniffed the odour of cheap scent on her husband's jacket. It was no more than she had expected. She was aware of the judge's passion for easy women: it had always been thus throughout their marriage. She had learned to tolerate it, because she loved to bask in the social limelight that came with the power of his position. The marriage was one of convenience.

She noticed the police car head down the winding drive of their home. It was different from the cars that usually formed their protection team. She knew them all. Then she heard the voices of the officers talking to Niall in the hallway below. A sixth sense warned her of impending doom. She watched as Hennessey climbed into the police car alongside one of the officers. The car pulled away.

*　　　*　　　*

It was a fine afternoon along the coast. The sun glinted off the bay at the rear of Noel Caffrey's mansion. He and his wife pottered in their well established garden, preparing for the summer season of flowers that would bloom and create a carpet of colour. The radio blasted out the news of the postponement of the talks until fresh ground could be sought. Caffrey whistled to himself.

His heart had sunk when the stories of the 'bomber' and the 'executioner' had flooded on to the television screens and into newspapers. But the man had died in the attempt. No one knew where he came from or his reasons. That would be an end to it. There was no link.

Caffrey looked out to sea. It was always gut-wrenching for him to think how Martin would have enjoyed a day like today. The plump, elderly housekeeper shuffled into the garden to tell Caffrey of his visitors – of the two plainclothes police officers who waited in the room where the eyes from a hundred photographs of a handsome young man stared down at them.

*　　　*　　　*

He slid the empty glass down the bar and demanded a refill of the thick black stout . . . and give him a whiskey chaser too. Derek Macnamara was fuelling his anger with drink. In his mind he had been proved right: the Brits and the Loyalists were never to be trusted. He had tried to tell the likes of Clancy, and they had ignored him and told him that his ways were outdated. But he was right.

The brothers joined him in the tiny corner bar in Turf Lodge where Macnamara often drowned his problems. They were all that remained of his command, but he could still strike one last blow before even they exiled themselves in the South. This time he would go with them; and the Brit with the drugs that had contaminated the children, the man that came with the Prod whore, would pay.

* * *

Ma Dillon took her usual seat in the front room and prepared herself for the ritual of watching her favourite television soap opera. The TV soaps were her friends, the companions that she had grown to rely on during seven years of loneliness, praying for her daughter's return. The routine was not about to be broken now. Noreen was busy preparing the evening meal in the kitchen and occasionally floated into the front room to see to the needs of her mother. She had resigned herself to the fact that this would be the path of her life for months to come.

Scala had attempted to contact her on numerous occasions, but she had always found a reason for not seeing him. She needed time. Her heart and body wanted the man, but her brain resisted. She had endured so much pain in her life. She had wanted to be certain about the man she thought she had known, but who was now shrouded in mystery. She fought to make herself trust him and believe in him; she had shared his bed and given herself in a way that she had never thought possible. Yet she still feared for the man who had come from England.

The meal was ready. She took the tray to her mother and sat beside her.

The street outside was deserted, and there was no one to see the battered Ford Sierra that crept along the road. Slowly casting shadows from the street lights, the car passed along the row of identical houses before coming to a halt outside the home with the light green paint. Kevin sat behind the wheel, while Billy, eyes bulging with the effects of the Speed tablet he had taken, sat in the passenger seat. It had been years since Derek Macnamara had taken part in an active operation. He had volunteered himself for this mission, and was sitting in the back of the Sierra. They could see the movement of figures behind the light curtains in the room. Gradually the front passenger and rear windows of the Sierra wound down. Macnamara held the M-16 assault rifle, while Billy was to make use of the pump-action shotgun.

Simultaneously, the barrels of both weapons were levelled at the figures behind the curtains. The clatter of the M-16 on automatic clashed with the repeated boom of the shotgun as the weapons exploded into action, riddling the house with bullets, splintering brickwork and shattering every window. The men in the car could see the figures behind the curtains being hurled to the floor as the bullets struck.

The attack lasted only seconds. Kevin fought to hold his nerve and began screaming for the two men to finish. Then Macnamara barked the command: 'Go . . . drive, yer little shit! Get us outta here!'

The engine erupted into life and the car disappeared at the end of the road, as curtains opened and neighbours too frightened to reveal themselves before ran into the street. Macnamara had fought his last action, and the brothers had achieved the glory that they had longed for.

*   *   *

Scala had packed, ready to catch the early morning flight to Heathrow. Matherson had attended to everything in his calm public school manner. But Scala still had one task to complete.

He walked the familiar route towards the Shankill Road. His stomach was in turmoil, his mind confused. As he walked, he practised a speech for the girl, but nothing he rehearsed seemed adequate. He wanted to tell her that he loved her and would look after her, that everything would be okay and that he would have to leave for a while, but that he would be back and they would be together. But the words still sounded false as they jostled in his mind.

Then, as he turned the corner of the road, the sight that greeted him took the breath from his body. A police cordon stood outside Noreen's house. Armed RUC men stood guard and a crowd of sightseers had gathered to view what they could.

Scala felt himself break into a run and charged headlong into the open doorway, past a stunned policeman who attempted to stop him. 'It's okay . . . I'm a friend . . . British intelligence . . . I have to come in' he heard himself saying to the officer. Scala took a deep breath to prepare himself for what he feared he would find within the house.

The body was shielded from view by the officer. He saw the woman's feet, and the pounding of his heart deafened his ears. He saw the blood that was seeping into the pile of the carpet. The officer moved, and he saw the pitiful sight of Ma Dillon sprawled before him. The bullets had crashed into the back of her head. He thought she would have died before her body had touched the floor.

His anxiety swelled. There was no sign of Noreen. He dashed into the back room where he could hear the voice of a woman police officer. Noreen sat upright in the corner chair, her eyes fixed on the blankness of the wall. There were no tears. She was unable to cry any more. She did not recognize Scala as he walked into the room and took hold of her hands. She looked past him.

'Oh, Christ! I'm so sorry, Noreen! What happened? It'll be all right, I'm here. Oh, God! Why darling? Why? I thought it was all over,' he babbled, wanting to comfort her.

Noreen was expressionless. 'I heard you, Jim Scala. I heard you tell the cop you're an intelligence man . . . I knew there was somethin' about ye! They came for you, didn't they? The men who killed Ma – they came for you,' she murmured.

'That doesn't matter now, does it? I'm here, and I love you, Noreen. I want to take care of you. Come with me, Noreen, there's nothing for you here any more. I want to look after you.'

She turned to him, her eyes accusing. 'I don't think that's what you want, Jim Scala. I've heard the lines before, you see. Nope! I don't think that's what you want at all. And I know it's not what I want any more, Jim Scala!'

Scala listened in silence.

'I thought you were different, Jim Scala. I gave more to you than to any man I've ever known. I thought you'd stay – every man I've ever loved has left me, you see! First there was me Da . . . then our Noel. They all left me, Jim. It was like I was cursed. The others had all just used me. But I thought you were different. And I wanted to believe in you . . . I wanted to love you . . . But you used me as well . . .'

Scala attempted to interrupt. 'Look, I know I was a bastard, but God help me, I didn't want to fall for you, I didn't want to actually care for you. But the truth is, I *do* care for you . . . I love you. And now I want to be with you.'

Noreen didn't hear. 'Noreen, believe me,' he went on desperately, 'I had to do this. But now I want to take you back with me. Despite what you might think at the present, I'm one of the good guys.'

Noreen snapped: 'There are no good guys, Jim Scala! The truth is, I would have gone with you. I needed your strength . . . and it's true that there's little here for me now. I thank you for the offer, but I'm staying. Whatever my life holds for me, I'll face it on me own . . . You see, I'm the only person I can trust. Now go!'

There was no persuasion. Scala rose and walked to the door. He felt in his pocket for the envelope of cash given to him by McConachie. He placed the envelope containing the £10,000 on the arm of Noreen's chair.

'You might find a need for that,' he said quietly as he kissed her on the cheek and walked into the night.

She examined the envelope and saw the money. Slowly she rose and walked to the kitchen boiler and lifted the lid. The flames licked the edge of the hatch. As if disposing of a piece of garbage, she dropped the envelope into the flames and watched as they engulfed the package.

*   *   *

The runway was visible now as the British Airways shuttle descended through the clouds on its final approach to Heathrow. The dark-haired man with the scar on his cheek finished his gin and tonic and looked at the scene below. The chief stewardess gave her final instructions to the cabin crew as the aircraft prepared to land. Scala looked at the copy of the first edition of the *Evening Standard* that had been given to him during the flight.

He scanned the pages. A short four-paragraph story on page nine revealed that the body of a distinguished former soldier from an old military family had been fished from the river near Cirencester. The man, a Colonel Aidan Massey, was thought to have committed suicide.

Scala did not linger on the article but returned to the front page – that kind of story always left him cold. According to the story, the government was in danger of losing a crucial Commons vote because of the untimely resignation of one of its brightest up-and-coming stars, Antony Hursley, and that of the Ulster Union extremist Declan Holmes – both for personal reasons. The Unionists traditionally voted with the government, so the result of the vote was now in doubt.

Scala had no patience to read any more. His thoughts conjured up an image of Noreen standing alone by the grave of her mother. The wheels of the plane touched down, jarring him back to reality. Another image, this time of Angie and the children, flashed before him. Then the words of Matherson took over, when he had warned him that 'the only way out is dead'. As he walked towards the arrivals lounge he wondered if that would be true for him. He still carried the newspaper, and casually glanced at the front-page lead story once more before hurling it in the nearest waste bin. It had nothing to do with him. Why should he care about a story like that?